"You're beaut   **he whispere**

The reverent hush in Jake's voice, the worshipful way his body was intertwined with hers, prompted Robin to ask, "Is tonight real?"

Jake considered the complex query. "No," he replied. "That's why we can say or do anything we want."

As though the pronouncement had granted her a license to steal, Robin reached out, touching his eyelids, his cheeks and finally, his lips. His parted, breathing lips.

In a primitive claiming, with a wild guttural sound, Jake yanked her to him in an embrace that went far beyond anything sexual.

Tonight wasn't real, he reminded himself. Tomorrow he'd tell her the truth about who he was.

Tonight wasn't real, Robin reminded herself. Tomorrow she'd deal with the guilt she knew she'd feel.

Whatever happened in the future, tonight they belonged to each other. Tonight there was nowhere to hide. For either of them.

D0564272

ABOUT THE AUTHOR

The secret to being able to produce nineteen blockbuster books in only seven years is a willingness to break new ground, as Sandra Canfield has proven. Time after time, she has dared to tread where few have gone before, and this adventurous approach has garnered her numerous awards, including best all-round genre writer of 1988. *Tigers by Night*, Sandra's fifth Harlequin Superromance, is yet another example of this author's ability to weave a powerful, sensuous love story with a unique twist.

Books by Sandra Canfield

HARLEQUIN SUPERROMANCE
213–CHERISH THIS MOMENT
252–VOICES ON THE WIND
278–NIGHT INTO DAY
338–MARIAH

Don't miss any of our special offers. Write to us at the following address for information on our newest releases.

Harlequin Reader Service
901 Fuhrmann Blvd., P.O. Box 1397, Buffalo, NY 14240
Canadian address: P.O. Box 603,
Fort Erie, Ont. L2A 5X3

Tigers by Night

SANDRA CANFIELD

Harlequin Books

TORONTO • NEW YORK • LONDON
AMSTERDAM • PARIS • SYDNEY • HAMBURG
STOCKHOLM • ATHENS • TOKYO • MILAN

For Betty Davis,
who so willingly shared
her knowledge of preemie babies,
and for Sue Royer,
who not only shared her nursing wisdom,
but also has given so freely of her friendship.
And for M—for always and forever

Published September 1990

ISBN 0-373-70419-4

CHAPTER ONE

GIVE OR TAKE A BABY-SOFT inch, Peter Gerald Bauer
was the size of Jake Cameron's hand. The fact bore
eloquent testimony to the smallness of the former and
the largeness of the latter.

"She's late," Jake said, the statement rumbling
quietly, deeply from the chest hidden beneath the
sterile hospital gown. Following regulations, he'd
donned the garment before entering the Neonatal
Intensive Care Unit—NICU—of Brigham and
Women's Hospital, one of Boston's finest medical fa-
cilities.

As he spoke, he checked the disposable diaper
spread beneath, but not fastened to, the baby's naked
three-pound-five-ounce body. Determining that it was
damp, Jake scooped the tiny hips into a single palm
and pulled the soiled diaper away, careful not to disturb the network of tubes and wires connecting the
infant to an assortment of lifesaving machines. He replaced the diaper with a fresh one.

"There. Better?" As if the baby had responded
around the tube taped to his mouth, Jake replied,
"Good. Now listen, you're not to worry about your
momma, you hear? There's a bad-weather bulletin out
and she just probably decided to stay put. Ten to one,
she'll be here in the morning at the crack of dawn."

The baby's eyes, a blue so dark it could be called navy, were wide and alert, as though the child were following every word of the conversation. The navy-blue eyes also seemed to say that they didn't buy a moment's worth of the flip attitude concerning the woman in question.

"I am *not* worried," Jake said, vehemently denying the baby's silent accusation, then recognizing the denial for the lie it was.

The truth was he'd been worried about Robin Bauer, with whom he had never exchanged so much as a single word, for the past three months. The police psychologist said that he had a fixation, which was just another way of saying that he was obsessed, which was just another way of saying that guilt did strange things to people.

The same police psychologist, one Dr. Daniel Jacoby, had strongly recommended—as in flat-out ordered—that he take a leave of absence from the department. Jake hadn't put up a fight—okay, maybe a small one!—principally because he knew the recommendation was sound. A police officer who couldn't draw his weapon was a danger not only to himself, but also to any other police officer depending on him in a crisis.

Jake wondered what the good doctor would say if he knew what Jake was doing with his leave of absence. Actually, he didn't have to wonder. He knew just what sort of invective he'd hear if Daniel Jacoby ever found out that he'd gone to the source of his guilt. But then, from his layman's perspective, it had seemed the only logical thing to do. He needed to satisfy himself that the mother and her premature child were all right, and then surely he could go on with his life. Couldn't he?

Deep in his heart, Jake wasn't certain he believed that, though he did believe that fate had directed him onto the path he should take. How else could he interpret his seeing the minuscule article in the paper that indicated Brigham and Women's Hospital's need for volunteers in its neonatal unit? For several reasons, the idea had appealed to him. One, he loved kids; two, he'd missed his two daughters terribly since the divorce; three, his sister Whitney had given birth several years before to a preemie who, regrettably, hadn't lived. All this, plus the fact that volunteering at the hospital two afternoons a week would be the perfect entrée into Robin Bauer's life, had made his decision an instant and easy one.

He'd been volunteering for a week now. Both afternoons—he'd signed up to work Tuesdays and Thursdays—he'd seen Robin Bauer, but had discreetly kept his distance. He didn't want to scare her off, and besides, he wasn't certain how to approach her...or even if, morally, he should. Maybe, he thought, he should just content himself with observing her. And worrying about her, he added as he once more glanced up at the clock.

It was almost seven. He'd already stayed two hours beyond his usual time. Even though the weather promised to be a first-class bitch this Tuesday evening, he could hardly believe that Robin Bauer hadn't driven the twenty-five miles from Lowell, Massachusetts, where she'd fled following her husband's death. The head nurse said she hadn't missed a day visiting her son since he'd been transferred here from the Lowell hospital.

A loud clap of thunder, nature's macabre applause for the approaching storm, reverberated throughout the neonatal ward. A baby began to cry; a nurse cooed gentle words. Jake looked down at Peter.

"Hang in there, pal. It's only thunder," he said in a soothing voice that, according to the bedside monitor, actually slowed Peter's heart rate. When she'd first noted the phenomenon, the head nurse had said that three minutes of Jake Cameron's voice was better than a bedtime story and a tranquilizer rolled into one. "That's it," he said. "Everything's gonna be all right."

In response, the baby kicked.

Jake smiled, erasing by half the wrinkles that forty-one years, and seeing too much of the dark, violent side of life, had etched into his face. Many of those wrinkles had seemingly appeared in just the past few months. "That's it. Fight back," he said, his thumb caressing the baby's small ivory-white leg, one of the few patches of skin devoid of tubes and wires, "and let the devil fend for his own."

The baby kicked again.

"Hey, have you heard the latest rumor?" Jake asked. "They're talking about taking you off the ventilator. And did you know that they started you on continuous feeding yesterday? That's what that tube to your tummy is all about. No, this does not mean you can have a Big Mac."

The fact that Peter might be removed from the ventilator and placed within an oxygen hood where he could breathe on his own was an encouraging sign, as was the institution of continuous feeding. The month-old baby was obviously improving and gaining weight, which warmed Jake's heart. In a way he couldn't explain, even to himself, his emotional survival and the baby's physical survival were inextricably linked. He intuitively knew that somewhere in Peter's softness lay his own salvation, that somewhere in Peter's innocence lay his absolution from guilt, that somewhere in Peter's courage, he could find his own.

"Speaking of food," Jake said, knowing that a long evening of loneliness awaited him, "I have this heavy date with a TV dinner. You think I ought to go for turkey and dressing or Swiss steak and mashed potatoes?" He waited the length of one response. "Yeah, I think I will have the steak and potatoes." He leaned lower and spoke conspiratorially. "Unless you wanna break outta here and get a Big Mac."

Thunder grumbled again, and the rain that had been falling all afternoon increased its tempo, hurling itself against the windows. Jake glanced outside, then up at the clock on the wall. She wasn't coming, which was a good thing in this weather.

"She'll be here tomorrow," Jake said, as though the baby's mind, like his own, had never strayed far from the earlier subject. He pulled forward a rattle even though the baby was far too small to play with it. "Be good," he added, patting Peter one last time and easing away from the radiant warmer bed that maintained a constant temperature. In silent protest at the disappearance of the soft, consoling voice, and because he couldn't cry with the tube in his mouth, Peter clenched his tiny hand into a fist.

At the nursery door, Jake shed the hospital gown and pulled the sleeves of his beige turtleneck sweater back down. Reaching for his watch, which he'd left at the sink when he'd scrubbed up, he fastened it around his wrist before slinging his long arms into his leather jacket.

"See you next time," he said to the nurse who was busily charting medication.

The nurse looked up. "You leaving?"

"Yeah."

"Stay dry."

"I'll give it my best shot," Jake answered, pushing on the swinging door.

"Hey, Mr. Cameron!" the nurse called out.

He turned, holding the door with his massive hand.

"Wee Care meets this Thursday—" the nurse glanced down at the note on her desk "—at seven o'clock in the conference room."

One of the nurses, herself the parent of a preemie, had formed a support group for parents going through the traumatic ordeal that went with giving birth to a premature child. Volunteers were encouraged to attend to gain knowledge not only about premature infants, but also about the parents' fears and concerns.

Jake nodded. "I'll be there."

"Great. Good night."

"Good night."

The door closed behind him. He walked to the empty elevator and rode it down to the garage. Although the parking area was semi-enclosed, the September wind drove misty sheets of cold, gray rain in at the open sides, making the concrete thoroughly wet. Even from where he stood, Jake could feel the moisture creeping into his jeans and the cold stinging his clean-shaven cheeks. He zipped up his jacket partway, rammed his hands into the pockets and, his dark head bent low, started jogging in the direction of his Jeep.

"Lousy damned night," he swore under his breath.

IT HAD BEEN A MISERABLE DAY, Robin Bauer decided as she pulled her car into the hospital parking lot. A miserable day that was fast turning into a miserable night. The cold she had awakened with that morning was worse, complete with runny nose, teary eyes and a stuffy, fuzzy-feeling head. Add to that the fact that the predicted storm was steadily, predatorily moving in. Because she felt so wretched, she'd fallen asleep on the sofa and had awakened less than an hour ago. She knew she ought to be home curled up next to a heating pad and guzzling orange juice, but it was unthinkable—even considering her cold, the weather, the world coming to an end—that she would let a day go by without seeing her son. Not that they would let her near him with this cold, but she could stand at the glass, look at him and think loving thoughts.

Then, of course, there was the matter of her daily delivery of the milk she pumped from her breasts. The hospital froze it, and when Peter began to take food into his stomach, they would thaw it and give it to him, first by tube, followed by a nipple when he was strong enough to suck. The nurse had explained that, at some point, probably right before he was sent home, Peter would begin breast-feeding.

There were two things that she passionately longed for: to hold her son and to have him suckling at her breast. Both happy activities were dependent upon everything continuing to go well.

Please, dear God, let my baby be all right, she prayed. The alternative was so painful that she couldn't even consider it.

A sudden sneeze brought her back to the achy present. Wiping her nose, she laid the tissue on the passenger seat next to the sack that held the jar of milk, and looked around for a parking place. Despite the fact that it was a cold and stormy Tuesday, the parking lot was surprisingly full. Nothing. She saw no available space. She was just wondering where in the world she was going to park when she saw a fire-engine red Jeep pull out from a slot at the far right end. Was it possible that the day's luck was about to change?

Stifling another sneeze, she inched the car forward and slowed it to a stop. She waited. The taillights of the Jeep, like scarlet sabers engaged in a fencing match, cut across her golden headlights. Needing to back up just a bit to get out of the vehicle's way, she started to shift gears. At the same instant, the jar of milk began to roll off the seat...and she sneezed! She reached for the jar, jerked the steering wheel to the left and skidded on the rain-slick surface all at the same time. The disastrous result was one vehicle impacting with another. The sound of glass shattering rent the chilled air.

No, please, Robin prayed, *don't let this be happening.* But the pounding of her head and the sick feeling in the pit of her stomach told her that it was happening. If these symptoms hadn't convinced her, the man spilling from the Jeep to check the damage to his vehicle would have. Wishing fervently that she could die on the spot—did feeling like death increase her chances?—she cut off the engine and threw open the car door. Immediately, the windblown rain splotched her jade-green corduroy skirt, slipped down the collar of the matching jacket and wreaked havoc with her uncovered, shoulder-length hair. She shivered.

"Are you all right?" The man, equally exposed to the elements, spoke to her without looking up.

"Yes," Robin answered, silently adding, *Just feeling like a fool.* "How bad is it?" she asked over the patter of persistent rain.

The man was hunkered down, the muscles in his thighs straining against the increasingly moist denim of his jeans. After checking the Jeep, still squatting, he swiveled on the balls of his booted feet in order to investigate her car. He still didn't look up.

Never having had a wreck before, Robin was uncertain about the protocol, but she felt obligated to check the damage too. This she did, though she had no earthly idea how to assess it. She did consider it a relatively good sign that nothing other than glass was strewn about the parking lot. But then, maybe all that meant was that something was internally, and expensively, jammed into something else. With the luck she'd been having today, it was probably one of those freak accidents where both cars looked intact, but had been completely totaled inside.

This last disturbing thought made her hasten to ask again, "How bad is it?"

Jake Cameron rose, his eyes at last finding the woman. Though usually in command of his reactions—a cop had to be—surprise streaked boldly across his face. He was spared detection by the fact that Robin was busy adjusting the angle of her head to accommodate his considerable height. The man just seemed to go on and on.

She observed rather absently that the stranger was probably in his late thirties or early forties, and had a face that managed to be appealing despite its craggy, blunt features. He had thick, dark brown hair, silvering at the temples, that tumbled onto a wide forehead, perhaps helped there now by wind and rain. His eyes were brown, as well—a deep, rich brown somewhere between hot coffee and polished mahogany. Incongruously, his eyes appeared both gentle and hard. Well, maybe not so much hard as filled with too much hurtful knowledge, Robin amended. It was a look that said he'd seen too much of life and no longer had any illusions. It was the same look she knew she wore.

At present those incongruous eyes were taking in her every nuance. Jake had never seen his obsession up close. He'd watched her from a distance, when he'd stood in the shadows at her husband's funeral, and he'd seen her across the neonatal ward of the hospital. At graveside, he'd been unable to see anything except a woman shrouded in a black veil, a woman who'd stood straight, despite the heavy burden that had been heaped upon her shoulders. Her petite shoulders. That much he had been able to determine, that much he had confirmed as he'd surreptitiously watched her at the hospital. But, sweet heaven, he thought as he realized that she came only midway up his chest, he'd had no idea how truly small she was!

Her size, combined with the long, kinky hairdo that so many young women wore—there was even a tiny section braided in front, pulled to the side and caught with a gold clasp—made her look as though she were in her early twenties, though he knew for a fact that she was in her mid-thirties. Her clothes—leather boots, calf-length skirt and baggy, belted sweater worn beneath a stylishly oversized jacket—added to her youthful appearance. Everything about her looked young. Except her eyes. Hazel green and flecked with gold, they looked tired, sad, as though they knew firsthand the meaning of the word *tragedy*. Jake couldn't even begin to guess how many tears those tired, sad eyes had cried. And all because of him.

Realizing with a start that Robin was watching him, waiting for an assessment of the damage, he replied, "You, uh, you broke your headlight."

"Is that all?" She was still filled with anxious concern, yet, curiously, the man's voice had a soothing effect.

"Seems to be," Jake answered, stooping to pick up the largest piece of glass near the now darkened headlight. She noted that his hand seemed large...very large.

Turning toward his vehicle, she asked, "What about your—"

"Just dented the bumper."

"I'm sorry. I sneezed, the milk fell, the car skidded—"

"It's okay. Bumpers are made to be bumped."

"I know, but I should pay for—"

Jake shook his head. "Just get a new headlight before you drive back—" He stopped himself just in time. He had come dangerously close to saying, "Before you drive back to Lowell." He couldn't very well tell her he'd snooped in Dr. Jacoby's file to find out where she lived...and he doubted she'd buy his being clairvoyant. "Get a new headlight before you drive very far. A garage, maybe even a service station, can put in a new one," he added.

Robin nodded. "Should we call the police?"

Jake had the sudden unsettling vision of one of his cohorts answering the call and spilling the beans about who he was...a mess that would drip all the way back to Daniel Jacoby. Then Jacoby would be on his tail asking that unanswerable question of just what in hell he thought he was doing.

"It's really too small an accident to report," Jake heard himself saying. "All you need is a headlight, which your insurance company isn't going to pay for, anyway. The frame of the headlight socket's not even damaged." He paused, then plunged, listening to his heart scamper at his blatant dare. "Of course, if you'll feel more comfortable calling the police..."

"No, no, that's fine. This is just my first accident and... Look, I'm sorry about everything. I—" She sneezed loudly, unexpectedly. "I'm sorry," she repeated, sniffing. "I've had this rotten cold all day and—" She sneezed again, reducing herself to a state of total embarrassment.

His heart returning to a normal rhythm at her dismissal of the police, Jake fished a handkerchief from his back pocket and handed it to Robin. She hesitated, then took it because she had little choice unless she wanted the additional indignity of a runny nose.

Jake noted that she was still wearing her wedding ring, a beautifully engraved gold band. The sight of it slashed at his conscience.

When Robin finished with the handkerchief, she started to hand it back, but stopped. She wasn't sure if you were supposed to give a man's handkerchief back to him dirty.

"Keep it," Jake said, settling her predicament.
"You may need it again. Especially if you stay out in
the rain much longer." He wanted to fuss at her for
coming out in this weather at all, particularly with the
cold she was sporting, but he didn't. He didn't have
the right, no more than he had the right to caution her
about driving back in the storm. But he'd worry about
her just the same. He knew he would. It was the pen-
ance he'd levied on himself—the current market price
of guilt.

Both were growing uncomfortably wet from the
blowing rain. Robin's hair kinked even more tightly,
fat droplets of water dripping from the coiled curls
onto her peaches-and-cream cheeks. Jake's damp hair
inched lower onto his creased forehead.

Drawing the scene to an abrupt close, he said, "You
can have my parking space."

The accident had blocked the slot and cars were
circling like vultures around a carcass.

"I'll get the Jeep out of the way," Jake said, already walking toward the vehicle.

"Thanks," she said as she opened her car door and
slipped inside.

In seconds she had started the car and, avoiding the
scattered glass as best she could, had pulled into the
parking space. Slinging her purse across her shoulder, she gathered up the milk. Once more she exited
the car, locked it and hastened toward the hospital
entrance.

"I'm sorry!" she called back over her shoulder one
last time.

"Forget it," Jake hollered through the open window of the Jeep. "And get that light repaired!" He
thought he saw her wave an acknowledgment.

With her quickened steps, her hips moved noticeably beneath the folds of her skirt, an alluring, womanly sway that put the final lie to her youthful appearance. Suddenly, she was showcased in the fluorescent lights near the hospital doors. They cast a glow that took her hair from light brown to sun-spun gold. Without needing to see it, Jake knew that the same glow gilded the flecks in her spring-green eyes, and accentuated the pain in their depths.

Oblivious to the cold rain stealing in through the open window, he watched long after Robin had disappeared inside the huge brick building. He wondered what she would have said had he told her who he was. Would she have cursed him? Would she have spat upon him? Or would she have just silently, loathingly condemned him to hell?

The last would have been redundant, Jake thought with a self-derisive smile, for hell was where he already dwelled.

When the nurse saw Robin outside the nursery, she glanced at the clock, then motioned for her to come on in even though visiting hours were over. Robin shook her head and held up the sack.

"I can't come in," Robin explained seconds later when the nurse opened the door. "I have a cold." The announcement was so profoundly nasal that it left no room for even the slightest doubt.

"Heavens, you are sick, aren't you?" Old enough to be Robin's mother, the nurse proceeded to scold. "You shouldn't have come out in this weather."

"I wanted to bring this," Robin said, holding out the sack of milk. "And to see my baby."

The nurse took the package. "A day or two won't make any difference with the milk," she said, then volunteered the information she knew would be asked for next. "He's had a good day."

Robin smiled, forgetting entirely that her head hurt and her body ached. "That's great!"

Ignoring the fact that the hospital staff members weren't supposed to get emotionally involved with their patients or their patients' families, the nurse smiled, too. "In fact, Peter's doing so well that we started him on continuous-tube feeding yesterday. We're going to try him off the ventilator and put him under an oxygen hood in a day or so." At the brilliance that bloomed in Robin's cheeks, the woman cautioned, "Note I said *try*. We might have to put him back on the machine if he isn't willing to start breathing on his own. And you're not to be disturbed if we do."

Robin's excitement didn't dissipate by even a sparkle. "I know, I know!" she said. "Step by step." It was the creed, the difficult creed, that a preemie's parents lived by.

"Right," the nurse agreed, adding, "Just roll with the punches."

Robin didn't reply, but she could have said that she'd rolled with more punches in the past few months than any human being should be asked to roll with. Actually, she'd fought them like the very devil in the beginning, but when she'd realized the fighting was doing neither her nor the baby in her womb any good, she'd tried to accept what she couldn't change. Even at that, because it had been a difficult pregnancy from the beginning, she'd almost lost the child as a result of the stress.

"It is a good sign, though, isn't it?" Robin prompted despite the nurse's caution.

Again, the nurse couldn't help but smile. "Yes, it is a good sign." Then, her voice taking on an exaggerated gruffness, she said, "Now, young lady, you go home and crawl into bed."

"May I see Peter first?"

"Sure. And stay home tomorrow if you're not better. You hear me?"

Robin assured her that she did hear and would stay home, knowing full well that she wouldn't, not as long as she could put one foot in front of the other. The nursery curtain had already been drawn for the night, but the nurse pulled it aside. Fortunately, the bed bearing Peter Bauer was closest to the window. The nurse smiled and went back to work.

As it always did, the sight of her son brought an instant, heavy warmth to Robin's heart. How was it possible to love one little pink, wrinkled bundle so very much? She'd loved before—her parents, her husband—but never had she felt this kind of love. She marveled at the depth and the beauty, the complexity and the simplicity, of the maternal instinct.

She also felt, again as always, the overwhelming urge to yank all the hideous, frightening wires and tubes from her baby's body. She had to remind herself constantly that these wires and tubes, regardless of how hideous and frightening they might appear, were keeping her child alive. The ventilator tube might soon be gone, however. Then she could hear her baby breathing on his own, could hear him cry, could eventually hear him coo and laugh. She could even hear him call her momma. This last thought brought a knot to her throat, and, stepping closer to the window, she pressed her open palms against the glass, as if by doing so she could feel the tender sweetness of her son.

"Hi, Peter," she whispered, her words absorbed by the empty hallway. "It's Mommy. I'm sorry I couldn't come see you today, but I have this terrible cold, and I didn't want to give it to you. Did you miss me?"

Peter's eyes were closed in sleep, but Robin imagined the response she wanted to hear.

"I miss you, too, baby. The nurse said you had a good day. I'm so proud of you for fighting so hard. You're Mommy's brave little boy. Oh, Peter—" her voice rose a note with excitement "—they're going to take you off the ventilator. You must try very hard to breathe. Please try hard, Peter, please. Okay?"

Robin's eyes misted and she swallowed deeply, adding a silent *please*, this one to a God she hoped was watching over her child.

For long minutes she stood quietly watching her baby. She could see his little chest rise and fall as the ventilator pushed air into his lungs. At birth they had lacked surfactant, the substance that gave the lungs their elasticity. Occasionally the baby's eyelids twitched, as if he were dreaming innocent baby dreams. Of what? she wondered. At four weeks old, what did he know to dream about? Dreams. Lord, she wished her own would stop! Or that they would mellow to the point where she would dream of Gerald alive and laughing, not splattered—

She recoiled from the thought, chasing it away. "Your grandparents called today," she said. "They said to tell you hello." A small, sad smile appeared at her lips. "I think they're still mad at me because I didn't go back to Tucson with them after the...after the funeral. I couldn't though, Peter. *You* do understand that, don't you? I mean, I had to get out of Boston, but I just couldn't go that far away. I couldn't leave your father.''

She had tried a thousand times to make her parents understand, most recently when they'd returned for Peter's birth. The truth was, she couldn't make them understand what she herself didn't. All she knew was that she had to get out of Boston and away from the unrelenting press, but she couldn't go far. Lowell, where she and Gerald had met seven years before, and where they'd lived briefly before the bright dreams of Boston had beckoned, had seemed the perfect place for escape. Besides, Boston was where her business was . . . sort of. The boutique to which she sold her exclusively designed sweaters was located there.

The thought of the unfinished sweater sketches on her easel made her grimace. ''The sketches aren't finished yet,'' she told her sleeping son. ''I just haven't felt like working. I don't sleep well, which makes me tired during the day and . . . I just haven't felt like working. Then I got this cold.''

She sighed, feeling her headache increasing and a chill, inspired by the dampness of her clothes, sluicing over her.

''Oh, Peter, it's been the most god-awful day. I ran into this man in the parking lot and dented his fender and broke my headlight and now I've got to get another one and my head hurts and I'm wet and—'' her voice cracked ''—I miss your daddy.'' She rested her forehead against the glass partition and closed her eyes before they betrayed her with the tears she already felt stinging her lids. The glass was so cool that she idly wondered if she had a fever. Just as idly, she decided she probably did. "Oh, Peter," she whispered, "it wasn't supposed to be like this."

The three of them were supposed to have been a happy family—laughing at life and loving each other. There would have been the sharing of first steps, first words, Gerald dressing up as Santa Claus. There would have been frisky puppies, father taking son to a Red Sox game, the three of them playing in the surf at Cape Cod.

Would Gerald have loved their son as much as she did?

Each time this question invaded, Robin felt guilty for having even posed it. Of course Gerald would have loved his son as much as she did. It was just that in the beginning he hadn't been as excited about the pregnancy as she had. He had thought it poorly timed. He had just taken on a new job as controller for Century Aeronautics; they had just bought a new house and a new car. Robin had pointed out that, since everything else was new, surely one more new thing couldn't hurt.

Pulling her forehead from the glass and opening her eyes, Robin said emphatically, "Your daddy would have loved you as much as I do."

Then, because her baby was so tiny and her fear for him so great, and because her husband was so coldly, so irrevocably dead, the tears finally made good their threat.

"Oh, Peter, please be all right. You're all Mommy has."

One tear, followed by another, plopped onto her fevered cheeks and ran down into the corners of her mouth. She sniffed, opened her handbag and rummaged around for a tissue. All she could find, however, was a man's handkerchief, which she again used out of necessity. As she did so, she noted that the handkerchief was initialed with a *C*. Conjuring up an image of the man in the parking lot, she thought of gentle eyes and a soothing-soft voice. Both, belonging to a stranger with a name that began with *C*, were somehow oddly comforting on a day that otherwise had been totally miserable.

THE POWERS THAT BE obviously did not intend that she get a headlight that evening. It was the only conclusion that Robin could draw after first stopping at a garage, which had been closed just as she'd feared, and at two service stations. The first station didn't deal in automotive parts, while the second could have supplied a light for everything from a motorcycle to a Mack truck. Unfortunately, it was all sold out of the more common item Robin needed. She had left the attendants snarling among themselves as to whose job it was to keep the shelves stocked and had gimped home, amid a torrential downpour, by the beam of a single headlight.

Why had she never known to appreciate all the little things that Gerald took care of—such as the replacement of headlights?

Weary to the bone, she forced down a mug of hot tomato soup, took an even hotter bath hoping to curb her chill and crawled into bed on the heels of a debate concerning whether she should take a couple of aspirin. Unable to remember whether the drug was on the list of medications a nursing mother should avoid, Robin opted not to take the chance. It was just she and the raw symptoms of a cold battling the night. Finally, at three minutes till a rainy twelve o'clock, she fell into a fitful sleep.

IN CONTRAST, JAKE ARRIVED home as Robin was fruitlessly searching for a headlight. He tossed a foil-wrapped TV dinner in the oven to heat while he took a quick shower. Thirty minutes later, he downed the Swiss steak and mashed potatoes—one tasted like cardboard, the other like paste—then settled down to a book that should have been good, but wasn't. Now lonely and worried—had Robin Bauer gotten the headlight repaired? Had she gotten home safely?—he called his daughters.

The sixteen-year-old was at some school function, but the twelve-year-old, all dimples and braces and lamentations about this really neato boy in her class who had eyes for her best friend, spoke nonstop for almost fifteen minutes. It was the highlight of his day.

But then, his ex-wife got on the phone. She refrained from asking how he was doing, as if so asking would push him over the edge that everyone was so damned sure he was teetering on. Instead, she talked on and on about how Ed was taking her and the girls skiing in Colorado for Christmas—if, of course, their taking the girls was all right with him. Jake had hung up feeling not only lonelier, but also depressed. Not that he minded about Colorado, not that he was still carrying a torch for his ex-wife, but because some man named Ed saw his daughters a hundred times more often than he did.

Maybe because at that moment he was well aware of how lonely a parent could feel, or maybe because the child in him just needed to hear his father's reassuring voice, he dialed his father's telephone number. The eighty-three-year-old retired and widowed police officer lived across town in a small brownstone. The woman Jake and his sister had hired as a live-in companion a year before when Henry—Hank—Cameron had had a stroke answered the phone. The captain had already gone to bed. Would he like her to wake him? Jake told her no, that he'd call another time.

Shades more restless, he ambled into the kitchen, where he drank a half quart of chocolate milk, his panacea for anything that ailed him, straight from the carton. He then went to bed. Miraculously, he fell asleep immediately.

The dream began immediately, as well.

The night was eerily quiet, and Jake could hear the adrenaline-rushed thumping of his heart. Robbery in progress. He could see the backup unit scattering to the rear of the office building. He could see his partner checking with him to coordinate their movement through the front door. Gun drawn, Jake nodded, flattened himself to the side of the wall and pushed through the door. Bright lights. Ransacked desk. Security guard lying dead on the floor. Suddenly, a man appeared in the doorway of the adjacent room. The man fired a gun. With trained precision, Jake steadied his own weapon and fired back, felling the man with a single shot.

"Got him...got him...got him..." echoed his dream partner.

"Got the punks coming out the back door," one of the officers from the backup unit announced.

"Then who...?"

"Oh, my God," came the voice of the newly arrived owner of the company, *"you've killed my controller...my controller...innocent man...innocent man..."*

Jake bolted upright.

Robin, too, jackknifed into a sitting position.

The dream was always the same. Black wreaths. A minister's monotone of "ashes to ashes, dust to dust." The image of a blood-splattered corpse. Blood... blood... blood...

Robin raked her fingers through her perspiration-damp hair, just as Jake raked his through his rumpled hair. Robin took a deep breath, just as Jake drew in an equally ragged lungful of air. Robin swung her legs to the side of the bed, just as did Jake. For a long while both sat thus, each unwilling to return to sleep, each unwilling to court further dreams, each unwilling to risk being stalked again by the tigers of the night.

CHAPTER TWO

HE WAS LATE, A FACT corroborated by the dozen pairs of eyes that expectantly looked up at him as he opened the conference room door Thursday night. Jake mouthed a silent and sheepish "Sorry," slipped to the back row of the circularly arranged folding chairs and slid into a seat. The woman presiding over the Wee Care meeting, presumably the nurse who'd formed the support group, smiled welcomingly, though she never missed a beat of what she was saying.

" . . . the purpose of the group is to offer the understanding that only someone who has walked, or is walking, in your shoes can provide. And to educate you concerning the preemie infant . . ."

Squaring ankle to knee, Jake unzipped his leather jacket, revealing the ivory, green and camel-colored sweater beneath. He ran his arm along the back of the vacant chair next to him.

" . . . so if you have any questions, feel free to ask them. If you have concerns, feel free to express them."

Jake glanced from the speaker, a woman in her early thirties, slightly dumpy, and with a face filled with compassion, to the other people in the room. The young couple at the front he recognized as the parents of one of the preemie girls. The older woman beside them was the same child's maternal grandmother. Same row, but farther around the circle, sat a couple he'd never seen before, which probably meant they visited their child in the mornings. Several other couples he saw occasionally, and the lone man he knew to be the father of the newest baby in the neonatal unit. So new was the baby, who'd weighed in at a relatively healthy four pounds, that the mother was still hospitalized.

Scanning the group, Jake methodically sought out the last figure, a woman who sat on the opposite end of the curve from him, a woman with shoulder-length, honey-brown hair. Hair that hung in fashionable and youthful ripples. Hair that swung full and free. Hair that belonged to the woman he'd prayed would be here tonight.

He'd hoped to see her during his volunteer session that afternoon, but she'd never appeared. All during his lonely dinner at a fast-food restaurant, he'd told himself that it would be best if he never saw her again, yet, as he returned to the hospital for the Wee Care meeting, he'd found himself hoping beyond hope that she'd be there. What he was engaged in was a subtle form of suicide—emotional suicide. He knew that...as well as he knew anything. But he couldn't help himself. The truth was that he was emotionally dying, anyway. From an overdose of guilt.

As though he'd willed it, Robin turned her head. Their gazes meshed. Slowly, Jake's lips curved into a smile. Robin, too, smiled in greeting, although her smile was tentative and shy. She immediately looked away, once more presenting her attention to the speaker.

Jake settled down to listen and watch...listening to the nurse and watching Robin Bauer.

"'Remember that it's okay to feel everything you're feeling. It's perfectly normal to feel cheated, frightened, angry—"

"What I hate the most," one of the women piped up, "is that I feel angry and that there's no one, nothing, to blame. David's being born early just happened."

Someone else agreed.

"I know," the nurse empathized. "You'd feel a whole lot better if you could go out and give someone or something a good swift kick, wouldn't you?"

Laughter followed, yet it was restrained. Jake supposed it was too heartfelt a subject to kid loosely about. He wondered if Robin Bauer was angry. Unlike the woman who'd just spoken, perhaps she knew exactly what to blame . . . or rather whom.

Jake had tried repeatedly to get Daniel Jacoby to give his professional opinion of just how much her husband's death had contributed to the early delivery, but the psychologist had dodged the question by saying he wasn't an obstetrician, nor was he familiar with the widow's physical condition. For that matter, he'd pointed out, he wasn't familiar with her emotional condition, for she'd firmly rebuffed his offer of assistance, an offer the department had made under the delicate circumstances. Dr. Jacoby hadn't had to answer Jake's question, however. The fact that he'd dodged it was answer enough.

Dr. Jacoby did share one thing with Jake, though. Curiously, possibly as some form of denial that only the grief-stricken woman understood, Robin Bauer appeared to have no interest in the police officer who'd shot her husband. It was enough that *a* police officer had shot him. For that reason, Jake had been advised not to contact her. But he had, anyway. Sick with the need to apologize, he'd phoned her, but the call had been intercepted by a man who'd identified himself as her father. Though polite, the man had asked him not to call back. Jake had then stammered an apology. The man had said nothing. Nothing! He'd just repeated his request that Jake not try to contact his daughter. Jake had hung up feeling like pond scum. He still felt that way, twenty-four out of every twenty-four hours in the dark day and darker night.

"But they're just so little," Jake heard another woman say and forced himself to turn his back on his guilt and pay attention to the meeting.

Someone else said, "My dog gave birth to puppies that were bigger than Sarah."

Again, titters of laughter skipped through the group. Again, they were laced with anxiety.

"Remember that a baby carried to twenty-eight weeks has everything in the way of body parts that it's going to have. They're just not fully developed. Remember also that each day, each week, your baby gets stronger, no matter how many weeks he was at birth."

"But some don't make it, do they?" The question came from one of the men and instantly cast a pall over the group. Jake noted that Robin's complexion paled from peaches and cream to ash-white. He also noted that her chin rose just a little bit in defiance.

"No," the nurse said softly but truthfully, "some are born so prematurely they're not viable. Some are viable, but develop complications. But by and large modern medicine, at least in this area, is in the business of doling out magic, and you just have to believe that your baby is going to get his or her share of that magic. You just have to take it step by step."

"Let's talk about when we can take them home," someone said, changing the subject to one that everyone, even Jake, was more comfortable with.

"Yeah," another agreed, "let's talk about taking them home."

The nurse smiled. "Somewhere around five pounds, if everything's going smoothly, which means that the baby is sleeping in an open crib, breathing on its own, maintaining its weight and body temperature . . ."

For the next few minutes, the room fairly glowed with expectancy, each parent fantasizing about that wished-for day. On that uplifting note, the meeting ended. Slowly, the people stood and began to talk among themselves.

Jake walked around the back of the semicircle of chairs and, his hands balled in the pockets of his jacket, headed straight for Robin Bauer. He told himself that what he was doing was tantamount to putting a loaded gun to his head. He did it anyway.

Robin, exchanging pleasantries with the couple nearest her, saw Jake approach out of the corner of her eye. Her pulse quickened, just the way it had when she'd seen him unexpectedly, yet so charmingly, sneak into the room. She really couldn't explain her altered heart rate, except she supposed it had something to do with feeling foolish about crashing her car into his. That and the fact that she had known he would say something to her before leaving. Did she want him to say something to her? She found it easier to just ignore the question . . . just the way she'd found it easier to ignore or deny certain aspects of what had happened during the past few tragic months.

"Hi," Jake said when the couple drifted away.

"Hello," Robin replied, tilting her head back to bring her eyes to his. She wondered again just how tall this man was. He was certainly taller than any other man in the room. Far taller than Gerald had been.

On the other hand, Jake was once more wondering just how short Robin was. She was also...the word *pretty*, straight from the shores of nowhere, sailed at full mast right into his mind. Abruptly, a grin nipped at the corner of his mouth. "I hardly recognized you without damp hair."

Robin returned his smile. No, Jake thought, he'd been wrong. She wasn't pretty, she was downright beautiful.

"I hardly recognized you without that disgusted look on your face," she said.

Jake's eyebrows, dark and full, arched in question.

"You know, the look a man always gets when a woman's just creamed his car."

Jake's smile broadened to dazzling. He couldn't remember having smiled so completely in a long while. "I was not disgusted. And I wouldn't exactly call denting my bumper creaming my car."

"Nonetheless, I'm sorry—"

"You've already apologized," he interrupted, adding, "Another isn't necessary." *Besides*, he thought, his smile waning, *I should be the one apologizing...for ruining your life.*

Robin could find nothing more to say, so she nervously fidgeted with the handbag strap that was slung across her shoulder. The action drew attention to the red cashmere sweater she wore.

Jake noted the attractive way the sweater fit her and the way it matched exactly the woolen skirt hanging in perfectly pressed pleats. The well-defined curves of both her breasts and hips, along with her high-heeled boots, suggested maturity, while the wide linen collar overlaying the sweater hinted at a youthful sweetness. Jake admitted that part of this woman's appeal rested in this seemingly incompatible duality.

"So, are you the parent of a preemie baby?" she asked finally when it became obvious that something was going to be necessary to fill in the silence that was looming larger and larger. She immediately answered herself with "Stupid question. Of course you're the parent of a preemie." She wondered where the child's mother was. Both times she'd seen this man he'd been alone.

"No, actually, I'm not. I'm a volunteer in the neonatal unit." At her look of surprise, he explained. "I'm relatively new...and the hospital encourages the new volunteers to attend the support group meetings. This, uh, this is my first meeting."

"Oh," Robin said, thinking that he didn't necessarily have a wife anywhere, then. Not that it mattered one way or the other. "I, uh, I haven't seen you in the nursery, have I?"

Because I've deliberately kept my distance, he thought, but answered vaguely with "I've only been working a couple of weeks."

She nodded, as if that explained everything. From there, silence once more descended. Again, Robin nervously shifted her handbag strap.

Abruptly, as though he needed to do it before he changed his mind, Jake pulled his hand from his pocket and extended it. "Jake Cameron," he said, envisioning the trigger of the gun, the one pointed at his head, cocked and ready to fire. A part of him hoped that Daniel Jacoby was wrong about her purposely keeping herself in the dark about the cop who'd shot her husband. That same part of him hoped that she recognized the name, hoped that she pulled the damned trigger, which was what he wanted—an at-last confrontation. Moreover, her pulling the trigger was what he deserved. It was obvious within heartbeats, however, that the name meant nothing to her. Another part of him breathed an inaudible sigh of relief.

Robin had no recourse but to take the hand offered her. She immediately felt her hand swallowed in the immenseness of his. The *warm* immenseness of his. "I'm Robin Bauer."

"I know," Jake said. "You're Peter's mother." *And why didn't I suspect that your hand would be as small as the rest of you?* Even as the thought crossed his mind, he felt the small hand leaving his. He fought the urge to draw it back.

At the mention of her son's name, Robin's face brightened. "You know Peter?"

"Know him? Your son and I are the best of friends." Robin's smile widened until its beauty caused Jake to feel as though he'd had a swift kick in the stomach. "Don't tell me he hasn't mentioned me," Jake teased.

It crossed Robin's mind that the laughing lights in this man's brown eyes looked a little incongruous next to the deep worry lines framing those same eyes. She also thought the laughing lights were irresistible. As were perhaps the worry lines, for they made a woman want to soothe them away with the tips of her fingers. This last she struck from her mind as she said, still with a smile, "You know, as a matter of fact, I think he has mentioned you."

"He probably mentioned that Big Mac, too, huh?"

Robin looked lost. Totally lost.

"I did not promise to bring him a Big Mac now that he's changed his eating habits," Jake said as though defending himself against serious allegations. "Although I can tell you he begged repeatedly."

Robin caught on quickly. "And for fries?"

"Of course. What's a Big Mac without fries?"

"And a milk shake?"

Jake gave a knowing look. "I can see he's hit you up, too."

The two adults laughed over the silly subject. Robin wondered when she'd last laughed. She honestly couldn't remember, although she knew it had to have been at least three months before. Something told her that it had been even longer than that, however. She and Gerald hadn't shared laughter in a while, principally because he'd grown quiet and serious, worrisomely moody. Then, too, he'd worked so much overtime that she'd rarely seen him. As always, the thought hurt, so she pushed it aside in order to savor the laughter a little while longer.

It was Jake who sobered first. "You must be very pleased that Peter's doing so well off the ventilator." Jake had checked first thing when arriving at the hospital to see if the baby had been removed as planned from the life-breathing machine. He had. Just that very morning.

"Yes," Robin said, equally serious. Several of the couples were ambling toward the door, bringing the evening to a conclusion. "I, uh, I was just on my way to see Peter. Well, actually, I can't go near him with this cold, but I can view him from the glass."

"I was just going to ask you about that cold."

"It's...it's hanging on," she said, adding, "My timing's lousy. I could hold him now that he's off the ventilator."

It dawned on Jake that this woman had never held her baby. He was certain that little on the face of the earth mattered as much to her. "Your timing is lousy, then, but look on the bright side, it'll give you something to look forward to next week."

She smiled. "Yeah."

The smile once more punched Jake in the stomach. "Look, I won't keep you," he said. "It was nice seeing you again."

"It was nice seeing you," Robin replied to the figure who was already taking backward steps toward the door.

"Tell Peter good night."

Robin nodded. "I will. And keep being firm on those Big Macs."

Jake grinned around a "You betcha" and walked from the room.

Minutes later, as Robin gazed down at her sleeping son, she realized that she still had the stranger's handkerchief, and that the *C* stood for Cameron. Jake Cameron. She had laundered the handkerchief on the off chance she saw him again. She had just had a golden opportunity. The question was, What had so preoccupied her mind that she hadn't remembered to give it back?

THE NIGHT WAS CLOUDY and held the promise of another cold, wet morn. Shuddering as the chilled air crowded about him, Jake dug into the small front pocket of his jeans and withdrew his keys. He had just rammed the key into the lock of the Jeep's door when he noticed the car parked across and over one. It was Robin's car and, though he couldn't tell clearly from where he stood, it looked suspiciously as if the headlight hadn't been replaced. Threading his way past the closely mated bumpers, he squatted in front of the car's grille. He frowned at the gaping socket that stared back.

Why hadn't she had the headlight repaired? A couple of legitimate possibilities presented themselves, but neither altered the fact that she was driving around without adequate headlights...and that in so doing was recklessly courting danger.

Coming to his feet, Jake stepped back to the Jeep, pulled open the door and, sprawling across the seat, unlatched the glove compartment. After a few seconds of rummaging, he found a grocery checkout list, the blank back of which would serve his purpose. After a few false starts, the pen he plucked from the compartment's murky bottom oozed enough ink to allow him to scrawl a terse message. He left the note, its ends flapping in the breeze, beneath the windshield wiper of Robin's car, then scrambled back inside his own vehicle and drove from the parking garage.

A SHORT WHILE LATER, snuggling deeper into her coat, Robin exited the hospital. Her mind was filled with warm baby thoughts. Was it her imagination or did Peter's thinly skinned bones suddenly look more padded with flesh? And was his hair, surprisingly thick even at birth, fuller and darker? He was going to have black hair like Gerald's with maybe that stubborn little cowlick....

The thought trailed off as she saw a slip of something trapped beneath the windshield. Frowning, she freed the paper. The message was simple and clear: *Stay put. Jake.* Robin's frown deepened as she eased into the car and out of the cold night. Though she must have asked herself *What's going on?* a thousand times during the next ten minutes, it never once crossed her mind to disobey the cryptic order.

She recognized the Jeep the instant it pulled into the parking garage and felt that crazy acceleration of her heart again. Sliding from the car at the same moment Jake slammed his door shut and started toward her, she watched him approach. Which was easy to do since he stood head and wide shoulders above the parked vehicles.

"Hi!" he called.

His voice, deep and rich and sounding as mellow as sunshine glazing a meadow, made her feel as if she'd suddenly been enveloped in a warm cocoon.

"Hi!" she called back. Seeing the bulb in his hand, she knew immediately what the note had been about. She felt oddly moved by the generous gesture. "You didn't have to do that, you know."

"I couldn't let you keep driving around with only one headlight. Besides, Peter asked me to take care of it." At the oh-sure-he-did grin that toyed with the corners of her mouth, Jake added, his own lips twitching, "I swear he did."

For seconds, they stood thus, almost smiling, but not quite. In that time, she noted the way the breeze tossed his silver-dusted dark hair about. He noted how the same breeze flirted with hers . . . and wondered if her hair was as soft as it looked . . . and if it was a lot of trouble to braid that single strip in front and draw it to the side. He'd never known a woman who braided her hair. It seemed old-fashioned. Endearingly old-fashioned.

"And did Peter tell you how I tried to get it replaced Tuesday night?" she asked around her almost-but-not-quite smile.

"It must have slipped his mind."

Robin recited her frustrating experience as Jake, nimbly and without invitation, hunkered down and began installing the new headlight. She absently observed the rippling play of thigh muscles beneath his tight jeans. Jeans that had been repeatedly washed to a comfortable, malleable, faded blue.

She went on to explain how she'd given in to the cold and fever Wednesday, bothering with nothing that wasn't absolutely necessary. Which translated to: she'd dragged herself out of bed solely to see her son. By that morning, she'd actually forgotten about the headlight and hadn't remembered it until she'd started into town for the Wee Care meeting that evening. By then it was too late.

"It's taken care of now," Jake said, completing the job in what seemed an incredibly short time.

"That's it?" Robin asked.

"That's it," he said, standing, gathering up the debris and rubbing his free hand down the length of his pants leg. "As much as I might like to show off my mechanical skills, I can't make the job any more complicated."

"I thank you as though it had been enormously difficult."

"You're welcome as though it had been enormously difficult."

Robin reached inside the car and picked up her purse. "Let me pay—"

"That isn't necessary."

"Oh, but it is. I ran into you, remember?"

"The answer is still no."

"But I insist upon paying at least for the part."

He stayed the motion of her fingers as they maneuvered the handbag clasp open. "No," he said softly, but with incontestable firmness.

As she had earlier when shaking hands, Robin got the impression of being buried beneath something far bigger than her. She also perceived warmth and a callused softness. Somewhere deep within her the stimuli registered as protectiveness. She intuitively knew that this man was good at protecting and because she needed—had needed for a long time now—to feel protected, she deliberately denied herself that comfort. Under the circumstances, with this strange man, it would be inappropriate. It was Robin who removed her hand from his.

"At least let me pay you for your time," she insisted.

"What time?" he asked, pulling back a hand that suddenly felt painfully empty. "It took less than a minute."

"But surely—"

"Look, if you want to pay me, buy me a cup of coffee."

Jake could see the wariness that jumped into her eyes, could hear her hesitancy in the long silence. He told himself not to push her, but push her he did simply by saying nothing.

Robin scoured her brain for a reason to refuse. She could find none, however. At least none that didn't sound petty in the face of his generosity. "Sure," she answered. "It would be my pleasure."

It would be less than that and Jake knew it, but he was going to take the coffee and her company any way he could get it.

"There's a diner right down the street," he said.

She nodded.

"You could ride with me," he suggested, motioning toward the Jeep.

"No! I mean, I'll follow you. That way you won't have to bring me back. Besides, I live in Lowell and this'll save me some time."

Jake acquiesced, knowing that he'd pushed as far as he could.

In the best tradition of diners, the establishment was small, quietly populated by a corps of loyal patrons and dedicated to a brief and simple menu. It was a place where time stood still, allowing one the rare opportunity to dawdle over a slow cup of coffee.

Robin shrugged her shoulders from her coat, and as though it were as natural as breathing, Jake reached up to assist her. Their gazes met briefly before he teamed her coat with his jacket and shoved both to the inside of the booth. He followed behind them, while Robin eased into the seat across the way. Within seconds, a thin, wiry woman wearing a ruffled white apron set two glasses of water before them.

"Evening," she said to Jake. "Your usual?"

"No, I'm going to trade chocolate milk for coffee tonight."

The waitress wrote the order on her pad as if it were too complicated to be remembered. "Well, now those cows are gonna be sorry to hear this. Unless, of course, you want cream with this coffee."

"My apologies to the cows," Jake said, "but I'll take it black."

"One black coffee," the waitress repeated, precisely making the notation before shifting her attention to Robin.

"The same. Except I'll take decaf."

"Black decaf coffee," the waitress said, and recorded this, too. She looked up from her pad. "Anything else?"

Jake glanced over at Robin.

"No, thank you," Robin answered.

"That'll do it," Jake said to the waitress.

An awkward silence descended the moment the two of them were alone. Jake could clearly see that Robin was having second thoughts about being talked into the outing.

"Are you from—"

"You obviously come here—"

They both spoke at once; they both smiled at the fact.

"Go ahead," Jake said.

"I was just going to say that you obviously come here often."

"Yeah. I live nearby." He didn't mention that he often stopped in at the end of a shift. That is, when he wasn't on leave waiting for the breakdown that everyone wondered if he was going to have. The one that he, too, wondered about. Just as he wondered how Dr. Jacoby would interpret his sitting across the table from Robin Bauer. Was this a sure sign that the breakdown was imminent?

Shoving the unsettling question to the back of his mind, Jake picked up one of the mugs of coffee the waitress had just left, took a sip and said, "You men-

tioned you had to drive to Lowell." He was lying. He
knew it. He knew, too, that it was the worst kind of
lie, the sneaky kind that implied you didn't know
something when in truth you did.

Robin nodded. "I live there. Actually, I was born
there, but I've lived in Boston the last few years. I
moved back to Lowell about three months ago after...after Peter's father was killed."

Jake's stomach knotted at the pain he saw on her
face, at the pain he'd heard in her voice. Like a true
masochist, he waited for her to say something more,
something that would give some inkling of how she
was coping, but she said nothing. It was as though she
crawled somewhere deep inside herself. Jake knew the
feeling. He spent a lot of time trying to find a peace-
ful spot within himself. Unfortunately, there didn't
seem to be one.

"I'm sorry about your husband," Jake said. *Sorrier than you can possibly imagine. Sorrier than I've
ever been about anything in my life.*

The sound of Jake's voice was warm and soothing,
and Robin let it wash over her like sun-kissed sea
waves. She didn't even question why it felt so good.
She only basked in the fact that it did. "Thank you,"
she said.

"How was Peter?" Jake asked, changing the subject to one that didn't hurt so much, and was guaranteed to bring a smile to Robin's lips.

The smile appeared. "Fine. He was sleeping." She
took a swallow of coffee, then asked, "You think babies dream?"

It was a provocative question that Jake considered
seriously. "Probably. Of warm. Of soft. And, in Peter's case, of Big Macs."

Robin's smile widened to match the grin suddenly teasing Jake's lips. She wondered when she'd ever seen such a captivating smile. Jake wondered pretty much the same thing about hers.

"So, tell me," he said, "is the support group helping?"

"Yeah, I think so. Just knowing there's someone else going through the same thing is a help. To be honest, though, I was reluctant in the beginning to join the group."

"Why?"

Robin idly outlined the handle of the mug with her forefinger. "I don't know, I just ... I just didn't want to talk about what had happened. I was so disappointed. Like most expectant mothers, I had pinned my hopes on a normal pregnancy, with my baby being full-term and healthy, and then when he wasn't ..." She shrugged gracefully, eloquently. "I was devastated. And I felt so sorry for Peter. He was so little and was struggling so hard, and I wanted to do something to help, but I couldn't. I couldn't even hold him."

"Were you angry?" Jake asked, remembering the discussion that had taken place earlier that evening at the Wee Care meeting.

"Yes," she said emphatically, even angrily. "I'd done everything the doctor told me to, I'd taken as good care of myself and my baby as I could, and still something happened."

"I, uh, I'm sure your husband's death didn't help." Jake held his breath, knowing the answer he'd hear and wondering why it was necessary to make himself feel worse than he already did.

Robin lowered her eyes and murmured, "No, it didn't."

Jake felt everything he knew he would—every dark shade, every hurting hue of the color of guilt. So immersed in his misery was he that at first Robin's next comment failed to make any sense.

"I felt sorry for that man tonight." At the inquiring look on Jake's face, she added, "The one who asked about some of the babies not making it. I could feel his pain."

"So could I," Jake said, remembering as well the palpable fear that had swum in the room. Phrasing the question as gently as possible, he asked, "Are you afraid for Peter?"

Robin raised her eyes to his and he thought how unfair that such beautiful eyes, green sprinkled with the purest of gold, should know such fear. She thought once more that his voice was probably the softest, the kindest she'd ever heard.

She took so long to answer that Jake thought she wasn't going to. "I'm sorry. I shouldn't have pried."

"Yes, I'm afraid," she said. "I know he's doing well, but I also know that he's still small and that complications can come out of nowhere. I'm just afraid that some day I'll go in and he'll be..." She didn't finish the statement...simply because she couldn't.

Jake longed to cover her hand, her oh-so-small hand, with his. Instead, he said, "He'll be all right. He has spunk. I can feel it."

Something in the consoling tone of Jake's assurance made Robin believe him. It, coupled with the other times she'd noted the gentle quality of his voice, stirred a memory of something she'd heard about a soothing, comforting voice, but she couldn't quite formulate it into a coherent thought.

"Yeah, he'll be all right," she repeated, imbuing the words with force, strength. "He's defied the odds all along, and he'll keep on defying them. He wasn't retarded, right?" Jake's raised eyebrow indicated his question. "The doctors thought he might be retarded," she explained.

"I hadn't realized that."

"My water started leaking a week before he was born, so they put me in the hospital and did everything they could to prevent his coming early. They were afraid that he'd be so premature he'd be retarded, but I guess the week I held onto him did the job, though he was still so tiny at birth. Only three pounds."

Even though the baby had weighed so little, Jake wondered how someone as small-framed as this woman had managed to give birth. Or had she delivered by cesarean? Jake realized just how intimate his thoughts were. At the same time, Robin realized how intimately she'd been talking to this stranger. She'd told him things about the birth of her child that a woman usually shared only with her husband.

Suddenly shy, she said, "Enough about me and Peter. Tell me how you got started working in the neonatal unit."

Jake momentarily hesitated in the act of bringing the mug to his lips. The request was as sobering as the dark brew. For a few minutes, as he'd listened to her speak of the difficulties with her son, he'd forgotten about his own problems. It had felt good. Now, however, his stomach tensed once more. Taking a slow swallow of the coffee, he did what necessity demanded: he hedged.

"I have some time on my hands right now and saw a piece in the newspaper about the neonatal unit needing volunteers. I thought it was something I'd like to do." *And I had this desperate need to see if you were all right.*

"They're lucky to have you."

"We'll see."

Jake sipped his coffee; Robin sipped hers. She wondered again why she'd shared so much with this stranger.

"I like your sweater," she said out of the clear blue.

Jake glanced down at the ivory, green and camel-colored sweater as if he'd forgotten what he was wearing.

"It's called a fisherman sweater," she offered. "According to legend, they were first woven in Ireland and the Hebrides. No two were alike in stitches or patterns so that, if a fisherman drowned at sea, the distinct design would identify the body if it washed ashore. The sweaters are also characterized by a textural openness."

Jake grinned. "You're a regular font of information concerning sweaters."

Robin grinned back. "That's what I do for a living."

"Make sweaters for men going to sea?"

Notes of Robin's laughter burst upon the air, and Jake thought how exquisitely lyrical the song was. "I design sweaters for men going anywhere. And for women. I sell them to a small boutique here in Boston." What she didn't say was that they sold for prices so high she could never quite believe anyone would pay that much for her work. Nor did she say that knitting had quite literally saved her sanity. After her husband's death, she'd knitted day and night because, in counting the stitches, she'd been forced to channel her mind away from her grief.

Old-fashioned. The word popped into Jake's mind. Yes, she was definitely, intriguingly old-fashioned. "My daughters gave me the sweater," he said.

"You have daughters?" Robin heard herself asking. She was keenly aware that it hadn't been the question she'd really wanted to ask.

"Two," Jake answered. "Rachel's sixteen, going on twenty-six, and Regan's twelve going on twenty-six." He paused, then volunteered, "I'm divorced."

Robin realized that he'd just answered the question she'd wanted to ask. She told herself that her curiosity was healthy and natural. She also told herself for the thousandth time that her marriage hadn't been coming apart at the seams. Sure, she and Gerald had had their problems, but they'd been working them out. Hadn't they? Yes, they had been. And Peter would have made everything perfect again. Equally for the thousandth time, she felt guilty even entertaining the notion that her marriage had been on the rocks. She also felt angry, angry at the circumstances that had taken him away, leaving her to feel forever that their marriage had been unresolved...and forever guilty that she felt that way.

"I, uh, I really ought to go," she said, sliding out of the booth with an unmistakable finality.

Her abruptness startled Jake—what had he said to bring such a swift end to the conversation?—yet he followed her lead and stood.

"Yeah, me, too," he said, reaching with one hand for the bill the waitress had earlier placed on the table, while with the other he gathered up their coats.

"No, that's mine," Robin insisted, plucking the bill from his big hand.

Jake didn't argue.

Less than a minute later, they were once more stepping out into the chilled night. Robin turned up her coat collar against the cold.

"Thanks for the coffee," Jake said, slipping his hands into the pockets of his jacket.

"Thanks for the headlight."

There was a slight pause before he added, "Well, I guess we'll see each other around."

"Right."

"Good night, then," he said.

"Good night," she answered, moving toward her car as Jake started for the Jeep. His fingers were already curled around the door handle when she called out a sharp "Wait!"

Jake turned.

"I keep forgetting to give you this." She rounded the hood of her car and handed him the handkerchief he'd lent her. At its wrinkled state, she said, "It's clean. I've just been carrying it around in my handbag."

He took what she offered. "It looks fine. You didn't have to bother, though."

"Yes, I did." She took a step backward. Then another. "Well, good night again."

"Good night," Jake said, watching Robin as she eased behind the wheel, started the motor and, without looking back, pulled out into the street.

Long after she'd disappeared, he crawled into the Jeep and stared down at the handkerchief. In that convoluted way the brain has, it suddenly reminded him of another handkerchief. That one he'd yanked from his hip pocket in an attempt to stanch the flow of blood from the man he'd just shot. But it had been too late. The man was already dead.

The man.

The stranger.

The innocent bystander.

As the sweet, subtle smell of perfume wafted from the handkerchief Robin had just returned, Jake wondered if guilt was as eternal as death.

CHAPTER THREE

THE NEXT EVENING, a long and lonely Friday evening, Jake heard the telephone ringing as he stepped from the steamy shower. Grabbing a towel and muttering darkly about someone's lousy timing, he made a mad, naked dash down the hallway. The bedroom, like the rest of the earth-hued apartment, was small, efficiently furnished and cleanly cluttered.

"Yeah!" he growled into the receiver in a tone that had been known to make criminals quiver and quake.

"Jake?" came a woman's voice.

"Hey, Sis," Jake said, his harshness immediately softening.

He shoved the towel through his wet hair before making several cursory swipes across his hair-covered chest. Then, lodging the receiver between his head and freckled shoulder, he wrapped the towel around his lean waist and secured it with a careless tuck. Heedless of the water still roaming through the spirals of hair on his legs, the same water puddling on the rust-colored carpet, he plopped onto the side of the bed.

"Let me guess," Whitney Ames began, and Jake could picture a mischievous smile jumping to her lips, "the length of time you took to answer the phone and your breathlessness mean I caught you in the middle of a torrid encounter with a flame-haired vixen."

Despite his mood, which was somewhere between hangdog depressed and angered-bear surly, Jake felt his lips twitch. "Try in the shower."

"Oh, that's delicious! You were in the shower with a flame-haired vixen. No," she said, immediately changing her mind. "I don't see flame-haired vixens as your type. How about blond-haired wenches? Nah," she said, discounting that idea entirely, as well. "Brunettes. I'm sorry, little brother, I see you only with brunettes. Tall and willowy brunettes. Buxomy brunettes."

An image of tawny-brown hair, a plaited strip clasped beneath a barrette, rushed to Jake's mind. Along with a petite stature and a figure that was full without being bosomy. He had no earthly idea why the image had invaded with such conquering force and, the truth was, he found it a little disconcerting that it had. He dealt with it by ignoring it.

"Try in the shower...alone," he said, thrusting his fingers through his hair and drawing a moist shag of it back out of his eyes.

"Ah, Jake, are you practicing for the priesthood again?"

"Ah, Sis, are you meddling in my love life again?"

"What love life? You haven't got anything that even resembles one. Hey, I'd like to remind you that even a penguin mates every year or so."

"And I'm sure if I wait long enough, you'll arrange a blind date with one."

"Funny. Real funny, *Father* Cameron. And listen, that last blind date I fixed you up with wasn't half bad."

"I thought you said it wasn't a date, that you just needed someone to, quote, socially round out a threesome, unquote."

"I said that?" Whitney asked sheepishly.

"You did. And by the way, Ms Not Half Bad spent the evening talking about her ex-husband."

"Oh. Well, listen, I know this penguin . . ."

Both Jake and his sister were grinning. God, he thought, what would he do without this crazy, meddlesome sibling? What would he have done without her these past few months? She'd been his Rock of Gibraltar when the world had spun out from under him. For that matter, she'd always been his anchor . . . just the way he'd always been hers. Four years his senior, forty-five to his forty-one, Whitney Cameron Ames had always doted on her younger brother. Oh, not that she hadn't screamed long and loud when he'd knocked over her dollhouse or when he'd smashed the sand castle she'd spent hours working on at the beach. The truth was, though, despite the normal sibling rivalry, they'd always been there for each other, during the good times and the bad. He'd been there for her when, in her mid-thirties and to the horror of their panicked parents, she'd decided to marry a man ten years older than she. He'd been there at the death of her firstborn. He'd been there five years later when she, her biological clock ticking dangerously fast, had given birth to a beautiful and healthy son. She'd been there for the birth of his two daughters and for the breakup, or rather burnout, of his eighteen-year marriage.

She'd also been the one to finally tell him straight-out that Daniel Jacoby wasn't merely suggesting he take a leave of absence from the police department, he was insisting upon it...and that she couldn't agree more with the good doctor's decision. She'd been the one to tell Jake, bluntly and cutting no corners, that he had to get his life back in order because, if he didn't get control, he was about to blow his distinguished career. Jake had hated hearing the words, but ultimately, had thanked Whitney for caring enough to say what had to be said. He knew she wouldn't approve of his insinuating himself into Robin Bauer's life, so he just wouldn't tell her...even if he could find the words to explain what he was doing.

Nor would he tell her that she was right about his love life. Hell, the penguin had him beat by a mile...by a year! Following the divorce three years before, he'd found it hard, and awkward, getting back into the dating scene. He'd never been good at casual sex, sex for sex's sake, especially coming from a long-standing marriage during which it had never crossed his mind to be unfaithful. It had stunned him to discover how much the mores had changed and just how willing women now were and just how much was expected of a man. In the beginning, he'd performed. He supposed he'd needed to prove that he still had what it took, but in the end it hadn't been his style. He'd discovered that he hadn't needed to prove himself, after all—at least not to himself. He'd discovered that he was looking for a relationship rather than a hot Saturday night.

Relationship.

His thoughts went back to the woman who was never far from his mind. What kind of relationship had Robin Bauer had with her husband? The perfect kind that came around once in a lifetime? The loving, adoring kind that turned kisses and caresses into sensual works of art? Had he worshipped her, cherished her, caused her to cry out his name in passion? Had he, Lieutenant Jake Cameron, with a single bullet, destroyed one of the world's great love affairs?

"Jake?"

He realized his sister had spoken.

"I said, how are you doing?"

A new wave of guilt, fueled by what he'd just been thinking, caused him to suddenly feel restless... explosive...ready to come apart at the seams. "Great! No breakdown as of yet. Course it's relatively early in the evening, so you might want to check the ten o'clock news."

His voice was laced with sarcasm, a sarcasm that, like a pair of shoes belonging to someone else, didn't fit him well. For all that he'd seen the seamier side of life, day in and night out as a cop, he'd managed to hang on to a basic optimism, believing that in the end everything worked out, that everything happened for the best, that there was some master plan to life. At least he'd managed to hang on to that optimism until three months ago.

"Cut it out, Jake," Whitney warned softly.

"You never can tell," he continued. "I just might go nutso, take my weapon and shoot up half the damned town."

"Stop it," came another quiet warning.

"Or, then again, and don't think I don't know this hasn't crossed everyone's mind, I might take the weapon and just pull a David Deliso." David Deliso was a Boston police officer who, two years before, had found himself in the exact same situation that Jake now found himself in—he'd killed an innocent by- stander in a bank shoot-out. David Deliso's way of coping had been to level the gray barrel of his gun to his temple and pull the trigger.

"Dammit, Jake, stop it!" Whitney's voice rang with equal notes of anger and fear.

Immediately, Jake felt contrite. The last thing he wanted was to upset his sister. Closing his eyes, he lay back on the bed, bringing his hand to massage his forehead as though the action would ease the headache that had burst across his brow.

"I'm sorry, Sis," he said, unaware that the towel at his waist had popped open to reveal the flat planes of his rock-hard stomach and the toned muscles of one thigh.

"Don't ever say that again," Whitney said, the order underscored with desperation. "I mean it, Jake, don't ever say that again." For a long while, neither spoke. Finally, Whitney said, "I've said this before, but I'm going to say it once more. The shoot was deemed a righteous one. The investigative board found not one thing to fault you for. You acted exactly the way any good police officer would have. You acted the way you'd been trained to."

"Yeah," Jake said, but the word was as flat as yesterday's promises. He was busy thinking that, for once in his life, why had he had to be so damned good?

"So, how's the volunteering going?" Whitney asked, obviously determined to leave the grim subject behind.

"Good," Jake said, thinking of Peter and his mother. "Actually, it's going real good."

"I'm glad," Whitney said, and, when she spoke again, her voice had once more grown serious. "Look, Jake, I hate to dump this on you now...I mean, I know you have enough on your mind...but..."

Jake could almost see his sister ruffling her fingers through her shorter-than-short, coal-black hair. "But what?"

Whitney sighed, a deep and weary sound. "I saw Dad today."

Jake's stomach knotted.

"Oh, Jake, I don't know what we're gonna do. Physically, except for being tottery, which heaven knows I guess he has a right to be at eighty-three, he's doing pretty good. He seems to have improved nicely following the stroke. He can speak again, he can use his right arm—"

"But," Jake interrupted.

"But," Whitney said, and he could hear her pain, "he's not an adult, anymore, but then again, he's not a kid. He can't balance his checkbook, but he gets all hurt and angry if I volunteer to do it for him. 'What do you think I am, senile?' he says. And he really isn't—senile, I mean—but sometimes he remembers more clearly what happened twenty years ago than he does what happened last week. I don't know, Jake. I don't know what we're going to do. The doctor keeps pushing for a nursing home, where he'd get medical attention twenty-four hours a day and have people his own age around him, but you know what Dad's going to say to that."

Jake knew only too well. The subject of a nursing home had been broached following the stroke. It had almost brought on another one. Yet, Jake also knew that with each visit he could see his father deteriorating, could see him unavoidably giving in to the ravages of time. The sight made Jake ache deep in his heart.

"I'm going to visit him tomorrow," Jake said. "Let me see if I can talk to him."

"I'm sorry, Jake. I know this is a bad time for you."

"Hey, we're in this together, Sis."

Jake heard his sister swallow and wondered if she were fighting at tears.

"Have I ever told you that as far as warty little brothers go, you're not too bad?"

"Have I ever told you that as far as bossy big sisters go, you're not too bad?"

"Hey, Jake, I know this penguin...."

Smiles on their lips, they hung up on that cheerful note. Jake's smile faded by sobering degrees. It was almost eight-thirty. The rain that had appeared off and on all week, now mixed with sleet, tapped at the windows. The light from the bedroom lamp whispered apologies for its frail paleness. Jake sighed. God, he was tired! Tired of worrying about his dad and tired of feeling guilty for an accident that had happened a quarter of a year ago. He was tired, as in weary to the bone, of wishing he could go back and change three seconds of his life. Three seconds. Dammit, that was all he asked for! Just three lousy seconds. He may as well ask for the moon, though, because life didn't oblige you by letting you correct your mistakes. It simply forced you to live with them.

He opened the drawer of the bedside table and stared down at the gun. It was an ordinary, plain-looking weapon, the weapon he'd had ever since he'd graduated from the academy, the weapon that had always been his best friend. Now, however, it was his enemy, an enemy that caused sweat to pop across his forehead and his pulse to race. Would there ever come a day when he and the metal beast would go back to their former amicable relationship?

He didn't know.

Dammit, he didn't know!

Flinging himself from the bed, Jake snatched up a clean pair of knit underwear and threw his legs into the clingy, soft cotton. He then slung his arms into a flannel shirt, which he left unbuttoned. Barefoot, he strode to the kitchen, where he opened the refrigerator and removed a carton of chocolate milk. The refrigerator door still ajar, the kitchen's coolness nipping at his unclothed legs and feet, he tilted the carton to his mouth. He drank long and hard. Chocolate milk might be a miraculous panacea, he thought, but he doubted that, if he drank every drop in the world, it could cure what ailed him.

For that matter, he was afraid nothing else could, either.

SOME THIRTY MILES AWAY, in the manufacturing city of Lowell—called the "spindle" city because of its textile beginnings—Robin stood at the window of her small rented cottage watching the same rain turn to bullet-like sleet. Despite the thick sweat suit she wore, a shiver skated down her spine. Even for the mature days of September, the weather had been cold, portending a blustery, frigid winter for the vulnerable Eastern seaboard. Gerald had loved the winter—the colder, the better. At least three or four times a season, he'd whisk her off to Vermont, where they would ski the snow-tipped hills and lounge before roaring fires, nursing cups of hot, buttered rum.

She recalled that as far back as the spring, he'd begun to make plans for the upcoming season. This year he'd wanted to invite his boss at Century Aeronautics, and the man's wife. He'd pointed out that it was good to hobnob with the people in power. While Robin hadn't shared this view, or for that matter, her husband's insatiable ambition, she hadn't argued. She had, however, reminded him that the baby was due in December and that she'd be breast-feeding, which eliminated the option of leaving the child with a sitter for any length of time. Gerald's reply, which he'd made without ever looking up from the column of figures he was adding together, had been that he guessed she'd have to stay home, then.

His response had hurt, though she'd told herself that he hadn't meant to be insensitive. His response had also left her feeling that somehow the baby was to be hers in a way it wasn't to be his. Robin let the sheer curtain fall from her fingers, blocking out the cold night as though it were a play that had ended. On a deep sigh, she turned away and walked toward the warmth of the stone fireplace. She deliberately avoided glancing over at the cardboard box that sat by the door, the box that the UPS carrier had delivered that afternoon. Instead, she forced her mind elsewhere.

To Peter.

She smiled. Even given the grief in her heart, it was so easy to smile when she thought about her son. Except this week she'd had a whole new set of frustrations to deal with in regard to him. Leave it to her to wait for four eternities to hold her baby and the minute she could, she comes down with a cold! Furthermore, she'd walked by the full-term nursery that morning, and the newborn babies there had seemed like giants compared with those in the neonatal unit. Predictably, the comparison had recharged her concern. Particularly since Peter hadn't gained any weight since being put under the oxygen hood, although the doctor assured her that he was responding normally. He had explained that babies often even lost weight at this point because breathing on their own consumed more calories.

Peter's doing fine, she told herself, though she felt the need to burn up some of the nervous anxiety that never seemed to fully sleep. In an attempt to do just that, she picked up the poker and jabbed at the fiery logs. The shifting wood hissed, while burnt-orange and scarlet-red sparks shot high and hot.

What would her son feel like in her arms? Soft? Warm? Cuddly? Would he be able to feel her love, a love she'd felt from the moment he'd been born? Actually, she'd loved him from the moment she'd realized that she was carrying him. Her love had increased with the swell of her belly, with each tiny kick, with each flutter of his precious life. Did this sweet, innocent infant have any idea how much she needed him? How desperately she needed to channel her love somewhere? How desperately she needed to know she wasn't alone?

As though her thoughts demanded it, her eyes strayed to the box.

It had arrived that afternoon by a route that was circuitous at best. It had gone from the hospital to the coroner's office to the police department to the Boston address that she and Gerald had shared. From there—possibly a neighbor had set it on its new, and last, journey—it had made its way to her in Lowell. The box, the accompanying letter explained in a cool, logical, unfeeling way, contained what her husband was wearing at the time of his death.

Funny, she hadn't even thought to wonder what had happened to his personal effects. Funnier still, she couldn't for the life of her recall what he'd been wearing that night. She wished she couldn't recall anything else about that night, either. She especially wished that she couldn't recall that they'd fought.

At the remembrance, Robin's heart grew as heavy as lead. She recradled the poker and stepped toward the box. Picking it up, she carried it to her bedroom, where she deposited it, unopened, in the bottom of her closet. She didn't want to look inside; she didn't want to remember that night; she didn't want to remember Gerald's needless death. No, murder, she amended. She didn't want to remember Gerald's needless murder. Because remembering that night, remembering that she'd never again see Gerald, remembering that her son would never know his father, hurt so badly that it literally took her breath away.

An hour later, forcing herself to finish a ham on rye sandwich that she didn't want but told herself she needed, she ambled back into the living room and the crackling fire. Easing onto the stool sitting before her drafting table, she scanned the sketches she'd made earlier in the day. All in all, they were good, but needed fleshing out. Taking pencil in hand, she started drawing, but stopped after only a few strokes. She just wasn't in the mood.

Damn, she hated the weekends! They were neverending. Reminding herself that this was only Friday night did nothing to sweeten her sour mood.

Restless, she moved to the sofa, kicked off her shoes and curled her socked feet beneath her. She reached for a knitting magazine. The first article extolled the virtue of 100-percent pure Irish wool; the second was an in-depth look at the Blackberry Stitch. Neither article held her fast-fleeing attention. Finally, in order to save her sanity, or what little was left, she scooped up the wicker basket of yarns that rested beneath the coffee table, selected one at random and positioned her needles. Without any purposeful goal she began to knit.

Knit...purl...knit...purl...knit...purl...

She could feel her tension ebbing as her mind focused anew. Somewhere in the far corner of her consciousness, she still wondered what it would feel like to hold Peter in her eager arms. In the same far corner of her mind—so far away that it in no way threatened her—she realized that the yarn she'd selected was brown.

Brown as in rich and dark.

Brown as in steeped coffee and shiny mahogany.

Brown as in the color of Jake Cameron's hair and eyes.

THERE WAS NO DOUBT whatsoever where Jake got his imposing height and sturdy structure. Even though age had warped his frame, Henry Cameron—Hank to everyone who knew him—still sat tall with shoulders that were admittedly swayed, but reminiscent of strength and solidity. That very reminiscence knifed at Jake's heart Saturday afternoon, achingly reminding him of the countless times his father had tossed him, then a squealing child, high in the air. That same man, never stingy with, or embarrassed by, emotion, had crushed him with a thousand loving bear hugs. The tossing days were over, however, just as were the crushing ones.

Not for the first time, Jake bitterly reflected that you ought to be rewarded for growing older, not penalized for it. Surely it was only fair, after years of hard work and raising a family and struggling to keep body and soul and principles together during a daily grind that chipped away at you, that you receive some compensation for having weathered the bastard called life. Instead you got just the reverse in the forms of deterioration and senility. In short, you got your teeth kicked clean down your throat. That is, if you were lucky enough to have teeth to kick.

"Hi, Pop," Jake said softly, uncertain whether his father, who sat in an overstuffed lounge chair with a colored afghan draped across his lap, was catnapping or merely had his eyes closed. In the background the television was playing, and Jake idly noted that the housekeeper, one very Irish Mollie Murphy, stepped toward it and turned down the volume. She then left the bedroom, discreetly pulling the door shut behind her.

At the sound of Jake's voice, the elder Cameron opened his brown eyes, focused them from behind bifocals and smiled. "Hey, Boy," he said, reaching out his hand in search of his son's.

Jake took the thin-skinned, prominently veined hand in his, thinking that his father had always called him Boy. He'd been a boy at six, he'd been a boy at sixteen—much to his dismay. Wasn't his father ever going to realize that he was a man? He'd been a boy at twenty-six and thirty-six, and Jake knew now that he'd be a boy until his father's dying day. At least in his father's mind. Jake knew, too, that he wished desperately that that were the truth. But it wasn't. Somewhere along the way—when had it happened?—their

roles had become reversed. He had become the father, his father the son. A jagged bolt of anger tore
through Jake, leaving him to hurt as if his flesh had
been ripped open. Dammit, he didn't want to be his
father's father! He wanted to be his father's son—his
father's boy.

"You behaving?" Jake asked, sitting in the chair
across from his father. He still held the elderly hand.

"At my age, what is there left to do?"

Jake grinned. "I thought I'd find you chasing Mrs.
Murphy around the bed."

Hank snorted. "You sound like your sister. She calls
Mollie my raven-haired wench. I'd like to know what
the heck you two think I'd do with Mollie the Wench
if I happen to catch her? By the time I got the equip-
ment working, I'd forget what I wanted it for." Jake
laughed and allowed his father to pull his hand away.
"That danged TV isn't nothing but racket, but Mollie insists I keep it on. She's got this mistaken notion
that I'm lonely." The older man reached for the re-
mote control and attempted to shut off the television.
Instead, he merely raised the volume to a blaring level.

"Here, let me, Pop," Jake said, taking the control
and bringing an instant, and blessed, silence to the
room. Was his father lonely? Hell, how could he not
be, going for weeks without seeing anyone but the
family and Mollie Murphy. Companionship with his
peers was but one of the many advantages that a
nursing home would offer.

"Want something to eat?" Hank asked.

"No, thanks."

"Mollie made a cake..."

"I don't want anything, Pop."

"...coconut, I think...no, maybe carrot..."

"I don't want anything, Pop."

"...coffee...she could get you some coffee...."

"Pop, I don't want anything!" Jake said firmly, then wondered if he'd spoken too firmly. "I just had lunch. I'm not hungry."

"Oh, you just had lunch, huh?"

"Yes, sir."

"I guess Mollie'll be bringing mine in a little bit."

The statement gouged at Jake. It was one-thirty. He knew his father had already had lunch. The housekeeper had told him so minutes before.

"You've had lunch, Pop," Jake said, trying to make his voice sound normal.

"Have I?" The senior Cameron looked perplexed, then added, for a moment sounding and looking like the younger man that Jake remembered so well, "Well, did I enjoy it?"

Jake grinned. "You must have. Mrs. Murphy said you ate all of it."

"Then, I guess I enjoyed it...or else the wench badgered me till I gave in." The twinkle disappeared from Hank's eyes and he said, though trying to make it sound as if it were no big deal, "Sometimes I can't remember things."

Again, pain, like a ruthless knife, sliced at Jake, but he tried to ease his father's concern. "We all forget sometimes." *At least the lucky ones,* Jake added silently, sarcastically. No matter how hard he tried, he could never forget for a minute that he'd taken an innocent man's life. Nor could he forget the grief-stricken widow that innocent man had left behind. Nor the child who would never know his father.

Sighing, the old man passed his age-dappled hand across his bleary eyes. Jake half expected him to say more on the subject, but his father didn't. Jake wondered if he'd already forgotten what they'd been talking about.

"Whitney said she came by," Jake volunteered.

Hank nodded his head, which was bald except for a thin white fringe of hair. In contrast, his eyebrows, the same snow-white, bushed thick and full.

"Rachel and Regan said to tell you hello. I have them next weekend. I'll bring them by to see you."

The senior Cameron nodded again, then said, "A man should see his kids more than every other weekend."

The words echoed Jake's own thoughts and feelings. Their honest truthfulness hurt. So badly that Jake rose from the chair and stepped to the bedroom window, where he stuffed his hands into the back pockets of his jeans. "I know, Pop, but that's the way divorce works."

How did you explain to a man who'd been married to the same woman for forty-two years that your marriage had ended after only eighteen? And for reasons you had only the skimpiest idea about? How did you explain that one day, without the slightest warning, your wife had come to you and announced that she needed to find herself and that she couldn't possibly make that voyage of discovery married to you? How did you explain that months after the divorce, she'd remarried? Jake had never had the nerve to ask if she'd been unfaithful to him. The truth was—and this had shocked him—he didn't much care if she had been. Somewhere along the way, some unguarded night when they hadn't held each other tightly enough, they'd drifted apart.

Not bothering to analyze why, Jake found his thoughts going to Robin Bauer. Intuitively, after only two meetings, he knew that she wasn't the kind of woman who'd leave a man to find herself. She wasn't the kind of woman who'd have to. She would have always known where to find herself. Women of substance always did.

"Your mother and I were married forty-two years," Hank said in a tone not so much accusatory as puzzled that the new generation didn't possess such marriage skills.

"I know, Pop," Jake said, staring out at the sun struggling to shine through a rain-washed sky, staring out at the yard where he and his sister had played as children.

This small three-bedroom brownstone, simply decorated, had been the only home he'd known as a child. Furthermore, it had been the only house that Hank and his bride had ever lived in. Daisy Cameron had been dead for ten years, yet Jake knew that her clothes still hung in her closet, just as her picture still rested on the mantel . . . right next to the distinguished service medals that the Boston Police Department had awarded her husband . . . right next to pictures of her children and grandchildren . . . right next to the endless bric-a-brac she'd collected over the happy years. Jake knew that in asking his father to go to a nursing home, he was asking him to give up more than his home. He was asking him to give up his past, to give up a way of life he'd known for almost half a century, to give up his life with Daisy Cora Cameron.

Did he, or anybody, have that right?

Yet didn't he have a responsibility to take care of his father as his father had once taken care of him? Even though it meant forcing unwanted things that were for his own good?

Dammit, Jake thought once more, he didn't want to be the father! He still needed his father's wise counsel. He wanted to say, "Look, Pop, Whitney and I have this problem. The doctor thinks you should go into a nursing home and we just don't know what to do. Advise us the way you have all these years. Tell us what the right and just thing is."

Jake sighed. He also wanted to discuss the shooting incident with his father, but wasn't even certain that his father remembered his telling him about it. He'd never mentioned it again, and Jake, not wanting him to worry, had never told him about taking the leave of absence. He longed, too, to tell him about hazel-eyed Robin Bauer and her blue-eyed son. He longed to have his father tell him that everything was going to be all right.

"Pop," Jake began, still peering out the window at the watery sun, "there's something I want to talk to you about." He took a deep breath and forced himself to speak around the sudden constriction in his throat. "Whitney and I spoke yesterday. She said that the doctor thinks you ought to consider moving into a nursing home."

There, it was out! Said and done!

Jake waited for a reaction. None came. Finally, he could stand the suspense no longer and turned around. His father still sat in the lounge chair. The afghan was still spread over his lap, with the tips of his worn house shoes peeking from beneath. His hands were placidly, prayerfully clasped together, while his head lolled gently to the side. His eyes were closed, and his breathing was soft and regular.

Hank Cameron was fast asleep.

For a moment, defying his age, defying his masculinity, Jake wanted to cry. Because his father hadn't heard a word he'd said. Because his father had grown old and there was nothing Jake could do to change that fact. Instead of crying, as silently as possible, he stepped forward and tucked the afghan around the sleeping, aged form. Leaning forward, he kissed his father on his furrowed forehead.

"I love you, Pop," he whispered, and walked quietly from the room.

CHAPTER FOUR

"HI," JAKE SAID TUESDAY morning to the woman wistfully peering into the nursery through the glass partition. He had expected to find Robin at the hospital—that was why he'd switched his volunteer session from afternoon to morning—but he'd expected to find her inside the nursery rather than outside looking in. Especially since she could now hold her son.

At the soft-spoken voice, Robin turned. Surprise danced across her hazel eyes, a surprise accented with pleasure.

Pleasure? Maybe he was simply reading into her reaction what he wanted to see because, the truth was, he was pleased to see her. The weekend had been hellishly long, with one tedious, boring hour crawling into another. Monday had been the bitter icing on the bitter cake. If Tuesday had dawned a half hour later, the men in white coats would have carted him off to the funny farm.

"Hi," Robin said, vaguely aware that her stale spirits had just been partially revived.

Jake nodded toward the nursery. "I thought you'd be inside rocking Peter."

Robin's recently revived spirits plummeted. "I thought so, too."

Jake heard every flat note of her disappointment. "What's the deal? I thought once your cold...your cold is better, isn't it? You don't sound stopped up like last week."

Robin's disappointment turned to thinly disguised sarcasm. "Oh, the cold's fine now," she said, absently swiping at a sprig of hair clinging to her cheek, "but leave it to me to get a fever blister. They have a whole list of things they won't let you in the nursery with. A fever blister's one of them."

The fever blister had appeared Sunday morning. The following morning, the nurse had explained that fever or stress could have been the culprit. Whichever, she couldn't go near the baby.

At the mention of the blister, Jake's gaze dropped to Robin's lips. Now that his attention had been called to it, he could see the blemish. Tiny though the cluster of blisters were, they nonetheless were there. Just at the corner of her mouth, hidden beneath a sheen of pale pink lipstick.

Was her mouth as soft as it looked?

The question startled Jake. Why in hell had that even crossed his mind? He rushed his gaze back to hers. "I'm, uh, I'm sorry. I know how much you'd been looking forward to holding Peter."

Robin shrugged her shoulders stoically. Her small shoulders, Jake thought. Her incredibly small shoulders that continually seemed to have one burden after another heaped upon them.

"In a few days," she said, then attempted a smile. "How long can a fever blister last?"

Jake's gaze dropped back to her lips. Yeah, he thought, they'd be soft...soft enough to destroy a man's sanity. If the question concerning her lips had stunned him, the conclusion he'd reached blew him away. Something deep within him told him that this whole line of thinking was inappropriate. Damned inappropriate!

"You're right," he said, his eyes once more firmly fixed on hers. "How long can a fever blister last?"

"End of the week, max, I figure."

"Max," Jake repeated. Despite her brave attitude, he could feel her frustration. Hell, it was a frustration he felt for her! He racked his brain for something that would make her and him feel better. He came up with nothing.

Robin nodded toward the door. "You'd better get to work." She smiled. "It looks really bad when they fire a volunteer."

Jake grinned. "They wouldn't dare."

Neither said anything for a few seconds. Finally, Robin spoke: "It was nice seeing you again." Strangely, she realized she meant it. For all that something in his eyes hinted that he himself might not be fully at peace, this man had the power to make her feel better. It had something to do with his voice. Again, there seemed to be something that she should remember about a soft-spoken voice, but she couldn't get the memory fragments to coalesce into a whole. It dawned on her that she didn't do her best, and clearest, thinking around Jake Cameron. It had taken her a while just to remember to return his handkerchief.

"Yeah, nice seeing you, too." He took a step, then another before reaching for the door handle.

"Wait!"

He halted. Turned around. Locked his eyes onto hers.

"Will you give this to the nurse?" Robin asked, holding out a paper sack.

Until that moment, he hadn't even realized that she'd been holding anything. Possibly because the sack had been lost somewhere in the folds of the coat draped over her arm.

At what must have been an inquiring look, she added, almost shyly, Jake thought, "It's milk. For Peter."

At first, he couldn't make sense out of what she'd said. Why would she be bringing milk— Suddenly, he understood. She was going to breast-feed. Which, now that he'd realized it, didn't surprise him at all. As naturally as breathing, just as his eyes had lowered to her lips when she'd spoken of a fever blister, so did they now lower to her breasts. She wore a pink clingy sweater that subtly sculpted her feminine form. The same color pink stole softly, prettily, into her cheeks. Jake's eyes once more found hers, but not before both of them felt that someone had siphoned a little of the oxygen from the atmosphere.

"Sure," he said, taking the sack. It made a crinkling sound that seemed loud within the empty hallway.

"Thank you," Robin said. "I appreciate it."

"No problem."

Jake's free hand wrapped again around the door handle. He pulled. The door opened.

"Jake!" she called out, this time stopping him with the intimacy of his name. For some reason, he was a little surprised that she'd used it. She was surprised, too. Maybe more than a little. "I, uh . . ." She took a step toward him. A beseeching step? "I was wondering if you'd . . . if you'd hold Peter for me."

The sweetness of his name on her lips had not had time to settle about his senses before the sweeter-yet request drizzled over him. Nothing that she could have said or done would have better defined a mother's love, nor would anything have more accurately given the measure of this woman. She was unselfishly asking something for her son, something that she herself longed to give him, but couldn't, something that it would hurt like hell to see someone else giving him. Jake felt suitably awed.

"I mean, if you have time," she added, as though now feeling that she'd been too presumptuous. "It's just that he's never been held...and I've read that human contact is important...and...and...I'll understand if you don't have time. I mean, I'm sure you need to tend to all the babies." She suddenly looked as if she wished she hadn't brought the subject up. "I'm sorry. I don't know what I was thinking of. You don't have time—"

"I have time," Jake interrupted, thinking that, even if he didn't have time, he'd make it—if he had to move heaven and earth. "That's what I'm here for. Look, you stay where you are, and I'll drag the rocker over by the window." He grinned. "What message do you want me to give Peter for you?"

"Uh, tell him hello...and that I want to come see him, but can't...and that—" she swallowed "—and that I love him."

And that you're about to cry because you want so badly to hold him.

Jake's grin faded. "Are you sure? Don't you want to wait until—"

"No. I'm sure."

For long moments, they just stared at each other.

Finally, Jake repeated, "I'll bring the rocker over by the window."

Robin nodded, then watched as Jake disappeared through the door. She stepped back to the wide wall of glass and looked down at her son. His eyes were open and occasionally his hand, the one still taped with intravenous tubing, jerked. The tube that continuously fed him her diluted milk ran down his throat. She still hated the tubes and wires, yet, little by little, they were changing to something more tolerable to look at or were disappearing altogether. The ventilator hose, which had been taped to his mouth, was gone—thank God!—leaving his mouth in plain view. Even as Robin watched, Peter pursed his tiny little lips into a tiny little moue.

She smiled.

"Hi, Peter," she whispered, tapping quietly on the glass. He didn't look toward her, but then she hadn't really expected him to. One day he would, though. One day soon. "It's Mommy, darling. I miss you. Listen, Jake—Mr. Cameron—you remember him?— well, he's going to hold you . . . just the way I would if I could . . . but I can't . . . I have a fever blister and . . ."

She stopped, feeling tears well in her eyes. No! she told herself, blinking, she would not cry. That was stupid. There would be plenty of times when she could hold her son. The important thing was that he was going to be held. She would not selfishly lose sight of that fact.

When Robin next saw Jake, he had traded his coat for a pale green sterile gown, which, incredibly, made him look taller, bigger, like a giant afoot in a small land. He was talking to one of the nurses. Robin saw her nod. Effortlessly, Jake picked up a rocker and carried it toward the window. He smiled at Robin as he set it down and mouthed, "Close enough?"

"Yes," she returned.

Still watching, she followed Jake as he stepped to Peter's bed. She saw his lips move as he spoke to the baby and wondered what he'd said. She could feel the gentleness with which he pulled back the fleecy blue blanket and felt the diaper spread beneath the infant.

Jake looked up and again mouthed, "Wet. Very wet."

"Sorry," she mimed back.

With movements that were speedy and sure, Jake rediapered the baby, this time molding the fabric to the child's lean hips and sealing the tabs. Even though the diaper was specially designed for preemie babies, Peter still looked lost inside it. Just as he looked lost in the little flannel shirt that fit over his frail chest. Abruptly, Robin was reminded just how small her baby was. She experienced a wave of panic.

He's doing fine. The doctor says he's doing fine. And he'll continue to do fine. He has to.

Forcing her thoughts in a more pleasant, positive direction, Robin looked on as Jake bundled the baby in the blanket. He gave her a thumbs-up, indicating that Peter was ready. She returned the thumbs-up...and felt her heart rate accelerate.

In seconds, Jake had called to the nurse, and she, stepping forward with a smile for Robin, helped Jake adjust the wires and tubes as he prepared to lift the infant. Slipping the oxygen hood, which resembled a clear plastic helmet, from the child, Jake scooped the swaddled baby into his hands. He also picked up the tube bleeding oxygen into the air and, sitting down in the rocker, immediately, deftly, adjusted the tube so that the oxygen blew across Peter's nose.

A dozen thoughts, all disjointed and disconnected, flitted through Robin's mind. She remembered one of the nurses telling her that babies breathed only through their noses. She was aware of thinking that Jake Cameron was a natural with a baby, that he obviously didn't feel the slightest bit awkward. Even Peter's smallness didn't seem to faze him. Had he had experience with preemie babies? She'd have to ask him sometime, a part of her noted, while another part watched, fascinated, yet frightened, as the nurse evaluated all the readouts from the machines to see if Peter had tolerated the move all right. She knew the nurse would also be checking the baby's color to make certain he wasn't turning blue from lack of oxygen. Robin hadn't realized that she'd been holding her breath until Jake smiled up at her. Even though the nurse simultaneously stepped away, indicating that everything was all right, it was Jake's smile that validated the baby's well-being. Robin let out a deep, relieved sigh.

She also wondered if anything on the face of the earth was as beautiful as Jake Cameron's smile. On the other hand, Jake was wondering if there was anything more beautiful than the glow on Robin Dauer's face.

As though it were vital to her very life, Robin peered through the glass, trying to see the baby's every movement. She took in every squirm of the blanket, every tiny kick of a tinier leg, every flutter of an arm. With each, she felt her heart turn over with pride, with love, with longing. How she wanted to be the one holding her son!

Jake watched as Robin, her hands flat against the glass, pressed herself as closely to the nursery window as possible, as though she were trying to absorb every sight, every sound, every *feel* of the baby. He sensed her maternal need, a need both sweet and savage—so sweetly savage that he could feel her gut-deep, her heart-deep, pain. She wanted desperately to be holding her child.

Drawing the blanket from the baby's crinkled face, Jake angled Peter where she could best see him.

Robin stepped closer, daring to become one with the window.

What does he feel like? her eyes asked hungrily.

"He's heavy," Jake mouthed.

"Is he?" Robin whispered back, knowing that he couldn't be truly heavy, but allowing herself to luxuriate in the fantasy that he was heavier than he looked.

"And wiggly."

She smiled.

"And soft."

Robin's smile widened.

"And he smells like baby powder."

Robin's grin turned into a giggle. Jake heard it through the glass. Or imagined that he did. On some far distant level of thought Jake acknowledged that the tube running down Peter's throat was carrying this woman's milk to his stomach. He remembered wanting his wife to breast-feed their two daughters, but she hadn't wanted to. Jake had never been quite sure why. Though he'd been absolutely sure of his disappointment.

Similarly, Robin was thinking about Jake—how strong and capable he was, how Peter seemed to just fit in the crook of his big arm, how his jeans-clad legs were squared in a way that looked decidedly masculine.

"He's doing fine," Jake said, this time uttering the words aloud. Robin could barely hear him, but hear him she did. The words brought another smile to her lips . . . as she let the thought about how masculine the square of his legs was slip comfortably from mind.

Time passed.

Jake rocked.

Robin watched.

The baby blinked, pursed his lips, made a little sound that was half whimper, half gurgle, and wholly heard by his mother.

Robin swallowed back the knot of emotion clotting her throat. Gerald would never hear that sweet sound, nor would he ever hold their son the way this man was. Oh, God, forgive her for being so selfish, but she wanted to hold Peter in her own arms, so desperately that the want was a coiling, curling pain!

Minutes later, when the child's eyelids drifted shut, Jake glanced up at Robin and mouthed, "He's asleep—"

Jake stopped, instantly registering the glassy sheen to Robin's eyes. His heart constricted. She was being so brave, so unselfish, but she was hurting. She wanted to be the one holding her baby. Slowly, her eyes connected with Jake's and for long knowing moments the two of them stared, sharing something that neither of them could have explained.

Don't cry, his eyes pleaded.

Hers just seemed to focus on him as though he were the only person left alive.

Suddenly, Peter stirred, shifted.

Jake glanced down. For just a second. When he looked up, Robin was gone.

JAKE WRAPPED HIS FINGERS around the wall telephone, but, as if it were bubbly hot, he jerked his hand away. No, he wouldn't call her! And that was definite! Final! Besides, what would he say? I've been worried crazy about you all afternoon, ever since you split from the hospital like a house afire? I've vacillated back and forth about calling until I'm dizzy? I've been dying inside at the thought of your eyes glazed with tears? Oh, and by the way, did I mention that I'm the policeman who shot your husband?

Groaning, Jake shoved his fingers through his already tousled hair. He looked over at the clock, which was mounted slightly askew above the refrigerator. The clock looked back, taunting him with the hour of eight-thirty. Eight-thirty. How could it be only eight-thirty? Surely that was a mistake. Surely it was later than that. Surely it would be appropriate to call and see if she was all right.

Wouldn't it?

Yeah, it would.

Sure, it would, he thought, reaching for the phone again and punching in the number he'd gotten earlier from directory assistance. In fact, she might think it strange if he didn't call. Certainly he wouldn't have to explain his concern. Anyone would have—

Dammit, no! he thought, slamming the receiver back onto the hook. He'd already violated the rules of common sense by getting involved with her as it was. To say nothing of what he'd done to the rules of ethics. At the very least, he'd bent them so out of shape that they, like him, threatened to crack any minute. No, he'd use what sanity he had left and—

The phone rang, splitting the silence wide open. Jake uttered a colorful profanity into the newly cleaved chasm of sound. He also yanked the phone from its cradle. "Yeah?" he barked.

"Well, I guess that answers my question," a man said.

"What question?" Jake asked, recognizing the voice of Dr. Daniel Jacoby. Despite himself, he felt his mood lighten. Officially, the psychologist might be the department's shrink, but, unofficially, he'd proven himself a friend.

"How you're doing. You're obviously doing tensely, leaning in the direction of clinically grumpy."

"Clinically grumpy?" Jake mimicked as he eased onto a bar stool and hitched a worn tennis shoe over one of the rungs. "Is that a psych term?"

"Yeah. And it's chiefly characterized by the crabby answering of the telephone. What's wrong, pal, haven't had your chocolate milk today?"

"Here, drink this. It isn't chocolate milk, but it'll have to do."

Jake could hear Daniel's order as though it had been given yesterday instead of months before. He could also hear the glass of amber-colored, warm scotch rumble across the doctor's desk. Less than an hour before, he'd shot and killed Gerald Bauer—not that he'd known his name then, but he had known that he'd been an innocent bystander. Following standard operational procedure, Jake had immediately been relieved of duty until the incident could be investigated. Just as typically, adrenaline had been pumping hard and fast through Jake's veins. Usually quiet and unnervingly steady in a crisis, he'd suddenly found that he now couldn't shut up, couldn't sit still and couldn't stop the shaking that seemed to be coming from the very core of his being.

"Hey, you there?"

The question drew Jake back from the grim past to the troubled present.

"Yeah," he answered. "As a matter of fact, I haven't had my chocolate milk today." Even as he said it, he thought that again scotch might be more suitable, that it was going to take something potent and strong to burn away the memory of gold-green eyes on the verge of crying.

"Okay, let's cut the chitchat crap," Daniel said. "How are you doing?"

"How do you think I'm doing? I'm tense and clinically grumpy. And bored. Are you sure taking time off is what I need? It gives a guy a lot of time to think."

"I thought you were doing some volunteer work."

"Two days a week," Jake replied, feeling a pang of guilt. He'd deliberately kept his volunteer activities vague, because the psychologist, knowing the Bauer baby was at Brigham and Women's Hospital, might be clever enough to put two and two together.

"Your taking it easy is the point, Jake," Daniel said seriously. "You need time to heal. You've already made progress."

And just how long was the healing process going to take? Jake thought. And just what progress would his friend think he was making if he knew what he had done?

"So how's everything down at the station?" Jake asked, deftly changing the subject.

For the next few minutes the two men discussed various individuals who were with the Boston Police Department. Jake even managed a couple of smiles and several "That sounds like him." Through it all, a feeling of restlessness gnawed at him. He wanted to be at work. That plain, that simple. Like his father before him, probably because of his father's positive influence, he was a cop. He could never remember wanting to be anything else. That hadn't changed. The only thing that had changed was that now he was emotionally crippled . . . and the last thing the department, and the good and trusting citizens of Boston, needed was a crippled cop.

"Yeah, well, tell the guys hello," Jake said, the restless feeling now doing more than gnaw. It actually took a few sharp, tearing bites.

"Will do. And, look, do yourself a favor. Take life easy right now, okay? Just lean back, relax and mellow out. It also wouldn't hurt to find a good-looking woman to occupy your mind and/or body."

"Is that your professional opinion?"

"Yeah. Sex is therapeutic."

"You've been talking to my sister, right?"

Daniel laughed. "Listen to her, Cameron."

"Yeah, well," Jake hedged, though his thoughts did roam to a woman. A woman with green eyes dusted with gold. A woman who wore her heart in those eyes. A woman valiantly fighting at tears. A woman valiantly fighting at life. Raking his fingers back through his hair, now under the motivation of a new restlessness, this one speaking directly to his male body, Jake added, "Thanks for calling, Dan. I appreciate it."

"Take care. And I'll be in touch. And remember, mellow out."

"Sure, like a dog in the sun," Jake said, adding a goodbye and stretching to rehook the receiver. Even after he had, however, he kept his hand on the phone. Suddenly, with a haste that said if he didn't do it now, he wouldn't at all, he yanked the receiver back off the hook and punched in a number. For a second, there was silence, punctuated only by the thrumming of his heart. Then, the phone began to ring.

Ring...ring...ring...

"Hello?"

Jake's thrumming heart found a faster, painful rhythm. For God's sake, what was he doing? one last vestige of sanity asked.

"Hello?" the voice repeated.

Say something, Cameron! You're the one who dialed the number! You're the one hell-bent on self-destruction!

"Uh...Robin?"

"Yes?" she answered, obviously not recognizing the caller.

"This is Jake. Jake Cameron."

There was a slight, startled pause before she replied, "Oh, hi."

"Am I interrupting anything important?"

"No...no...I was just sketching." Or trying to, she thought, brushing back the hair that had fallen forward as she'd leaned over the drawing board. Why hadn't she recognized his voice? How could there have been any mistaking its calming softness? And why was he calling her?

"I, uh, I was just calling to see if you were all right," Jake said as though he'd read her mind.

She knew fully the source of his concern. "I owe you an apology. I shouldn't have run out on you like that. It's just . . ." She hesitated. "I'm not sure I can explain. Suddenly everything seemed to close in on me. Suddenly the disappointment of not being able to hold Peter . . ."

"You don't have to apologize for anything. You don't have to explain anything. I understand."

Do you? she wondered, answering her own question with *Yes, he does understand.* She wasn't certain how she knew he did, but she did know it. And for some inexplicable reason, she was glad he'd called. Things—life, in general—always seemed a little bit better, a little more tolerable, when Jake Cameron was around.

"Look," Jake said, turning and in so doing twisting the telephone cord across his chest, "Peter asked me to call and give you a message."

A smile tugged at the corners of Robin's mouth. It was the first time she'd smiled since . . . since the last time this man had made her smile. "Did he?"

"He did," Jake returned with the utmost earnestness. "He said to tell you that, while I did reasonably well holding him today, he would much rather it had been you."

The words curled themselves around Robin's heart. For a moment, she couldn't speak. In that moment, Jake feared that he'd gone and done something stupid. Something stupid like make her cry. Which was the one thing he'd wanted to prevent.

"Robin, I—"

"Thank you," she interrupted. She'd never met any man quite like Jake Cameron. His sensitivity caught her off balance—delightfully caught her off balance.

"Thank Peter. He said it. He also said to tell you that the two of you have a date next week. Listen, tell him tomorrow that I told you. I don't want him chewing my rear Thursday.''

Jake could tell that Robin was smiling. He liked the idea that she was.

"I'll tell him," she said.

"Good. You know how he is."

"A petite tyrant."

"Exactly."

There was a pause, as though each was trying to decide what to say next. Jake told himself to hang up, not to push the conversation. Curiously, for a reason she didn't understand and didn't care to investigate, Robin didn't want him to hang up. It had something to do with his soothing voice, which washed over her like warm honey. It made her feel as though she were sheltered in a safe cocoon. It was a feeling that had been sorely absent from her life of late.

"Were either of your daughters premature?"

The question took Jake by surprise. "No, they were full-term. Why?"

"It's just that you're so good with Peter I thought you must have had experience with preemies. I would have been terrified of moving him with all those wires and tubes. I'd have been afraid I'd disconnect something."

"My sister gave birth to a preemie," Jake answered. "And the wires and tubes aren't that easy to disconnect."

"That explains your experience, then. And I'm still intimidated by those wires and tubes."

And frightened by them? he wondered.

"How old is the child?" Robin asked.

Jake wished she hadn't asked the question because he knew the answer would unquestionably frighten her. "The child didn't live," he said softly.

"Oh," Robin said, audibly swallowing. "I'm sorry."

Wanting to turn her attention to something brighter, Jake said, "Listen, Peter did great today. He breathed like a real champ."

"Did he?"

"I swear it. He did great. Even the nurses said so."

Robin was smiling again. He could tell. He could easily envision men killing for that smile. It was that precious and rare.

"I'm glad."

"Me, too." There was another hint of silence. "Listen, I didn't mean to keep you this long. I know you have things to do... like sketching... or making sweaters for fishermen... or—"

"You're the one, aren't you?"

Jake's heart stopped. Cold. Or maybe it was the sweat that seemingly in an instant popped across his brow that was cold. Ice-cold.

"Your voice is the one that slows the babies' heart rates." Robin sounded triumphant. "I've been trying to figure out what there was about your voice that kept nagging at my memory."

Jake's heart started beating again. The rush of blood was painful. He leaned his head back against the kitchen wall, willing his soothing voice to just sound normal... or somewhere thereabouts. "Yeah, we all have talents. Mine is putting people to sleep."

Robin smiled. "Your voice is very—" she hesitated, surprised the word *sexy* came to mind "—nice," she said instead, adding something she had no problem with at all, "*You're* nice."

Nice?

Yeah, lady, I'm a regular saint!

"Like I said, I didn't mean to keep you," Jake repeated, suddenly feeling the need to terminate the conversation, as if somehow his hypocrisy—and what else would you call posing as something you weren't?—might taint her.

"Thanks for everything today," Robin said.

"Right. G'night."

"Good night."

Jake stretched to hang up the phone, only then realizing that he'd tangled himself in the cord. The symbolism was unmistakable and made him want to both laugh and cry. Just as he'd tangled himself in the cord so, too, had he tangled himself in his own lies…in his own dark deception.

ROBIN HELD THE DEAD PHONE in her hand for long seconds before slowly slipping it back onto its cradle. A multitude of conflicting emotions warred within her. She wished he hadn't called, yet she was glad he had. She wished he hadn't appeared in her life, yet she couldn't deny that his presence had smoothed a rocky way. She didn't want to need anyone, yet Jake seemed determined to be her, and Peter's, friend. Which was maybe what confused her the most. She had no quarrel with Jake Cameron being Peter's friend, but she wasn't certain that it was right for him to be hers.

The realization startled her. Why shouldn't she need a friend every bit as much as Peter did? Why was it okay for him to have one, but not her? *Guilt,* came the immediate answer. She felt guilty accepting a friendship for herself.

But why?

Because you don't deserve a friend. Because you don't deserve to feel better about life. Gerald is dead and you deserve to hurt... hurt... hurt...

Robin frowned. Now, why on earth should she feel that way?

Because you killed your husband.

I did not! Even as she vehemently denied it, though, she felt as if she had killed Gerald. At the very least, she'd been an accomplice. If she and Gerald hadn't fought that night...

"We're spending too much money, Gerald."

"You let me worry about the money."

"But I do worry. You have a new bill for a five-hundred-dollar suit and we haven't even paid the old bill for the patio furniture.... Where are you going?"

"Back to work. Where I won't have to listen to you bitch about money."

"Back to work? But it's Friday."

"I know it's Friday, but I've got some things to catch up on."

"But you've worked two nights this week already."

"Get off my back, will ya, Robin?"

"That job is all you care about, isn't it? You don't care about me or our baby—"

"You were the one who wanted to have a baby. Now, we're going to have to pay for one. Grow up, Robin! You can't have your cake and eat it, too!"

"But you can damned sure have a five-hundred-dollar suit! Gerald, wait! I didn't mean—"

Robin winced, as though she could still hear the slamming of the door. She'd replayed that night, that conversation, a thousand times. Why, why, had she brought up that damned suit? If she hadn't, maybe he'd have stayed home, maybe he wouldn't have gone and gotten himself killed.

As always at this point in the reasoning process, tears filled her eyes. Unlike the other times, however, these tears seemed to wash away some emotional fogginess and, for one clear second, a provocative question posed itself. Was the fact she felt she'd contributed to her husband's death the reason she refused to deal with it, at least the specifics of it, except to try to adjust to the reality of his absence? Did this account for her not wanting to know specifically who had killed her husband, because she was unsure she wasn't guiltier than he? She didn't know. All she knew was that it hurt too badly to dwell too long on Gerald's death. Swiping the teardrops from her cheeks, she reaffirmed that Gerald would have loved Peter as much as she did. And again, as always, she felt guilty for even entertaining the notion that he wouldn't have.

That night tigers once more stalked her. That night the blood-splattered dream recurred. This time, however, a voice came from out of nowhere, telling her that she hadn't been the one to kill her husband. The voice was soft and soothing. The voice almost made her believe. It wasn't until morning, as she dawdled over a bowl of cereal, that Robin realized the voice had belonged to Jake Cameron.

CHAPTER FIVE

ON THURSDAY, JAKE REVERTED to his afternoon hours. That evening, he decided not to attend the Wee Care meeting. His reason for both actions was the same: he was distancing himself from Robin. Her comment about his being nice had slashed at his conscience, making him feel more a heel than he had before, a feat he'd thought impossible. He had no right to involve himself in her life. Observing her and Peter in order to put his mind at ease was one thing, but violating her trust by choreographing a friendship was altogether another matter.

Not even he was heel enough to do that!

Or so he told himself as he rode the elevator up to the floor where the neonatal unit was located. But part of him wasn't buying any of it, and wouldn't be ignored. So okay, Jake ole buddy, tell me this, prodded a small voice. If you're distancing yourself from Robin Bauer, if you're too nice and noble to continue this charade, then why are you here at the hospital bright and early on a Monday morning?

Well, you see, it's like this. I need to take Pop to the doctor tomorrow for his regular checkup, and so I'm swapping days—a Monday for a Tuesday—and I'm here bright and early because I've got a whale of a list of errands to run this afternoon and, if you believe any of this, then you're stupider than I thought!

The truth was he could have volunteered a couple of hours after his father's appointment, and the list of errands he needed to run that afternoon numbered all of three. The further truth was that, despite having had his daughters for the weekend, he'd thought the two days would never pass and that they, coupled with the rest of the week he hadn't seen Robin, were beginning to feel like forever.

The blaring, glaring truth emerged—he was obviously heel enough to keep up this charade!

This he concluded with great self-disgust as he shoved himself away from the wall of the elevator and started down the hallway. He spotted Robin as soon as the nursery came into view. She was inside, standing over Peter, a smile as radiant as three suns at her lips. It was then he made the admission. What he was doing might not be right, but it was necessary...to him...in some elemental way he couldn't begin to fathom. The bottom line, nitty-gritty truth was he'd willingly forfeit his soul for just this glimpse of her.

Robin glanced up, saw Jake at the window and smiled widely. She cradled her arms in a motion that indicated she was preparing to hold the baby. Jake was struck yet again by how disarmingly youthful she looked at times. Now, for example, her eyes flashed a childlike excitement that proclaimed it was Christmas morning, Easter afternoon and the last day of school all rolled into one. Jake lowered his gaze to her mouth. The fever blister was gone. The only thing that remained was the softness, the sanity-destroying softness of her lips, lips that were the perfect mature foil to her youthfulness.

Yes, he resolved, he'd willingly forfeit his soul for just this glimpse of her.

"I'm going to hold him," Robin gushed minutes later as Jake, scrubbed and gowned, stepped toward her.

Her smile was so contagious that there was no way he could have kept from returning it. "No joke," he teased. "I would never have guessed."

Robin's grin turned sheepish. "Am I acting totally ridiculous?"

"Not at all. Even if you were, I'd say you're entitled."

The smile erupted again, in such proportions that her face could barely contain it. "I feel like I've had a magnum of champagne...and I haven't even held him yet."

Interestingly, Jake felt just as intoxicated as she, and all he was doing was soaking up her effervescence. "Better sit down then, Mom, before your knees buckle. I'll hand Peter to you."

"Good idea," Robin said, easing into the rocker. "His mother dropping him first time out might traumatize him for life."

"Yeah, we're talking years of serious counseling," Jake said, looking over at the nurse who stood nearby checking the monitors. "Is he ready to travel?"

"All ready," the nurse returned.

"Okay, then, partner," he said to the tiny form he tucked the blanket around, "let's take a little trip to Mommy's arms." The baby made a cooing-gurgling sound. "Yeah, you think you'd like that, huh?"

The nurse helped to negotiate the wires and tubes as Jake lifted the infant from the bed and, cupping the child in his huge hands, gently nestled him in Robin's arms. For one instant, Jake was aware of his knuckles grazing against the fullness of one of Robin's breasts. The maleness in him appreciated the gentle curve, while the hospital volunteer in him said, "Relax. He won't break. And, look, keep this air tube just at his nose."

Robin heard without hearing, saw without seeing. All that registered was feeling or, more precisely, the feel of the precious weight in her arms. She felt the softness of baby skin, the ebony silk of hair, the flutter of a small hand. Two navy-blue eyes, framed by a fringe of black lashes, looked inquiringly at her, as though trying to decide just who this pretty person might be, while a rosebud-pink mouth puckered into a pout, relaxed, then puckered again. When Robin thought she could receive no more sensory input, one little leg kicked her in the stomach. She laughed and looked up at the man squatting before her. Jake had taken over the tubes and wires from the nurse, who'd now stepped in the direction of a crying baby. Robin vaguely noted that one of Jake's knees rested against the floor and that the jeans he wore were stretched tightly, daringly across his masculine form.

"He just kicked me," she said, as amazed as she was delighted.

"I told you he was strong."

"And he's heavy," she said, her eyes sparkling like diamond chips. "I mean, heavier than I thought he'd be."

"I told you."

"And he's gorgeous, isn't he?"

"Gorgeous."

"And he's squiggly."

"I told you so."

"And he does smell like—" Her voice cracked as she tried to say baby powder. She was as startled as

Jake by the sudden hitch in her breath and the tears that rushed to her eyes. She was going to cry! Right here, right now. And all because of the baby in her arms. There hadn't been much right in her life for the past few months, but this wee bundle of wiggly baby was right. As right as anything in the world had ever been ... or ever would be. And that kind of perfection left one filled to overflowing with emotions sweeter than a god's nectar. "I think I'm going to cry," she announced.

The announcement had been needless. Jake already saw the plump tears plunging from her diamond-dazzling eyes. With both her hands filled—one with Peter, the other with the air tube—the crystal teardrops ran unheeded. She angled her head, trying to swipe her cheek across the sleeve of her sweater. The attempt met with only limited success.

"It's okay," Jake whispered consolingly. "Happy tears are permissible."

Without any conscious intent, he wiped at her damp cheek with the pad of his thumb. Her skin was warm and silk-soft. Just as was the tear that bled across his flesh. He suddenly had the most irrational urge to bring his thumb to his lips and taste the moistness. Would it be salty? Undoubtedly, but he knew that it would also be sweet and pure, as sweet and pure as the woman herself.

"I'm sorry," Robin whispered, sniffing

"It's all right," Jake returned, removing his hand because the thoughts he'd just had confused him. Thoroughly. These very thoughts, combined with the realization that Robin probably wanted some time alone with her son, prompted him to say, "I'll give you

two some time together." He spoke as he started to rise
to his feet.

"No, don't go!" Again, as she had with the tears
earlier, Robin startled herself. "I mean, the wires and
tubes—"

"They're fine," Jake said, lowering himself back
into a squatting position. "Nothing's going to come
unplugged or untaped or—"

"Stay," she repeated. She was aware that part of the
reason for her request did, indeed, center around her
fear of the wires and tubes, but she was aware of another reason, as well, a shadowy reason that she felt
more comfortable not exploring. It was simply enough
to recognize that Jake made things better when he was
around. "Unless you need to be doing something
else," she added.

If he'd fried in hell for it, Jake could not have refused her plea. "No, I'll stay."

For heartbeats, their eyes held. Neither was quite
sure why, except that some powerful force deemed that
they should. Shyly, Robin averted her gaze first. She
glanced down at Peter. Her heart flooded with renewed feeling.

"He really *is* beautiful, isn't he?" she asked.

"He really is," Jake agreed.

The next fifteen or so minutes were characterized by
both conversation and quiet interludes. During the
latter, neither seemed bothered by the silence, neither
seemed obligated to fill it. It was as though they'd
often sat this way, sharing space, sharing time, sharing an occasional smile. On the other hand, when it
occurred, their conversation seemed natural and relaxed. Perhaps it was because it wholly centered on
Peter.

"He really does breathe well," Robin said during one such verbal exchange. "The doctor said that he's doing remarkably well for a boy. They explained at Wee Care Thursday night that boy babies have more breathing problems than girl babies. Something about hormones. Anyway, every time a boy baby is put through stress, it strengthens its lungs, which I guess happened to Peter during the week I kept going into labor and they kept stopping it." She smiled. "At the time, I thought the on-again-off-again routine was awful, but now I'm grateful for it."

Jake sat on the floor, at Robin's feet. The hem of her khaki skirt brushed the toes of his boots in a gesture of subtle intimacy. He wondered again how anyone as small as Robin had given birth, at all. If she'd been his wife, he'd have been scared to death. If she'd been his wife—

He heard her say something and glanced up. "I'm sorry. What did you say?"

"I looked for you Thursday night at Wee Care." She hoped the statement sounded casual enough...just the way she'd casually dismissed her disappointment that night.

"I, uh, I'd had a rough day and thought I'd pass," Jake answered. It was a lie, but what was one more entangling lie among many?

"You probably did the smart thing by staying in. It was so cold I almost froze my fanny off." She blushed when she realized what she'd said, quickly adding, "Figuratively speaking, of course."

The color stealing into her cheeks totally captivated Jake. He grinned despite his earlier dark thoughts. "Do you always blush so easily?" he teased.

Robin grinned, too. "Yes. And, if you keep looking at me, it's only going to get worse."

Jake kept looking at her. He also kept grinning. "I
like it. Blushing is charmingly old-fashioned."

As might have been expected, his remark only
deepened the rose in her cheeks. She groaned as she
felt her skin growing warmer. "Will you stop—"

Suddenly, the baby whimpered.

Robin glanced quickly down at her son, only to see
his face scrunch into a fretful cry. His wailing dented
the blissful silence.

"Oh, my God, what have I done?" Robin asked,
panic swimming through her bloodstream.

"You haven't done anything," Jake reassured her
as he pushed to his knees and leaned into her. The
hardness of his thighs, connected with the softness of
hers, a fact both noted subliminally. "Babies cry, remember? That's how they communicate."

"Yeah, well, I think he's saying I broke him."

Jake laughed. "You did not break him." As he
spoke, he peeled back the blanket and felt the baby's
diaper. "Aha, I've found the problem. Haven't I,
partner? No guy can be expected to endure such an
indignity. How's a guy supposed to retain a macho
image if he's wet?"

Robin smiled at Jake's crazy, softly delivered ban-
ter. Even Peter stopped crying and sought out the
quiet, comforting voice.

"You couldn't bottle that voice so a new mother
could take some of it home, could you?" Robin asked.

"Nope, but I make house calls," Jake said, saying
it so nonchalantly, so innocently, that Robin knew he
meant nothing threatening by it. At least she thought
she knew that. Yes, yes, of course, she knew that be-

cause Jake wasn't even looking at her. Instead, he was realigning the wires and tubes so she could get out of the chair with Peter. Which she did and placed him back in his bed, his head once more within the oxy hood. In seconds, with a little help from Jake, she'd changed the baby's wet diaper.

Just then one of the nurses called to Jake.

"You're being paged," Robin said.

Jake waved an I'll-be-there-in-a-minute signal to the nurse, though his eyes never left Robin.

"Thanks for everything today," Robin said, smiling. "It looks like I'm always thanking you for something."

"No thanks are necessary," Jake said. "It was my pleasure. Hey, I've got an idea," he said with such spontaneity that it was impossible to tell that he'd been planning his strategy for the past ten minutes—all the while telling himself that he was asking for trouble. Big trouble. "Why don't I take you out Friday night? In celebration of the momentous occasion of your holding your son for the first time. We could have a little dinner—"

"No, I couldn't."

"You already have plans for Friday night?"

"No, but—"

Jake smiled. "You're not going to give me that old 'I've got to wash my hair' routine, are you?"

"No, it's just..."

It was clear as the button-cute nose on her face that Robin had suddenly built a wall between them. It was just as clear why.

"Look," Jake said, his kidding tossed aside, "all I want is to be your friend." When Robin said nothing, he added, "Just think about it, huh?" Leaning down to Peter, he whispered loudly, "C'mon, pal, give me a character reference."

Jake gave Robin one last look before turning and moving toward the nurses' station. As though she had no will, Robin watched him go. How was it possible that he always seemed taller than the last time she'd seen him? How could his shoulders always look broader? And maybe she did need a friend.

They were heady questions.

She glanced down at her son as if he, and he alone, had the answers.

ROBIN GLANCED AT THE bedside clock—it was almost seven—then at her image in the antique oval cheval glass. No, the dress was all wrong. Just the way the one before it had been all wrong. And the one before that, to say nothing of the discarded dozen that now lay scattered across her bed in a rainbow of colors. She needed something not too casual, not too dressy. She needed something that could be appropriately worn anywhere, because Jake hadn't really said where they would be going. She needed... She groaned and eased to the side of the bed. What she needed was to have her head examined for accepting Jake's offer of dinner.

Had she really agreed to go out with him?

What could she possibly have been thinking about? Except that his suggestion of an evening out had seemed tempting beyond words. Tempting, too, was the friendship he was offering her. An uncomplicated, no-strings-attached friendship.

"Look, all I want is to be your friend."

As though drawn by a powerful magnet, Robin's gaze drifted to the box stored in the bottom of her closet, the box containing the clothes her husband had been wearing that fateful night, the box she'd never garnered the emotional strength to open. As always, guilt washed over her. She may not deserve a friend, she thought, but it didn't keep her from wanting one or needing one. It hadn't kept her from accepting Jake Cameron's offer to dinner.

Oh, God, had she really agreed to go out with him?

What in the world could she have been thinking about?

And was it already seven o'clock?

Wrestling herself out of the dress, she stepped from it and tossed it onto the growing stack. Clad only in beige silk underwear, she rushed toward the closet. Her hand had just closed around another hanger when the doorbell pealed.

Robin groaned. Her heart, like corralled stallions set free, went crazy-wild.

Jake's heart, weighted with disappointment, dropped to his feet when Robin opened the door. The old chenille robe that she clutched to her said only one thing: she'd changed her mind about going out.

"Hi," Robin said softly, shyly.

Jake, his fists hidden in the pockets of a three-quarter woolen coat, the nighttime cold curling about his legs, managed to say, "Hi."

"C'mon in," Robin said, stepping back. "I'm running late."

At the realization that he'd misinterpreted the robe, Jake felt his heart rise from the ground and settle back in his chest. He was startled to discover just how much this evening meant to him. Startled and unnerved. He was also startled that he couldn't take his eyes from the woman before him. She looked like a waif lost in the

robe's voluminous folds of fabric. A sexy waif lost and
just begging to be found? He let the question, only one
of many improper ones that seemed to plague him of
late, slip away. "Take your time. There's no rush."

"I'll, uh, I'll only be a minute," Robin said, starting back toward the bedroom. She still clasped the
robe to her; her feet, bare except for stockings, moved
silently over the polished, knotted-pine flooring.

Jake nodded, repeating, "There's no rush."

"Make yourself at home," Robin called over her
shoulder as she disappeared down the hallway.

After she'd vanished, Jake simply stared at the spot
where she'd last stood, as if he could still see fragments of her energy that had been left behind. A loud
pop of a burning log finally distracted him, bringing
his attention to the white-stone fireplace. At the
warmth that lapped about him, he shrugged from his
coat and laid it across the arm of a chair whose fabric
looked like old-fashioned mattress ticking. The sofa
was done in the same rustic material. Before it sat an
early American oak coffee table and beneath it peeked
a basket burgeoning with brightly colored balls of
yarn. In front of the fireplace sprawled a hand-
braided, scarlet rug, while adjacent to the sofa re-
clined a dainty rocker, its wood ash, its fabric a red
plaid. The only modern thing in the room, and one
that appeared anachronistic, was a drafting board.

Despite the furnishings, the room had a Spartan
look, as though the cottage had been hastily rented
and filled only with necessities. This feeling was sup-
ported by the empty space at the far side of the room
that had been designed for a dining table. Further
corroboration lay in the fact that only a minimum of
accessories lay scattered about. Aside from two brass

candlesticks with swirled hurricane glass globes that rested at each end of the mantel, there was only an occasional utilitarian object: a tambour clock of mahogany that measured time from the middle of the same mantel, a table lamp with a pierced tin shade, a wrought-iron shovel, poker and tongs for the fireplace, a—

Jake's gaze came to rest on the picture frame that sat on an end table. Pewter. The frame was of pewter. With a flower—an iris, he thought—sculpted all along one side. Jake made these inane observations as though the making of them prolonged his having to deal with the picture itself. Stepping forward, reluctantly, but as though he had no choice, he picked up the frame. The man in the picture was dark-haired, dark-complexioned, a perfect smile at his perfect lips. Jake had never seen Gerald Bauer alive . . . unless you counted the minutes that he'd watched the man's life drain from him, minutes in which he'd tried to hold in that life with one thin cotton handkerchief, minutes during which he'd prayed as he'd never prayed before.

But the prayer had fallen on deaf ears.

Gerald Bauer had died . . . because of him . . . and now, here he was, standing amidst the man's earthly possessions, waiting to take his widow to dinner. Suddenly, the magnitude of his deception struck him. Suddenly, he felt lower than a belly-crawling snake. Suddenly, he knew he had to tell Robin who he was. Now. Before the passage of another minute. Now. While he felt an ounce of human decency. Now—

"I'm ready."

Preoccupied with his tormenting thoughts, Jake hadn't even heard Robin enter the room. The framed

picture in his hand, he turned. Robin's eyes lowered to
the photograph. Subtle though the action was, a
shadow drifted across her eyes. She said nothing, as
though her grief were too profound to verbalize, as
though she'd hidden too deeply within herself to
dredge up the words.

Later that night, as he was trying to explain and excuse his silence, Jake blamed the shadow that had fled
across her hazel eyes and the silence that had sealed
her taupe-tinted lips. He told himself that he couldn't
find the courage to inflict even the smallest bit more
pain. Yet, he suspected another truth. It, too, had to
do with hazel eyes and taupe-tinted lips. In short, he'd
never seen eyes so goldenly beautiful, nor lips that
promised to be more silky soft. In short, he could not
remember ever wanting anything as badly as he
wanted to spend the evening with this woman. So
much so, in fact, that he was willing to damn human
decency.

"IT'S VERY NICE. Very... quaint," Robin said, glancing around the small restaurant that nestled on the
outskirts of Boston.

A fish net, like a nautical tapestry, hung on a nearby
wall, while scrimshaw collected dust and praise from
row upon row of shelves. The atmosphere suggested
that the decor hadn't changed since the restaurant had
opened for business in 1958, the year being proudly
proclaimed on an aged life preserver. The atmosphere
further suggested that the restaurant would lose a siz-
able chunk of charm should the decor be modern-
ized.

"The seafood's excellent," Jake said, knowing that
the quality of the food had little, if anything, to do

with his choice of where to dine. A far greater attraction of the restaurant was the fact that it was off the beaten path, his own little secret hideaway. He'd been patronizing the establishment for years and only rarely had he run into anyone he knew, which was perfect for this evening because he didn't want to have to introduce the woman he was with. Suddenly, a disturbing thought crossed his mind. "You do like seafood, don't you?"

At the panic that raced across Jake's dark eyes, Robin couldn't help teasing. "Actually, I hate it."

Jake looked like a little boy who'd been told to pack up his toys and go home. "Oh, hell, I'm sorry. I didn't even ask. I just assumed—"

"I'm only kidding," she interrupted. At his skeptical look, she said, "I swear it. You just looked so deadly serious that I couldn't resist."

So deadly serious and so...so sad, she added silently. She had sensed right from the beginning that this man shared his life with some sadness. What it could be he'd never so much as hinted at. Not that he owed her any explanation. After all, they were nothing more than friends...and new friends at that. Even so, and just as she had once before, she felt an urgent, almost painful need to smooth away the worry lines crinkling his eyes. So urgent, so painful was the need that she removed her hands from the table and folded them in her lap.

"I really do like seafood," she stated again.

Jake grinned. "You really better because I'm not taking you anywhere else now."

In seconds, she proved her point in spades by ordering a shrimp appetizer to be followed by crab au gratin. Jake dittoed the shrimp appetizer, but deviated from her entrée by ordering lobster.

"Oh, and we'll have a bottle of champagne," he tacked on.

"No, please—" Robin began, but was cut off with Jake's "We're celebrating, remember?"

"But I can't. I mean, I shouldn't. Not with—" A blush crept into her cheeks. "Not with Peter."

The pink color, like the shade of a sweet summer rose, said what her words had not. Jake understood that she'd been referring to nursing the baby the moment he'd seen the blush. As always, he found the blush endearing...and somehow sexy in a way he didn't want to dwell on.

"I'm sorry. I wasn't thinking." Turning to the waiter, he asked if the restaurant had a specific brand of mineral water. It did. "We'll have a bottle of that, then. And two champagne glasses."

"I've spoiled your evening," Robin said as the waiter stepped from the table.

"How?"

"Mineral water?"

"Bubbles are all you need to celebrate."

"But—"

Jake's teasing edged away. "Quit worrying about spoiling my evening, okay?" When Robin said nothing, he repeated, "Okay?"

"Okay," she said, thinking, and not for the first time, that this man truly was nice.

He was also handsome in an imperfect, rugged kind of way. She supposed she'd known this all along—that he was handsome—but the fact had hit her over the head with the force of a sledgehammer earlier that evening. When she'd reentered the room after dressing, she'd been struck by the man standing there. He'd seemed so very different from Gerald. Gerald, who seldom went out without his designer logo. On the other hand Jake looked as if he'd spent all of thirty seconds donning an ordinary pair of olive-green cords, pants that did far more than ordinary things to his long, lean legs, and even less time matching the cords with a sweater that he'd pulled over a starched but plain white shirt. The effect was one of...touch-ableness.

The hands in her lap folded about themselves. She immediately channeled her thoughts into another vein, this one having to do with Jake's scrutiny of Gerald's photograph. Why hadn't he asked about it? He was obviously curious. Whatever the reason, she was relieved that he hadn't. Gerald's death was something she didn't want to talk about. Not now. Possibly not ever.

"So, how was your week?" Jake asked, sensing that, for whatever reason, Robin was pulling into herself...and away from him. Maybe she was even regretting having accepted his offer. Actually, he'd been surprised she had.

"Fine," she said, her face suddenly lighting up. "Peter gained another ounce."

"I know. Pretty soon you won't even be able to carry him around."

Robin laughed. "I think we still have a ways to go before that."

"I don't know. You'd be surprised what a few Big Macs will do."

"He's still bugging you for Big Macs?"

"It's embarrassing," Jake teased.

Into the middle of two smiles, the waiter returned with a bottle of mineral water and two champagne glasses. In seconds, Jake had filled the glasses with effervescent spring water. One he handed to Robin, who, he noted, took her hand from her lap for the first time since sitting down. He also noted that she went to great lengths to keep her newly freed hand, the one reaching for the glass, the one still wearing her wedding ring, from brushing against his.

"To Peter's new ounce," Jake said, raising his glass aloft. "To holding Peter for the first time, which is the real purpose of this celebration. And," he added, "to Peter's mother. May she always be as happy as the first time she held her son."

The toast, delivered in a voice whose texture was that of crushed velvet, enfolded Robin in the most glorious warmth. She again felt this man's innate kindness and wondered how any woman could have been stupid enough to let him slip through her fingers.

"Thank you," she whispered as she clinked her glass against his.

Jake watched as she brought the glass to her mouth. He watched as bubbles broke against her glossy lips. He watched and he wondered. He wondered how in the world her lips could look as soft as the clingy sweater-like dress molding her body. Angora, he thought the knitted fabric was. A pale yellow angora. The color of early morning sunshine. The feel of soft warm rays of dancing light. Soft like her honey-toasted lips. Would those same lips be warm? He raised his eyes to hers. Curiously it was there, in her eyes, that he found his answer concerning her lips. Yes, they would be soft and warm, because everything about this woman was soft and warm—small, soft and winter-fire warm.

Robin's eyes scurried away.

"So," she said, the rapidness of her speech betraying a sudden nervousness, "tell me about yourself."

Jake had the distinct feeling that she had thought he was on the verge of asking something about her personal life. He had the distinct feeling that she was beating him to the punch. He also suspected that she was wondering what he did for a living. On this score, he was no more eager to talk than she.

Shrugging, he said, "There's not much to tell. As you already know, I have two daughters, both of whom have nothing but clothes and boys on their minds. I have an ex-wife, who may or may not have been unfaithful to me. I have a sister who'd love to marry me off to the first available woman—I'm not even certain she's picky about whether she's breathing or not. And I have a father who needs to be placed in a nursing home, although when I finally had the guts to tell him so, I discovered he'd fallen asleep and hadn't heard a word I'd said."

Jake's response hadn't been at all what Robin had been expecting. Certainly not his comment about his wife. Was this the source of his sadness? Robin heard herself answering with the same honesty Jake had shown. "Your daughters sound perfectly normal, your ex-wife, if she was unfaithful, sounds crazy, your sister sounds as if she's simply exercising her sisterly prerogative, and your father sounds like a victim of modern-day longevity."

Out of everything she'd said, Jake zeroed in on her observation about his ex-wife. He told himself it was a normal thing to do. He also told himself to leave her comment untouched, to let it lie the casual remark she'd intended it to be. Her next question proved that he'd acted wisely.

"How old is your father?"

"Eighty-three."

"Is he in good health?"

"Reasonably good for eighty-three, but he's unable to take care of his own needs now. He's had a live-in housekeeper ever since a minor stroke about a year ago. Live-in help is expensive, though. I don't know how much longer we can afford it."

"What about your mother?"

"She died years ago."

"I see." Robin ran her fingers up and down the thin stem of the champagne glass. "It must be hard telling your father he has to give up his home."

"No, it's not hard. It's impossible."

Robin saw the pain in Jake's eyes. Strangely, in some metaphysical way, she felt his pain. It was raw and sharp-edged, very much like her own. She sensed that the two of them were kindred spirits, wounded spirits searching for a healing. Robin realized that, for one brief moment, she'd thought of someone's pain besides her own. She had to admit that it had felt good.

Dinner was a pleasant affair, the talk amicable, the food delicious. Robin, who admittedly at the last second had developed cold feet about going through with the evening, now almost hated to see it end. Jake was good company, neither pushy nor aggressive. And, most of all, he didn't insist upon a lot of questions about her personal life, which she at one and the same time found comforting and curious.

At last, she said, "It's been a nice evening. Thank you for asking me."

"It was my pleasure. Thank you for accepting."

Robin grinned. "Thank Peter. It was his character reference that tilted the scales."

"I knew I could count on him," Jake said, unable, the way he'd been unable all evening, to take his eyes off Robin's lips, lips that were now curved in mirth. "You, uh, you sure you don't want dessert?" he asked, dragging his eyes back to hers.

"After what I just ate?"

Jake grinned. "For a speck of a thing, you really do know how to consume food."

Robin tried to act offended. "Thanks a lot. I'll have you know I weigh exactly what I did before I got pregnant. Well, give or take a pound or two."

"I'd say that close to perfection, a pound or two doesn't matter."

It was a simple compliment. The kind Jake might have gallantly made to any woman. Even so, Robin's face flushed with heat. "Perfection it isn't, I assure you. Look, I really should be getting home. I have to be up early in the morning. I've sworn to get some work done on my sketches, and I want to go to the hospital to see Peter first." As tactful as her remark had been, it nonetheless clearly signaled that the evening was over.

Jake motioned for the waiter and in due time paid the bill, via a credit card, while still seated at the table. He then stood, crossed to Robin and pulled back her chair.

"Here, let me," he said, holding her coat as she slid her arms into it. As he did so, his gaze naturally drifted about the room. Here...there...there...here...

Suddenly, his heart stopped. A silent swear word rushed to his lips as he noted two fellow police officers, in uniform, seated near the doorway. He recognized them as nice guys, but with overly active mouths.

Don't panic, Cameron. Just take it easy...and play it smart.

Looking back over her shoulder, Robin smiled. Jake managed to reciprocate. He even managed to sound halfway normal when he asked, "Ready?"

His hand at the small of Robin's back, Jake adroitly guided her toward the door. As he neared the table where the two officers sat, he took that moment to put on his coat, exaggerating the procedure so as to use the garment as a shield. He slipped unnoticed into the restaurant's foyer. Congratulating himself on his brilliant strategy, he threw open the restaurant door. Cold air rushed in. As did a woman. A black-haired woman. She stopped just inches short of plowing into him.

"Jake?" the woman said in surprise.

Jake recognized the voice immediately. A thought simultaneously crossed his mind, a grumbling, sarcastic thought. The next time he dined out, he'd do so in Grand Central Station and be done with it!

CHAPTER SIX

"HI, SIS," JAKE SAID in a resigned tone that reflected his having come to terms, albeit reluctant terms, with climbing the last few steps to the guillotine.

Whitney Ames's eyes, as dark as her close-cropped hair, sparkled from beneath the sassily slanted rim of a woolen beret, first revealing astonishment, then out-and-out pleasure. "Jake," she repeated, throwing herself into his mammoth arms and brushing a kiss across his cheek, "what a pleasant surprise."

"Yeah, what a surprise," he concurred, wondering if the bright flash in the night was the light of the full moon or just the gruesome glistening of the guillotine's steel blade. His left arm automatically encircled his sister's waist, while his right hand just as automatically stretched to greet the man beside her. "Michael," he acknowledged.

Michael Ames, though considerably older than his wife, was lean and trim and consummately fit for a man his age. He also had sandy-brown hair that revealed not even a sliver of gray, a fact the man always good-naturedly held over Jake, who, though much younger, had silver wings tipping his temples. Jake had always been fond of his brother-in-law, a speech-communications professor at Harvard, and was always glad to see him. Well, almost always.

"Hey, Jake, how are you?" Michael said in congenial reciprocation.

"Fine." *For a man about to lose his head.*

And with that thought, as though it had programmed the action, two pairs of eyes sought out the woman silently standing at Jake's side. Jake could almost hear his sister's "Well, well, and just who is this fair-haired wench?"

Jake's eyes found Robin's. Even under the stressful circumstances, he noted how the moonlight played across the golden-green landscape of her irises. "This is my sister and her husband, Whitney and Michael Ames." His gaze then shifted to his sister. A pause. A heartbeat. The sound of the steel blade racing downward to lop off his head. "This, uh, this is Robin. Robin Bauer." Jake's eyes narrowed, willing his sister to understand the significance of what he was about to say. "Robin and I met at Brigham and Women's Hospital. She has a son in the preemie unit."

To Whitney's credit, aside from one stark, startled second during which she hurriedly glanced toward her brother, she managed to act as though nothing out of the ordinary was happening, as though the name Bauer meant no more to her than Smith or Jones. "Nice to meet you," she said, extending her hand.

"Nice to meet you," Robin countered.

It was obvious that Michael, too, had recognized Robin's name. He, however, was not as adroit at handling the situation as his wife. He appeared at a loss for something to say. In fact, Jake thought, he looked as though he'd rather be anywhere but where he was. Jake knew the feeling.

Finally, Michael Ames, who was renowned for his great elocutionary skills, stammered, "I, uh, we, uh,

I didn't know anyone knew about this restaurant but us."

A mirthless smile nipped Jake's lips. "Just the two of you, me, and half the population of the western hemisphere." Jake looked behind him to see if half the population of the western hemisphere, or more precisely two men clothed in police uniforms, were about to add insult to injury. He saw no one. At least for now. Although that could change with the swing of the door. "Look, we don't want to hold you two up," Jake said.

"Right," the great orator began again, "...need to get a seat...if it's as crowded as you say...don't be a stranger, huh?...bring the girls by...c'mon, Whitney," the professor said, nudging his wife forward, "let's let these two get on their way...nice to have met you."

Robin expressed a similar sentiment.

Whitney, balking at her husband's overzealousness to get inside the restaurant, leaned close and kissed her brother's cheek again. "We'll talk," she said, looking deep into his eyes.

Soon. Jake would bet money that they talked soon. Too soon. Pushing the thought away—he'd deal with the call when the time came—he headed for the Jeep parked nearby, guiding Robin by resting his hand at the small of her back. Overhead, a starlit sky spanned the heavens, while the moon, looking like a platinum balloon that had escaped its earthly bounds, beamed downward. A blustery wind cut through the crowded parking lot, chilling all in its rimy path.

Robin shivered.

"Cold?" Jake asked. His heartbeat was beginning to return to normal. Their running into Whitney and

Michael had been unnerving, unsettling, but it was over now. He'd escaped with his deception intact.

"A little," Robin admitted, the wind whipping her hair into a wild frenzy and dousing her cheeks in a cheery red.

Shoving the key into the Jeep's lock, Jake opened the door on the passenger side. "I'll have the heater on in a minute—"

"Hey, Cameron!" a deep, male voice hollered.

Jake's heartbeat, the one that had begun to quiet down, erupted into an erratic rhythm. A swear word, this time viler than the last, silently jumped to his lips, along with the question, Why were the gods making sport of him? He whirled, knowing whom he'd find.

Two men, both well over six feet, both dressed in the uniform of Boston's finest, advanced toward him. Both men wore smiles a mile long.

The stockier of the two, the one who'd spoken seconds before, spoke again as he thrust out his beefy hand, "Hey, man, how're you doing?"

The greeting was unquestionably sincere, and Jake knew a moment's worth of guilt at wishing that these two men, his cohorts, would suddenly, but surely, drop off the face of the earth. He extended his hand—what choice did he have?—first to one man, then to the other.

"Dammit, Lieutenant," the second man said, "it's good to see you! It's too quiet down at the precinct."

"Frazier's right," the other man, whose name tag identified him as Benedaries, and whose dark hair was kinked as if it had been permed, agreed, "it's too quiet without you. Course Fraz and I are raising our usual hell, but it just isn't the same."

The man named Frazier laughed. "Yeah, we're raising hell, but it isn't the same."

"How've you been?" the curly-topped Benedaries asked. Neither man apparently thought it odd that Jake had yet to utter a single word. His body language, however, was fairly screaming. He stood as though shielding Robin from the wind, when in reality he was instinctively shielding her from the men, from the truth.

"I'm fine," Jake answered.

As had happened before with Whitney and her husband, two pairs of eyes leveled on the woman at Jake's side . . . well, actually, the woman standing just behind his wide shoulder. Jake knew he had to say something. He also knew that by noon tomorrow it would be all over the station that he'd been seen . . . and that he'd been seen with a woman.

"This, uh, this is Will Frazier and Curly Benedaries." He turned toward Robin and vaguely introduced her. "This is a friend of mine." He forced himself to grin, hoping that by doing so he could draw attention away from the fact that he hadn't mentioned Robin's name. "C'mon, you guys, be something other than your usual uncouth selves."

"Hey," Curly Benedaries said, "cut us some slack, huh? You know we got couth. Hell, I bought a pint of it just last week." He glanced over at Robin. "Nice to meet you, ma'am."

"Yeah, nice to meet you," Will Frazier added.

Robin smiled, though Jake thought her smile as faked as his. But then, he could imagine the turmoil tumbling through her mind. Her husband had been killed by a Boston police officer and—poof!—two appear out of nowhere, smothering her in painful memories. Not only that, they deliver the unexpected news that the man who'd been a tiny part of her life for the past few weeks, the man who'd virtually slipped in through the back door, was also a cop. Jake could see her almost visibly drawing into herself and wanted desperately to protect her from that cold, dark, lonely corner she crawled into. Which he supposed was just another way of saying that he wanted desperately to protect her from himself...after all, it was because of him that she crawled into that cold, dark, lonely corner.

"It was great to see you guys," Jake lied, gently, though effectively terminating the conversation by assisting Robin into the Jeep.

"When you coming back to work?" Curly Benedaries asked.

"I, uh, I'm not sure." As he spoke, he tucked Robin's heavy coat inside the vehicle.

"We'll save some of the bad guys for you," Will Frazier said.

"You do that," Jake said, closing the door. He started around the back of the Jeep. The wind sliced through him like a saber. The cut was almost as clean as the one made by the guilt he was feeling. Robin hadn't been the only one inundated with painful memories.

"Call for an ambulance!" Jake could hear himself screaming.

"He's already dead."

"No, he can't be dead! He can't—"

"Hey, Jake," Curly began...awkwardly, "about what happened. It could have happened to any one of us, man. To any one of us."

Jake's chest tightened with tension. He rushed his gaze to Robin, who sat enclosed within the Jeep. He knew she couldn't hear, yet paranoia demanded he check to see if she had.

"Yeah, man, you did what you had to," Will tossed in adamantly.

"Yeah, sure," Jake said, adding as he edged toward the driver's side, "You guys take it easy, huh?"

"You, too."

"Good to see you, man."

Jake curled his fingers around the door handle, hesitating for a second. In that second, he turned his head upward, closed his eyes and took a deep breath. He could feel, hear, his heart, like a battering ram, slamming against his chest. Slowly, he opened his eyes. Not only were the gods making sport at his expense tonight, but he could have sworn that the man in the moon was laughing.

"So, is that the sister who's trying to marry you off?"

Minutes had passed; long, quiet minutes during which the Jeep had filled with warm air, minutes during which Jake had steered the car toward home, minutes during which Robin had composed her scrambled thoughts. Or at least had tried to.

Jake cut his gaze from the street to the woman beside him. The question wasn't the one she really wanted to ask, but then, the one she wanted to ask was the one he didn't want to answer, so he willfully contributed to its delay.

"The same," he said, sounding as casual as a summer stroll when he felt as tight as a drum at a Fourth of July parade.

"She seems nice."

"She is. Even if she is my big sister."

Robin grinned. It wasn't a true grin, not the type that spelled the total involvement of one's spirit. It was the kind given absently. "You're her little brother?"

Jake's mouth slid into a similar, only half-sincere smile. "Yeah. And she never lets me forget it."

"I think that's an older sister's role—to tease and torment her little brother."

"Obviously. What about you? Do you have any brothers or sisters?"

"No, I was an only child." Robin's smile, what there was of it, disappeared altogether. "I didn't want Peter growing up an only child."

There was a starkness to her words that crushed the breath from Jake. He wanted to shout, "I'm sorry I killed your husband! It was an accident! A damned accident!" Instead, he deliberately kept his eyes trained on the road, wondering if she thought it strange that he asked no questions about her husband's death. But then, she'd never seemed eager to volunteer anything.

As Jake was dealing with these thoughts, Robin was trying to imagine Gerald's reaction to a second child. Unlike her pregnancy with Peter, the next one would have been planned for after they were financially secure, after Gerald was firmly ensconced in his new job, and he'd have thought it perfectly timed. Wouldn't he? Yes, of course, he would. Without the slightest doubt. Then why did she feel the need to flee from the subject?

"You're a policeman," Robin heard herself saying.

It was what she'd wanted to say ever since she'd made the realization. Or rather, ever since she'd had the realization foisted upon her. The words, however, had seemed reluctant to be spoken. Just the way her heart seemed reluctant to slow to a normal pace following the unexpected encounter with the two police officers. Her reaction had surprised her. She had expected to feel anger, a kind of proxy anger aimed at any policeman. Instead, the sight of the uniforms had terrified her. She'd been afraid that the men would recognize her. Which was stupid, she knew. How could they have recognized her? And why should she have been the one terrified, anyway? Simple. Because she didn't want to talk about what had happened. She just wanted to hide away. Even so, learning that the man beside her was a policeman was such a jolt that she had to say something. She had to hear him confirm or deny it.

This time Jake couldn't keep his eyes from her. "Yeah, I'm a policeman," he said as though nothing could have been more unimportant.

She glanced over at him. It suddenly crossed her mind that he might know of her husband's death—just how fluid was the gossip that flowed back and forth in the police department? With all the news coverage, most of which she'd considered yellow, sensational journalism, how could he not have heard about it? Maybe he even knew the policeman who had shot Gerald. Again, she felt as if she were skating on thin ice. The subject was one she could easily fall through and drown in.

"I hadn't realized you were," she said.

Jake shrugged. "I guess I never mentioned it." *Liar! You know damned well you never mentioned it!*

"I'm not sure what I thought you did." She smiled, again only with half her heart. "I guess I thought you were one of those rich types that spent your idle hours volunteering at the hospital."

"Hardly," Jake said, adjusting the heater. Was it hot in the car or did squirming in one's seat cause one to sweat?

"But you *are* taking some time off? I mean, it sounded as if you were on vacation or something."

Or something, Jake thought, but said, "Yeah, I had accrued a lot of leave and . . . well, this seemed like a good time to take it."

Robin's look said, "Why now?"

Jake grabbed at the first logical reason that came along. "My dad . . . he needs some extra attention right now and . . . well, I had the time to give him that attention, so . . ." He let the sentence trail off.

He'd always heard that lies got easier, but that wasn't true. Lies didn't get easier. They just got darker. He'd also heard that everyone had a price. That he did believe. Everyone had the potential for being a liar. All you had to do was find the right button to push. All you had to do was establish an individual's price.

Jake steeled himself for at least a dozen other uncomfortable questions, but, surprisingly, none came. Instead, Robin merely stared quietly out into the night. It struck him that she really didn't want to pursue his being a policeman any more than he did. Which he thought a little strange. Unless, of course, she'd chosen to blank everything out because of the pain. Whatever, or why ever, he allowed himself to feel a measure of relief. The only thing that concerned him, and equally heaped guilt upon him, was the fact that

Robin, now that she knew he was a cop, seemed to draw even deeper into herself. It was no more than he expected, yet the sight of her huddled all alone, her small shoulders stoically squared, hurt. Badly. So badly that he surprised himself by wanting to reach for her and haul her into his arms. Instead, he tightened his hands on the steering wheel.

In less than forty-five minutes, Jake turned the Jeep into Robin's driveway. The squat cottage sat on the shallow outskirts of Lowell. As the vehicle's headlights slashed through the darkness the house's isolation jumped out with crystal clarity. Woods, shadowed with the color of night, hugged one side of the small structure, while the other side just seemed to plunge down toward a deep ravine. The nearest neighbor was a good mile away.

"You don't mind being out here all alone?" Jake asked, cutting the engine and the car's headlights. Dim lights, a faded gold, beckoned from the cottage porch. In contrast, the moon beamed brashly.

"Actually, it was the solitude that appealed to me," Robin said, unable to ignore the way the moonlight draped across Jake's broad shoulders. Shoulders that she intuitively knew would be filled with strength and security. She forced her gaze from those wide, strong shoulders and to his eyes. His kind-looking eyes.

"You're never afraid?" he asked.

She grinned. "Never of bogeymen."

Her phraseology, which surprised her, implied that there were things that she *was* afraid of. What were those things? she wondered. She was, of course, afraid for Peter. She also realized that she was afraid for herself. Afraid of growing old alone. Afraid of enduring so many lonely nights that her heart would shrivel up and die. Afraid that the memories of Gerald would always taunt her, haunt her. Afraid... Afraid of the arm—Jake's arm—that now lay nonchalantly across the back of the seat, his fingers almost, almost, brushing against her shoulder. Afraid? Surely not. Yet why had her heart quickened its pace? And why was she pulling her shoulder away in order to eliminate even the merest possibility that her shoulder and his fingers might meet?

Jake saw her pull away. Was she afraid of him? Furthermore, was he afraid of her? Of the way the moonlight spilled across her porcelain skin? Of the way it splashed across her oh-so-vulnerable-and-soft-looking lips?

"I had a nice time," Robin said, now avoiding Jake's eyes altogether, her gaze resting, instead, on the square angle of his chin. A chin that hours earlier had been clean-shaven, but was now bearing the faintest trace of shaded stubble.

"So did I."

"Thank you. For asking me."

"My pleasure."

She clasped her purse to her as though it had become her lifeline. Still her gaze did not meet his. "I, uh, I should go in. I have a busy day tomorrow."

In response, Jake reeled in his arm from the back of the seat.

"No!" Robin said, her gaze now jumping to his. Forcing her voice to a lower pitch, she added, "It isn't necessary for you to get out."

"I'll walk you to the door."

"You don't have—"

"I'll walk you to the door," Jake said, giving her no choice in the matter.

She watched as he slipped from the vehicle and rounded its hood. She also felt her heart burst into a wilder pace. Stop it! she told herself. Jake Cameron had said he wanted to be her friend . . . nothing more. And his behavior had been of the strictest propriety. What harm was there in a friend walking another friend to her door?

In seconds, Jake was reaching to assist her down. At first there was the pressure of his hand on her arm—a minuscule pressure. His hand then moved to rest ever-so-slightly, but with a complete naturalness, on her shoulder. The guiding gesture loosely resembled having his arm about her. It also dramatically pointed out his height and her lack thereof.

Jake was aware once again of a strong, basic urge to shield this woman. He told himself that the urge had been built into the species and involved nothing more than instinct.

The gesture reminded Robin, too, of his having his arm around her. It equally reminded her that there would be strength and security in his embrace. For one brief and reckless second, she gave herself permission to enjoy the feeling of being protected. She excused her actions by telling herself that he was merely acting as a buffer against the blunt coldness and that, as such, she'd be stupid not to avail herself of it.

At the door, she turned . . . still within the shelter of his body. Her gaze traveled up his coat-wrapped chest, to the hollow of his throat, to his chin, past his lips and nose, before settling on his eyes. His night-black eyes. Her gaze quickly skittered away.

"Well, good night," she said, starting to turn around.

"Robin?" Jake heard himself calling her name. He'd had no idea that he was going to do that. Neither did he have any idea what he was going to say now that he had. He simply knew that he couldn't let her go. Not just yet.

Robin turned back, her expectant gaze lifting to his.

Jake, however, said nothing, did nothing. He simply stared at her. For long, long moments.

Suddenly, a gust of wind washed out of the west.

Suddenly, a swath of tawny-colored hair blew across Robin's taupe-tinted lips.

Suddenly, Jake's gaze lowered to those lips.

He was going to kiss her. Somewhere in the back of his mind he acknowledged that fact even as he brushed aside the errant strand of hair. He felt his heart pick up speed as his head slowly began to angle and lower.

He was going to kiss her. Somewhere in the back of her mind Robin knew this the instant his fingers trailed across her cheek, drawing back the wayward wisps of her hair. She knew it, yet her brain was reluctant to register it, possibly because it was preoccupied with processing the fact that his fingers, though rough-tipped, slid so smoothly across her skin. When his head began to lower, however, her brain was sharp enough to signal her heart to begin a savage thumping.

His mouth took hers with a gentle, simple uncomplicatedness. From the beginning, from the very second that his lips merged with hers, a grazing of the subtlest magnitude, he was aware of her passiveness. She wasn't kissing him back. But neither was she drawing away from him. This last he recognized as important, but he couldn't hold on to the thought. He was too busy realizing that her lips were softer, warmer than he'd ever imagined them. But how could he have imagined a soft as fleecy as airy clouds, a warm as drizzly as buttery sunshine? And how, dear God, could he keep his hand from splaying against the ivory smoothness of her cheek?

Robin, her hands still clutching her purse, had no recourse but to acknowledge the sweet pressure of Jake's kiss, the tender framing of her face by his oversized palm. Likewise, she felt warm ribbons, like silken kite streamers snapping in a breeze, flutter through her. The feeling proclaimed that she was alive, a fact she had seemingly forgotten, or perhaps chosen to ignore, during the past miserable months. Even as she felt guilty about being alive when Gerald was dead, she couldn't help but glory in the rebirth. So much so that she heard herself moan. At least she thought it was she who'd made the provocative sound.

Jake heard the moan spilling from her. He deepened the kiss, slanting his mouth across hers and opening his lips slightly. Warmth met warmth. Wetness met wetness. He felt her lips tremble to life beneath his—a slow awakening that died as quickly as it had been born. Curious, he withdrew his moist mouth from hers.

Confusion.

He instantly saw the startled confusion in her eyes He had taken her completely by surprise. Perhaps she'd even taken herself by surprise by responding, albeit her response had been guarded. What wounded his very soul, however, was the betrayed look in her eyes, the look that said she'd betrayed herself and her husband, the look that said he, Jake, had betrayed her. He'd promised her friendship, then had broken that promise.

"I'm...I'm sorry," he whispered, drawing his hand from her cheek. "I hadn't intended...I didn't plan...I..." He trailed off, his eyes beseeching her to say something that would ease his own self-reproach.

She said nothing.

"Robin," he pleaded.

Still she said nothing. She simply stood clenching her purse to her as the frigid, fiery wind tangled her hair about her.

The picture she made, one of abject vulnerability, hacked at Jake like a dull knife. "Dammit, I said I'm sorry! What more can I do?"

"Leave," she said softly, unemotionally, adding, "Please just leave."

Jake opened his mouth to say something—what, he wasn't sure—but closed it without saying a word. What was the use? What the hell was the use? Whirling on his heels, he tramped across the yard, wrenched open the Jeep door and hurled himself on to the seat. He ground the engine to a start and, burning rubber, peeled out of the driveway, not certain with whom he was angry, her or himself, or perhaps both. The last thing he saw in the car's headlights was Robin still standing at the front door. A look of betrayal still glazed her beautiful eyes.

"ARE YOU OUT OF YOUR MIND?"

The phone had been ringing when Jake entered his apartment. Maneuvering in the dark, he had groped his way to the bedroom, turned on the lamp and plopped down on the side of the unmade bed. Dragging the receiver to his ear, he hadn't had a chance to utter a word before the question was hurled at him. He'd instantly recognized his sister's voice.

"Is this one of those telephone surveys?" he asked, threading his fingers through his winter-chilled hair. If age were measured by weariness, he felt as old and grizzled as Methuselah.

"Cut out the cuteness and just answer the question. Are you out of your ever-loving mind?"

Jake lay back, closed his eyes and said, "Probably. No make that a definitely."

There was a pause as Whitney picked up on the fatigue in her brother's voice. Her tone had softened considerably when she said, "Oh, Jake, how could you? Don't you know it's the worst thing you could have done?"

Actually, it had been easy to infiltrate Robin's life, he thought, and no, it wasn't the worst thing he could have done. Kissing her was the worst thing he could have done. God, how could he have kissed her? How could he have so callously betrayed their friendship? And now that he had kissed her, how could he ever forget the taste of her lips? A sound came from somewhere. He recognized it as a groan. His own.

"Are you all right?"

"Yeah," Jake answered. "Just ducky."

"She doesn't know who you are, does she?" Whitney asked.

"Of course not. You think she'd go out to dinner with me if she did?"

"What happens when she finds out?"

"She won't."

"How can you be so sure—"

"She won't. I just need to see that she's all right and then . . . and then I'll disappear just the way I appeared." The thought brought an unexpected streak of pain to his heart. "Look, Whitney, I don't expect

you to understand. It's just something that I've got to
do, all right?''

"I do understand," Whitney said quietly. "At least
I think I do. I know for certain that I'm trying to."

"I appreciate that," he said, wondering if she'd explain it to him then.

"Jake—" Whitney paused, as though searching for
the right words "—you're not getting...involved, are
you?"

The question surprised Jake, particularly since it
brought such vivid images to his mind, images of soft,
warm lips. He ignored the images, though, at least as
best he could, answering with, "You mean as in man
and wench?"

"Exactly."

"What do you take me for, Sis? A complete fool?"

"How about just a human being?" his sister responded softly.

THE CONVERSATION STAYED with him for the next
three weeks. In fact, every sleepless night, every restless day, it hounded him. Was he getting involved? He
never seemed able to arrive at an answer. Or maybe he
just always defensively stopped short of one. One dark
night toward the end of the three weeks, he forced
himself to admit that maybe Robin hadn't responded
to him, after all. Maybe her moan and the trembling
of her lips had merely been in protest to the liberties
he'd been taking. No, dammit, she had responded to
him! A man couldn't misinterpret signals that sen-
sually clear.

So? he'd asked as he'd lain awake, his hands stacked
beneath his head, the cover midway up his bare, hair-
dusted chest despite the chill of the room.

So... in answer to the question he'd asked two thousand times... yes. Yes, he was getting involved with Robin. And, furthermore, Robin was getting involved with him. Interestingly, he'd known the answer all along. Why else hadn't he tried to call or see her? Why else had he worked so hard to avoid running into her at the hospital? Why else had he stopped going to the Wee Care meetings? A fool he may be, a jerk he may be, but he wasn't an unfeeling, uncaring sonofabitch. While it was true that she needed someone in her life to help her heal from the tragedy she'd lived through, the uncompromising truth was that she didn't need him. In fact, he was the very last man on the face of the earth that she needed.

And yet, he couldn't forget the taste, the feel, the tender trembling of her lips. Nor the fact that maybe his sister was right. Maybe he wasn't a fool, a jerk or a sonofabitch. Maybe he was just a human being.

Peter's progress during this period of time gave Jake something positive to focus on. The baby continued to breathe normally under the oxygen hood and almost visibly gained precious ounces. In the appropriate stages, he was taken off continuous tube feeding and placed on gavage. This, too, consisted of a form of tube feeding, although the tube was removed after each feeding... only to be inserted again two hours later when the hungry baby was refed. Then, with a dexterity that delighted the nurses, Peter began to nipple. A large hole was cut in an ordinary-sized nipple, allowing the child to suck the milk easily. Jake, who still talked to the baby as though the blue-eyed infant understood every word he said, longed to share Peter's progress with Robin. Did her eyes light up like golden sparklers at the sight of him nursing from a bottle? Was she only living for the day when he would suckle at her breast? Was she still scared that something would go wrong?

SOMETHING HAS TO GO WRONG, Robin thought every day when she visited Peter. Things were going too smoothly, too wonderfully. She longed to talk to Jake about this subtle, insidious fear that never seemed to go away entirely, just the way she longed to share these happy moments with him. She had missed seeing him the past few weeks, though, to be honest, she had needed the time alone. Jake Cameron confused her. Not only didn't she think clearly around him, she no longer thought clearly period.

"Leave. Please just leave."

The words, her words, harsh despite the quiet way in which they'd been delivered, played themselves over and over again in her mind. She could still see the hurt look in Jake's eyes, could still see the anger in his clipped stride. She could still feel his lips pressed to hers.

No!

The way she always did, she banished the tender vision of his kiss, but it, like her words, came back night after night to haunt her. Curiously, the dream of Gerald's blood-splattered body hadn't recurred. But then, how could it? You couldn't dream when you were wide awake.

Had she really wanted to kiss Jake back?

She never let herself answer that question. To keep from doing so, she'd fling herself from the bed and knit on the brown sweater she'd begun weeks before. Or she'd sketch. Or she'd simply roam from one room to another. One night, rather than face the question, she even opened the box of clothes that Gerald had been wearing when he'd been shot. She wasn't sure where her courage came from. She strongly suspected that courage wasn't involved at all, but rather cowardice. She'd do anything—anything—to keep from facing the question of whether she'd really wanted to return Jake's kiss.

Looking, touching the familiar clothes, clothes splotched with stiff, rust-colored bloodstains, had produced a surreal feeling. Which had thankfully resulted in a numbness. She was aware of everything she was doing. It was just that it was happening to someone else. Between the khaki pants, which Robin thought Gerald had paid a fortune for, and the striped shirt, which had cost only half a fortune, she had found a bloodstained handkerchief. It wasn't Gerald's. Of that she was certain. For one thing, he carried them only rarely and, when he did, they were always of the finest cloth. This handkerchief, though nice enough, was quite ordinary. Its only distinguishing characteristic was that it was initialed with a *C*. As though tapping on her shoulder, the monogrammed handkerchief beckoned some memory, but she couldn't conjure it up. She did, however, know one thing with a macabre certainty: it was Gerald's blood dried upon the fabric.

That night she hadn't slept at all, but rather had tossed and turned and fretfully sighed. Images of Gerald had bombarded her. There had been other images as well. Images equally potent, equally powerful. Images of broad shoulders that could shelter her from nightmare-gray memories. Images of lips that could make her forget everything except their warmth.

She moaned.

"I'm sorry...I hadn't intended...I didn't plan...I'm sorry...sorry...sorry..."

Robin gave a long sigh and grudgingly made the admission that she'd fought for days, weeks. Jake might have startled her, surprised her, confused her, but she wasn't sorry he'd kissed her. Furthermore— and this she could no longer deny—she'd wanted to kiss him back.

The following Tuesday afternoon, as she rode the hospital elevator upward, Robin wondered if Jake would be in the nursery. And had she unconsciously overslept and busied herself with a string of errands just so she'd arrive at the hospital during the hours she thought he volunteered? The question was one she never answered because the second the nursery came into view, Robin's heart exploded within her chest.

Peter's bed was empty.

CHAPTER SEVEN

PANIC, LIKE A SCALDING river, rushed through Robin, searing all rational thought. On the other hand, a remnant of clearheadedness tried to surface, reminding her that surely the hospital would have called had Peter's condition worsened. While they probably wouldn't have given her any bad news over the phone, they at least would have asked her to come to the hospital. But they hadn't called. A new wave of blistering panic washed over her when she realized that she hadn't been home for a couple of hours, that she'd been out running errands. What if they'd tried to reach her then?

Oblivious to the startled glances within the nursery, Robin burst through the door, recklessly banging it against the wall. The jarring noise ricocheted around the quiet room. Wild-eyed, her heart racing, Robin grabbed the first nurse she came to.

"Where is he? Where's my baby?"

As quickly as she seized the nurse, she released her and, driven by a powerful, frantic instinct, began to search for her son. Her gaze darted from one radiant warmer to another.

A second nurse caught Robin by the arm. "Mrs. Bauer—"

"Where is he?"

"...please, Mrs. Bauer, calm down—"

"Where's Peter?"

"...please," the nurse repeated, trying to restrain Robin, who now fought like a she-tiger to free herself.

With a superhuman strength, she broke away, screaming, "Dammit, where's my baby?"

From out of nowhere, two strong hands gripped Robin's upper arms, stilling her against her will. She was vaguely aware that the pressure produced by the hands intimately bordered on pain. She was also vaguely aware of a familiarity. The hands were familiar. As was the wide chest her gaze scaled. Along with the angular chin. And the nut-brown eyes.

"Peter's all right," the soft, velvet-smooth voice said. The *familiar* soft, velvet-smooth voice. When Robin said nothing, but continued to just stare up at Jake, he shook her...gently. "Robin?"

She blinked, as though trying to bring life back into focus.

"Do you hear me?" he asked, repeating, "Peter's all right. They moved him from the radiant warmer to an isolette. He's breathing on his own. Look."

Robin followed the line of Jake's vision. It led to a tiny crib, where Peter, dressed in an outing flannel gown, slept peacefully despite the scene his mother had just created. Gone were all the frightening tubes. Gone was the scary, outer-space-looking oxygen hood. Robin watched as her son's small chest rose and fell, its regular rhythm regulated by nothing more than the baby's own breathing. Considering that her own breath was caught somewhere between fear and hope, breathing was a feat that her young son seemed far more adept at than she.

"See, I told you he was all right."

All of a sudden, the relief that flooded Robin was more than she could bear. Her every muscle going limp, her legs liquefying, she slumped against Jake. Her arms slid around him, while she buried her cheek against his wide chest. Beneath her ear, she heard the reassuring beat of his heart. She didn't question why being in his arms felt so normal, so natural. It simply did. And that was more than enough for her.

Likewise, Jake didn't ponder why his arms tightened around her, nor why it felt so right for her to be burrowing into him. He also felt her breasts cozying against his chest. That, too, felt right. Good. And as natural as his own heartbeat.

"It's okay," he said as his hands caressed her back. "There's nothing to be frightened of." He spoke low and softly, his words audible only to the woman he held.

The rest of the room returned to normal. Everyone kept his distance, except the head nurse who slowly made her way toward the couple.

"It's okay," Jake repeated, finding the small of Robin's back and pulling her more deeply into him. She fit. Exactly. A fact that didn't surprise him at all. Somehow, he'd known from the first that she would.

As her body began to ease its quivering, as her breathing began to return to normal, Robin became aware of Jake's arms...of his body and how it was pressed intimately, protectively against hers...of what a fool she must have made of herself. Thinking of the latter, the fool she'd made of herself, made her want to lose herself all the more in the refuge of his body.

"Mrs. Bauer?" the nurse called quietly.

Robin jerked her head upward.

"Are you all right?"

It came as a shock to Robin to realize that there was another person within a hundred miles. When she did, she glanced at the nurse, then at Jake, then back at the nurse. With a faint blush to her cheeks, she stepped from Jake's embrace. Was it her imagination, or did he seem slow releasing her? Brushing back a swath of hair from her eyes, she answered, "Yes, I'm fine. I thought...when I didn't see Peter...I'm sorry, I guess I went a little crazy."

The nurse smiled. "It's understandable. I just regret we frightened you. We'd wanted it to be a wonderful surprise, not something that scared you half to death."

Robin grinned—sheepishly. "Obviously I'm just one of those hysterical types that jumps to a conclusion."

"Actually," the nurse said, "we thought you'd be in this morning, and we were going to move Peter while you were here. When you didn't come in, we decided to go ahead and try him on his own."

Robin glanced over at Jake. Was it written across her forehead that she'd waited until she suspected he might be at the hospital? And how did he feel about seeing her again? Nothing in his eyes gave her any clue as to how he was feeling or what he was thinking. "I, uh, I had some errands to run," she said, pulling her gaze away.

Jake couldn't decipher the look she'd given him. For one brief moment he'd entertained the notion that Robin had changed her hours in hopes of finding him there, but he quickly told himself that was foolish thinking. It was also dangerous thinking. Her showing up this afternoon, or a thousand other afternoons, didn't alter one basic fact: their relationship—

if what they had could be called that—was going nowhere. No couple had a future when they had their
past.

At the sudden whimpering sound, all three adults,
in one chorus of motion, pivoted. The fleecy blue
blanket tucked around Peter began to move as his legs
kicked and scrambled. One minuscule hand clenched
into a fist and wedged itself into one little mouth. The
little mouth sucked hungrily. When nothing nourish-
ing was forthcoming, the whimper turned into an out-
and-out wail.

The three adults smiled. "I'd say he's very much all
right," the nurse said, "that is, if you don't count
being a little fussy. What is it, fella?" she asked, stepping forward and automatically checking the baby's
color, then the state of his diaper, "are you hungry?"

The wail grew.

"Sounds as if he has his mother's sense of histrion-
ics," Robin said.

"Sounds as if he has his mother's appetite," Jake
said softly.

Robin turned. A grin hiked one corner of Jake's
mouth. Robin's mouth followed suit. It was funny, but
she never thought to smile anymore unless it was
around this man. Before she could verbally respond,
Jake's smile faded.

"Are you all right?" he asked, remembering how
her body only minutes before had been quaking with
fright.

"Yes," she answered, her manner now as serious as
his. She, too, remembered what had happened minutes earlier—how her body had felt thick with fear,
how Jake's body, hard and muscular, had held her.

Each was so caught up in the other that it took several seconds for them to realize that the nurse was speaking. "...log in the feeding in the chart, Mr. Cameron, if you would, please. I'd like to introduce breast-feeding and see how Peter does. He may not have the strength he needs yet, so don't be disturbed if he doesn't suckle properly. In fact, he might not be able to get any milk at all. Remember he's used to a large hole in a plastic nipple."

These last comments were said to Robin and in a tone that suggested the caution had been given routinely innumerable times before. The nurse also scooped a blanket-clad Peter, who was still fretting loudly, into her arms and started for the small room set aside for mothers to nurse their babies.

Robin stood rooted to the spot, as though she were uncertain she'd heard correctly, as though afraid to believe she had.

"Go on," Jake said quietly, gently.

Something in his eyes told Robin that he knew what the moment meant to her. It was a dream coming true, but, as so often happens, the realization of a dream can be a scary thing.

Giving a thumbs-up sign, Jake smiled and said, "Go for it."

Robin returned his smile, wondering how he always knew just what to say.

THIRTY MINUTES LATER, Robin stared lovingly down at her dark-haired son. His eyelids, framed in raven-black lashes, lay shuttered against his baby-pink skin. Though he was asleep, his mouth was still loosely fitted around the nipple of her breast. Occasionally, instinctively, he suckled. Robin felt each movement of his mouth at the very core of her mother's heart. Smiling softly, she drew a crooked finger across his cheek. If he'd been graded on effort alone, he would clearly have earned an A—he'd sucked his little heart out. Conversely, if he'd been graded on milk produced, he would have earned substantially less. Robin was convinced that, though he must surely still be hungry, he had fallen asleep out of sheer exhaustion.

"We'll do better next time," she whispered. "I'm new at this, too."

The nurse had instructed Robin on the elemental skills of breast-feeding, then had left mother and son alone, checking occasionally to see if they were all right. Robin took comfort in the fact that the nurse didn't seem in the least disturbed at Peter's inability to draw milk. On the contrary, she seemed pleased at what strength he'd displayed.

Once, when the nurse opened the door, Robin saw Jake working with one of the other babies. For a reason she couldn't explain, she felt very much alone when the nurse left minutes later. It was then that she'd noticed that the room had been designed for two—a mother and a father. Though she knew it was inappropriate, she imagined Jake beside her, then was immediately overcome with guilt. Why hadn't she imagined Gerald? She had no answer to that. The fact that she did not troubled her.

"How are we doing in here?"

Robin glanced up to see the nurse standing at the door. Grateful for the interruption of her murky thoughts, she smiled. "He wore himself out," she said quietly so as not to wake the baby. Even so, Peter squirmed, released her breast and blew a sweet sigh across her exposed skin. A bubble, composed of air, saliva and milk, formed at the corner of his mouth.

"He might have gotten more milk than we thought," the nurse said, easing the infant from his mother. He whimpered before sliding back into the sweet oblivion of sleep.

After the nurse left with Peter, Robin rearranged her tangerine-colored sweater. She was just refastening the last button of the garment as she opened the door. Jake stood nearby, making notes in a chart. At the sound of the door, he looked up. His eyes met Robin's. Robin's hand, still at the button, hesitated, as did her heart.

At the exact same instant, Jake's heart hesitated, as well. Actually, he wasn't certain it didn't stop altogether for a second. He fought to keep his eyes from lowering to her hand, to her breasts. He lost the battle, however, simply because lowering his gaze to her breasts seemed natural. Just the way it had seemed natural for him to join her and Peter in the private room. He'd had to keep reminding himself that his joining her would have been grossly improper. To say nothing of how it would have shocked the nurses. Would Robin have been shocked? Undoubtedly.

"How did it go?" he asked, closing the chart and rehanging it. He forced from his mind the image of the gentle curves that lay beneath the clinging sweater.

Robin lowered her hand from the button and shrugged. "For two amateurs, okay, I guess."

Jake smiled. "The nurse said it'll take a little time."

"Right," Robin answered, a million thoughts clashing in her mind. Why hadn't she imagined Gerald with her? Why had she imagined this man? And why did the look he was giving her make her skin feel fevered?

Moments passed, filled with heartbeats and heartaches and memories that neither could get to die despite the passage of three weeks, memories of warm, soft lips on a chafing-cold night.

Jake thought of the betrayal he'd seen in her eyes.

Robin thought of the harsh words she'd spoken to him.

"Look, I'm sorry..." he began.

"I'm sorry about..." she said at the same time.

They both stopped, each knowing what the other was referring to, each knowing that standing in the middle of NICU was hardly the place for such personal apologies.

Frustrated with their timing, Jake thrust his fingers through his hair and asked, "When are you leaving?"

Robin rerouted her gaze from his massive, hairdusted hand to the clock on the wall. "In a few minutes."

"I'll walk you down."

She didn't argue. For two reasons. One, she didn't think it would have done any good; two, she didn't want to.

A short while later, after a quiet elevator ride during which both stole glances at the other, Jake pushed open the door that led to the parking garage. A blast of cold air struck Robin full in the face. As she was snuggling into the woolen scarf wrapped around her neck, Jake, his coat collar turned up, stepped to her side. He matched his stride to hers.

"Where are you parked?" he asked. In the cavernous garage, where cars were stacked tier after tier, his voice echoed softly, huskily, as did their footsteps. Evening shadows were beginning to fall, casting the area in a gray, gauzy gloaming, creating a lone and lost world.

"Over there," she answered, pointing several rows to their right.

Jake followed her directions, spotted the car and selected the path they took by placing his hand at the small of her back. Despite the multilayers of her clothes, Robin was very much aware of his touch. And of the need to finish what she'd started earlier. While she still had the courage.

"I'm sorry," she said, not glancing up at him, but rather keeping her eyes trained straight ahead. It made saying what she had to say easier. "About that night...about telling you to leave, I mean."

Jake, he too keeping his eyes from her, wanted to hear her apology, though he knew he didn't deserve it. "You had a good reason to tell me to leave. You were angry. Which you should have been."

"You're right, I was angry, but not with you. I was angry with myself."

Jake glanced down at her, and she up at him. His surprised look demanded an explanation. It was an explanation she thought he'd earned.

"I was angry with myself because...because I wanted to kiss you back." Her words were whisper-soft—almost as soft as the lips speaking them. For all the words' softness, however, they jabbed Jake in the stomach like a pair of iron fists.

He stopped...vaguely aware that they had reached her car. It was clear he hadn't expected her admission...and didn't know what to say now that she'd made it. She, too, looked bewildered, as though she

couldn't believe what she'd just said and had no idea
what to say next. Consequently, each just stared at the
other, she into his dark brown eyes, he into her paler
hazel green. Each vividly remembered the kiss that was
now under discussion.

Robin swallowed.

Jake spoke. His voice was as gravelly as sea-tossed
sand. "I had no right to kiss you. I had no right to
presume. I...shouldn't have broken my promise to
you."

"It, uh, it's really a moot issue now, isn't it?" Robin
asked, her voice little more than a moonlit mist. "You
did kiss me and I did want..." She trailed off into a
vaporous nothingness. In a few moments, she said,
"Please understand. I've been a widow for only a few
months. Feeling what I felt, wanting to—" Jake could
see the blush crimsoning her skin "—wanting to kiss
you made me feel guilty."

"No!" Jake growled, the single word thundering
through the hollow-sounding stillness. He wouldn't let
her feel guilty! God, didn't he know how guilt could
coil your insides until you thought you'd die? He
couldn't stand the thought of her enduring that kind
of pain. "No," he repeated, this time more reasonably. "Don't feel guilty. It wasn't your fault." *Don't
you see? None of this is your fault. All of it's mine.
Mine, dammit!*

"That isn't true," she whispered. "It is my fault."

"No—"

"Yes," she interrupted, softly, but sharply. Her eyes
never wavered from his when she added, "Because
I've wondered every night for three weeks what it
would be like if you kissed me again. Because even as

we stand here, I wonder that same thing. I also wonder if I'd want to kiss you back.''

Her words, like a clever knife, whittled Jake's breath. They were so sweet, so honest, so contrary to the lie he was living. He wanted to tell her to run from him, to run hard and fast and never look back, but he didn't, couldn't, wouldn't. As the cold nipped their noses and slapped at their cheeks, he stood staring down at her...and wondering. He wondered the same thing she wondered. Would she kiss him back if he kissed her? And, whether she did or not, would he have the strength to resist her?

A sudden breeze sighed, temptingly, seductively scattering her tawny hair.

Damn me to hell! Jake thought, lowering his head as his finger tipped her chin upward. He didn't pause, but rather took her mouth as though it had been made exclusively for his, as though he was merely claiming his property. Even as he pressed his lips to hers, however, he felt the guilt, like black bilge, rise within him. He also felt a repeat of her passivity. He hadn't realized until just that moment how desperately he'd wanted her to return the kiss.

Despite the stillness of her lips, Jake continued his gentle assault. Taking her mouth from one angle, he tilted his head to take it from yet another. Then another. Sipping, supping, he rubbed his lips across hers, tasting her delicious essence as it burst upon his tongue. As though he had no control over his actions, his tongue flicked lazily across the fullness of her bottom lip. He then nibbled at the same spot—slowly, sensuously, as though eating the sweetest of sweetmeats.

At the feel of his teeth gnawing—erotically gnawing—at her lip, the last remnants of Robin's reserve
slipped away. Fire-hot feelings blasted through her,
singeing the edges of her guilt. To hell with guilt! To
hell with everything! She just wanted to feel alive!
Moaning, her lips quivered beneath his—tentatively,
shyly, but with certainty.

No kiss had ever stirred Jake's emotions more. No
kiss had ever stirred his body more. He felt as if he'd
been struck at the back of the knees. Wonderfully
struck. To counteract the toppling feeling, he leaned
against Robin's car. Groaning, he pulled her deep into
his arms as he parted his lips above hers. He felt her
lips melt against his—giving, taking, participating.
Her breasts brushed his arms, breasts that her son had
recently suckled at. Jake wondered, not lewdly, but
with an innate naturalness, what they'd feel like filling his hands, his mouth.

Robin flowed into Jake's body, her hands slipping
inside his coat and splaying wide against his chest, his
hands easing to her back and tugging her against him.
He tilted her pelvis until she fit perfectly against him.
Even through the layers of two coats, the position was
intimate. Man-woman intimate. And wholly erotic.
She could feel his thighs hard beneath hers, could feel
the possessive moves of his hands as they roamed over
the swell of her hips, could feel his mouth hot on hers.
She could feel him and everything that made him so
seductively male. She could feel...life. Glorious life!

But the traitor within taunted that she didn't deserve to be alive. Not with Gerald dead. Gerald. My,
God, how could she so easily forget him in the arms of
another man? Fighting the thick sensualness spread-

ing through her, Robin suddenly wrenched her mouth from Jake's.

He looked thoroughly startled.

"I have to go," she whispered, trying to pull from him.

Jake saw the return of her confusion, the revival of her guilt. But he also saw the passion clouding her eyes. That passion, and the urge to assuage her guilt, caused him to hold on to her.

"No, wait!" he said.

Her eyes met his squarely, pleadingly. "I have to go. Please."

Slowly, grudgingly, he released her. She stepped away from him and, unlocking her car door, opened it. She slid onto the seat and started the engine. Briefly their gazes touched as she began to back the car out of its slot.

Jake, his hands in his pockets, watched her drive from the parking garage. Long after she'd vanished, he still stood staring after her. One question kept repeating itself like a worn litany. How could someone so wrong for him feel so right?

THOUGHTS OF ROBIN'S sweet mouth were still on Jake's mind the following evening when the phone rang.

"Hello?"

"That's more like it," Daniel Jacoby said. "I knew finding yourself a woman would work a miracle."

Jake, dressed in gray sweats, a towel draped around his neck to absorb the sweat he'd broken while working out, dropped onto the kitchen stool. A quick vision of Robin flitted through his mind. For a fraction of a fantasy second, he could feel her crushed in his arms, could feel her lips responding to his.

"I take it I no longer sound clinically grumpy."

"You sound a helluva lot better than you did the other day. By the way, what's her name?"

Jake transferred the phone to his other ear, leaned down to open the refrigerator and pulled out a quart of chocolate milk. He ignored the sudden tightening of his stomach. "What makes you think there's a woman?" he asked casually.

"Benedaries and Frazier said they saw you with one."

Jake hesitated in bringing the milk carton to his mouth. Instead, he set it on the Formica cabinet. The tightening in his stomach could no longer be ignored. "Yeah, and what else did Curlylocks and the Fraz say?" He was still trying to sound casual, though it was a long way from what he felt.

"That she's a looker. Even if she is on the small side." Jake could feel his friend's sudden smile. "What're you two playing, Ken and Barbie?"

The teasing was part of the masculine camaraderie that men engaged in all the time. "Did I ever tell you you sound like my sister?"

"As a matter of fact, you did."

"Yeah well, Jacoby, I didn't mean it as a compliment."

"My, my, is that clinically grumpy I hear?"

"Stuff it, Doc."

Daniel Jacoby laughed. "All right, all right. I'll back off." Jake could actually hear his friend's smile fading. "I've got some interesting news."

"Yeah?" Jake asked, his stomach uncoiling as he reached for the chocolate milk. "Like what?"

"It appears that Century Aeronautics may not have been a simple robbery."

The milk carton stopped en route once more. "What do you mean?"

"Evidence now suggests that a sensitive set of plans for a new, revolutionary aircraft is missing."

Jake's mind reeled with all the implications of what he'd just heard. "Is that what the robbery was all about? Someone stealing the plans?"

"We don't know yet, but a quiet investigation's begun. It might turn out that the robberies were unrelated."

"That one was an inside job?"

"Possibly. Maybe even likely," the psychologist replied.

"What about Gerald Bauer?" Jake asked, quickly going to the heart of the matter like the methodical cop he was. "Is he a suspect?"

"At this point, everyone is."

Good God, how would Robin react if her husband were guilty of robbery? Jake thought, not even realizing that his first concern had been for her and not the possible easing of his own guilt.

"Anyway, I just thought you'd like to know," Daniel said, breaking into Jake's reverie.

"Yeah," Jake said, ruffling his hair with his fingers, "thanks for calling. I appreciate it."

"Oh and by the way, that reporter called again."

At the mention of Phil "the Bloodhound" Markham, Jake spat out an obscenity that would have earned him a considerable number of Hail Mary's if he still went to confession. Which he didn't. And hadn't in a long while. Ever since he'd learned that it

NO RISK, NO OBLIGATION TO BUY...NOW OR EVER!

GUARANTEED

PLAY "ROLL A DOUBLE" AND GET AS MANY AS SIX GIFTS!

HERE'S HOW TO PLAY:

1. Peel off label from front cover. Place it in space provided at right. With a coin, carefully scratch off the silver dice. This makes you eligible to receive one or more free books, and possibly other gifts, depending on what is revealed beneath the scratch-off area.

2. You'll receive brand-new Harlequin Superromance® novels. When you return this card, we'll rush you the books and gifts you qualify for ABSOLUTELY FREE!

3. Then, if we don't hear from you, every month we'll send you 4 additional novels to read and enjoy. You can return them and owe nothing, but if you decide to keep them, you'll pay only $2.74* per book - a savings of 21¢ each off the cover price! And, there's no extra charge for postage and handling!

4. When you subscribe to the Harlequin Reader Service®, you'll also get our newsletter, as well as additional free gifts from time to time.

5. You must be completely satisfied. You may cancel at any time simply by sending us a note or a shipping statement marked "cancel" or by returning any shipment to us at our expense.

DETACH AND MAIL CARD TODAY!

"ROLL A DOUBLE!"

PLACE LABEL HERE

SCRATCH HERE

SEE CLAIM CHART BELOW

134 CIH KA9E
(U-H-SR-09/90)

YES! I have placed my label from the front cover into the space provided above and scratched off the silver dice. Please rush me the free book(s) and gift(s) that I am entitled to. I understand that I am under no obligation to purchase any books, as explained on the opposite page.

NAME

ADDRESS   APT.

CITY   STATE   ZIP CODE

CLAIM CHART

🎲 🎲	**4 FREE BOOKS PLUS FREE 20k ELECTROPLATED GOLD CHAIN PLUS MYSTERY BONUS GIFT**
🎲 🎲	**3 FREE BOOKS PLUS BONUS GIFT**
🎲 🎲	**2 FREE BOOKS**

CLAIM NO. 37-829

HARLEQUIN "NO RISK" GUARANTEE

• You're not required to buy a single book - ever!
• You must be completely satisfied or you may cancel at any time simply by sending us a note or a shipping statement marked "cancel" or by returning any shipment to us at our cost. Either way, you will receive no more books; you'll have no further obligation.
• The free book(s) and gift(s) you claimed on this "Roll A Double" offer remain yours to keep no matter what you decide.

If offer card is missing, please write to: Harlequin Reader Service®, P.O. Box 1867, Buffalo, N.Y. 14269-1867 didn't much matter if God forgave him if he didn't forgive himself. "What'd he want?"

"The usual. A story. Said he'd heard you'd taken a leave of absence."

"What did the chief tell him?"

"To go snoop around another tree, that that kind of information was confidential. Then Markham got me on the phone wanting to know if I knew where the widow had fled to."

"What did you tell him?"

"Something considerably more colorful than go snoop around another tree."

Jake grinned. He could well imagine what the imaginative psychologist had said.

"So, what's the name of the woman you're seeing?" Daniel Jacoby asked, trying one last time.

Jake's grin disappeared. "She doesn't have a name."

"Okay, okay! Be gallant." As once before, Jake could sense his friend's flippant mood sobering. "Whatever her name is, keep seeing her. She's good for you."

Later that night, after consuming an entire quart of chocolate milk, Jake lay awake considering everything that Daniel Jacoby had said. Was it possible that the robbery had been more complex than once thought? Was it possible that Gerald Bauer was involved? And, if so, would the knowledge completely destroy Robin?

Robin.

No, Jake thought, remembering the last thing Daniel had said, Robin Bauer wasn't good for him. Or, more to the point, he wasn't good for her. He was a box of salt just waiting to be poured into a very raw wound. He rolled to his side and uttered an explicit profanity.

What in hell do you think you're doing, Cameron, letting this thing go on with her? Don't you know what you're doing is stupid, ridiculous, the craziest damned thing you've ever done?

The dark night his only companion, Jake admitted that, yes, what he was doing was stupid, ridiculous, the craziest damned thing he'd ever done. But it didn't alter the fact that Robin Bauer had the sweetest mouth he'd ever tasted.

CHAPTER EIGHT

TWO DAYS LATER, PROVING the theory that things can always get worse, Hank Cameron fell and broke his hip. Both Jake and Whitney were at his side when he came to following lengthy surgery.

"Hi, Pop," Jake said softly as his father tried to focus his drug-bleary eyes. Jake sat on one side of the bed, while his sister sat on the other. Each held an age-gnarled hand. The one Jake held had the tube of an IV feeding taped to it.

The elder Cameron, his face pale, his white hair mussed against the pillow, sought out the familiar voice. When he found it, he announced simply, groggily, "I fell."

"I know," Jake said, his heart constricting with pain.

"I told you to be careful chasing those wenches," Whitney said, drawing her father's attention.

Jake wondered if the old man heard the unshed tears that thickened his daughter's voice. They had been there ever since the doctor had said an hour before that, in his best professional judgment, his patient should be put in a nursing home to convalesce. The doctor had then restated that, if the patient were his father, he'd commit him to a nursing home permanently. It was nothing more than Jake and his sister had heard before, yet both knew that the time had come to make a decision. No longer would the situation wait for another day.

Hank attempted a weak smile with dry, cracked lips. "I almost had the wench, too."

Somewhere along the way, the senior Cameron's smile became a wince, then an outright grimace.

"Daddy?"

"Pop?"

"It hurts," he said, struggling to sit up despite the pain.

Jake jumped from his chair and, using all the strength he had, pressed his father's shoulders back onto the bed. "Lie still, Pop. You're going to hurt your hip."

"I want up," Hank said, wrestling with his son. "It hurts."

Jake fought the hands pushing against his chest. "I know," he said, "but you have to be still."

"I...want...up...!"

"Daddy, be still," Whitney pleaded, trying to keep the hand that had the IV dripping into it immobile. She couldn't however, and the needle tore from the thin skin. A stream of blood began to trickle down the age spotted arm.

"Daddy!" she wailed.

"Get the nurse," Jake ordered through gritted teeth.

An hour later, Hank Cameron lay sedated and restrained. The restraints, thin strips of cloth fastened around both wrists and tied to the bed, looked innocuous enough...to all except loved ones. It was all Jake could do to keep from ripping them from his father. It hurt, all the way to the quick of the heart, to see this man, once so fit, always so proud, forcibly bound. Jake had thought he wouldn't be able to stand another second of hearing his father beg to be untied. Thankfully, the sedative had done its job quickly.

Jake glanced over at his sister. She stood at the foot of the bed just staring at their father. She hadn't shed a tear. Not one. Jake wished she would. She needed to release the tension coiled inside her. Just the way he needed to. Interestingly, he thought that tension might ease if he could only share his heartache with Robin, if he could only feel her arms wrapped around him. He pushed the thought of Robin away, the way he had a thousand times since they'd kissed in the garage two days before. Or, rather, he tried to push the thought of her away.

After a few quiet words to Mollie—the live-in companion had insisted that her duties included staying at the hospital—Jake laid his hand on his sister's shoulder. "C'mon, let's go. Pop's out till morning."

Whitney, as though just landing back on Earth from some far planet, looked up at her brother. Wordlessly, she bent and retrieved her coat from the chair. Slipping into it as Jake slid into his own, she walked toward the door, which he held open for her. Neither spoke as they traversed the silent halls of Massachusetts General Hospital. Neither spoke as the elevator quietly carried them to the garage. Whitney's composure lasted until she reached her car. Then fat tears gushed to her eyes.

"Ah, Sis," Jake whispered, taking her in his arms. He held her, his hand cradled at the back of her head, as she cried for both of them.

"I can't stand...to see him...that way," she squeezed out around gulps of air.

"I know."

"The restraints... Oh, God, Jake, they tied him down!"

Jake tightened his hold. "I know," he said roughly. "I know."

Finally, her tears spent, Whitney raised her head. "I'm sorry," she said, sniffing and swiping and stepping back.

"Are you okay?" Jake asked, releasing her.

She nodded, once more the strong woman she'd always been when circumstances demanded it. It was the same kind of strength he'd seen in Robin. Maybe women, despite their fragile size compared with men, were really the stronger of the sexes, after all.

"Yeah," Whitney said. "I'm fine. Look, I'll take off a few hours early tomorrow," she added, referring to her job as a legal secretary, "and we can start shopping around for a nursing home."

"Just let me know when. I'm flexible."

"I'd like to get a home close by, so we won't have to drive far to visit."

"I agree."

She mentioned several nursing homes near where they both lived.

"Those sound like good places to start."

"Can you come by and see about Dad in the morning?"

"I'd already planned on it."

"I'll stay tomorrow night."

"You can't work days and stay up here at night. I'll stay."

"But that isn't fair to you," Whitney insisted. "You'll be assuming more of the burden than I am."

"I'm flexible right now. Remember?"

"I know, but—"

"You're not going to work days and play nurse at night. Mollie and I can switch out, or we can hire a relief sitter."

Whitney smiled faintly. "Yes, sir." Her smile faded. Laying her gloved palm against his cheek, she asked, "How about you, little brother? Are you all right?"

"Yeah."

She studied him, as though verifying the truth of his answer. At last she asked, "Have you seen her again?" She didn't need to clarify about whom she was speaking.

Jake rammed his hands into his coat pockets and leaned back against his sister's car. He crossed one booted ankle over the other. "Two days ago," he answered. *A lifetime ago. A breathless kiss ago.*

Whitney evaluated the tortured tone of her brother's voice, the agonized look in his eyes. "Just how deep are you in?"

Jake glanced over at his sister. She hadn't asked *if* he were in, but rather how deep he was. "I don't know." Even as he responded, however, he thought that maybe he did know how deep he was in. Maybe what he was feeling could legitimately be called love. "I, uh, I'm not going to be seeing her again."

Perhaps he should have been surprised to hear himself saying the latter, but he wasn't. It was the unavoidable conclusion he'd been slowly heading for for two days. Whatever he was feeling for her, whatever strong emotion, demanded that he protect her. Even from himself. Most particularly from himself.

"I'm sorry, Jake," Whitney whispered. "So sorry."

THE NEXT TEN DAYS WERE a nightmare for Jake. He spent practically every waking moment at the hospi-

tal at his father's side. He alternated every other night
with Mollie. When he wasn't at the hospital, he and
Whitney were searching for a nursing home. He had
expected to find them dark, dingy, foul-smelling in-
stitutions. They were not, however, and that greatly
relieved him. Even so, how could he muster the courage to move his father into one?

It was a question he asked repeatedly, either as he
sat by his father's bedside or lay restlessly in his own
bed. There were also other questions that relentlessly
plagued him, such as: What was Robin doing? Had
she missed him? Had she even cared enough to ask the
neonatal nurses why he'd been absent from the nursery?

As always, thoughts of Robin added to his frustration, leaving him wider awake, leaving him to toss and
turn and swear, leaving him to recall the taste of her
mouth, the feel of her body, the brush of her softly
curved breasts. He'd promised himself that he
wouldn't see her again. Not personally, anyway. Not
on door stoops or in darkened garages. Not where he'd
be tempted to shed his resolve and kiss her again.

On the tenth day, the nightmare worsened. Jake,
feeling like a child who'd misbehaved, told his father
that he'd been released from the hospital, but that he
wouldn't be going home. Instead, they were putting
him in a nursing home. A nice home. A clean home.
A place with good food and friendly staff. A place
where he could find companionship among people his
own age.

Hank Cameron, looking as though he'd been betrayed, had responded with only one question: "How
could you do this to me?"

Jake had wanted to throw up his hands and storm out the door. He'd wanted to scream, to shout, "Pop, don't you know this is killing me?" He'd wanted to beg his father's forgiveness. What he had done, however, was to pack up his father's things at the hospital, just as Whitney was packing some things from the house. Throughout it all, the packing and the ambulance ride to the nursing home, Hank Cameron was silent. It was as though all the fight had gone out of him. Jake had remained at the nursing home throughout the afternoon. His father spoke not one word, made not one gesture toward him. He simply did what he was told to do by the staff; he simply ate what was placed before him. At seven o'clock, Jake, weary and worn, left the nursing home. His father hadn't said goodbye. He'd just turned his face toward the wall and away from his son.

His heart breaking, Jake returned home. He heated up some leftover spaghetti, but realized as he tried to force it down that he wasn't hungry. In fact, he wasn't much of anything beyond tired and hurting. Unbuttoning his shirt on the way to his bedroom, he heaved it from his shoulders and, wadding it into a ball, tossed it in the corner. Hauling down the zipper of his jeans, he shucked them, letting them lie where they dropped. His black briefs followed. He stretched, turned on the faucets of the shower and crawled inside the stall. Pressing his palms against the tile, his head drooping, he let the hot water pummel his tension-tight neck and shoulders. At last, he dragged himself from the shower, dried himself off and, naked, crashed into bed.

Darkness glided over him, making him feel part of the winter night, yet curiously separated from it ... from everything ... from everyone. Sounds, though soft and subtle, rushed at him like great noises. He heard the angry blare of an occasional car horn, the rhythmic tick-ticktock of the bedside clock, the voice of his father.

"How could you do this to me?"

Groaning, Jake rolled to his side. He and Whitney had done what had to be done. It hadn't been easy, but it had been the right thing to do. Hadn't it?

"How could you do this to me?"

Jake jabbed at the pillow. Yes, it had been right. And in time his father would adjust. Wouldn't he?

"How could you do this to me? ... How could you do this to me? ... How could you—"

The ringing of the phone sliced through the discontented silence. Jake jumped, fumbled for the receiver and brought it to his ear.

"Hello?" he answered, fully expecting to hear his sister's voice.

Instead, he heard a hesitation, then a shy "Jake?"

His breath caught. Conversely, his heart lurched forward.

"Jake?" Robin said again, her own heartbeat less than stable.

The repetition of his name reminded him that he had yet to give a response. "Yeah," he said, pushing himself to an elbow and adding, "Hi."

"Hi," she returned—again, shyly. There was another hesitation. "Is now a bad time?" She shouldn't have called. She knew she shouldn't have called. But she hadn't seemed able to stop herself.

"No. Now's fine." *Actually, maybe you're just in time to save my sanity,* Jake thought.

"I, uh, I tried to call you earlier, but you weren't home. In fact, I called you several times this week, but...but you weren't home." She gave a self-effacing sigh and thought what an idiot she was making of herself. "Of course you know you weren't home. That was a stupid thing to say—"

"I've been with my father at the hospital. He fell and broke his hip."

"I know. One of the nurses in NICU told me."

So she had asked. The realization that she had pleased him. Far more than it should have.

"How is your father?" she asked. She was vaguely aware that she was clutching the phone so tightly that her hand was beginning to ache.

"Mending," Jake answered, "but we, uh, we put him in a nursing home. That's where I've been most of the day. We transferred him there this morning."

"Is he settled in?"

"Physically, but not emotionally."

"I'm sure he'll adjust in time."

"Yeah," Jake said, but his tone suggested he wasn't at all certain.

Robin heard every doubtful nuance. She also heard the pain in his voice. "Are you okay?"

"You want the truth?"

"Always."

For a moment Jake thought he was getting hysterical, because it was all he could do not to laugh. The truth? *Lady,* he thought on a sneer as he raked back his damp hair, *that's the last thing you'll get from me, the Master of Lies!*

"Lousy," he answered roughly, gruffly. "I feel lousy. Like heel of the year. Like the worst son ever born. And that's the truth. For once."

His answer, at least the last of it, didn't make a lot of sense, although his mood she could interpret perfectly. She knew that there would be worry lines radiating from his eyes and across his brow. As always, and for a reason she would have been hard-pressed to explain, she wanted to soothe them away. Maybe even kiss them away? She shifted the phone to her other ear, dispersing the last troubling thought as she did so.

"You did what you had to do," she said. "You did what was best for your father. You did... Oh, Jake, I'm so sorry. I know how difficult it must have been for you."

Jake lay back in the bed, closed his eyes and let her warm voice drizzle over him. Miraculously, he felt the pent-up tension flowing from him. Miraculously, he felt the day's hurt healing.

"Keep talking," he said when a silence fell between them.

"What?"

"Keep talking. About anything." When she still said nothing, he asked, "How's Peter?"

As predicted, the question produced the desired effect. A smile wreathed Robin's face and words seemed not in the least hard to come by. "He's fine. In fact, he's coming home next week."

The announcement was the kind of news that Jake needed to balance out a grim day. At least something good was happening somewhere in the world. Not in his world, but in hers. The jubilation he felt caused him to momentarily pose an interesting metaphysical question: Were her world and his slowly merging? Was that why he could feel happiness at her good news? "I'm glad Peter's going home. Congratulations."

"Thank you." Her smile widened. Jake could hear her joy oozing through the phone lines. "I can't believe it. They told me today, and I just can't believe it. I guess I was afraid to hope...." She let the words drift away. "Anyway, he's coming home next week. Which is one reason I called." Jake could hear the shyness edging back into her voice. "Next Thursday is Thanksgiving, of course, and I'm certain you have plans to spend it with your family, but I was wondering if you could maybe come to dinner Friday night...sort of my own Thanksgiving celebration...my and Peter's way of saying thank you for all you've done...it would be real simple, but if you didn't already have plans...well, maybe you could come." All the words blended together until they formed one gigantic, breathless sentence.

"You don't have to thank—"

"That's a matter of opinion," Robin interrupted.

Jake closed his eyes again. Oh, God, how had he gotten himself into this mess? Not only did he want to see her more than he wanted anything else in the world, he *needed* to see her. He needed her softness, her gentleness, her strength. But what did she need? Right now, she needed an answer.

"Robin—"

"I've missed you," she whispered.

Jake closed his eyes again as the admission snuggled next to his heart. Laden with guilt as she was about her husband, what had those three words cost her? Enough to humble Jake as he'd never been humbled before. Enough to make him want to reach out and yank her into his arms. Enough to assure his response.

"I'll be there," he said hoarsely.

Though Peter was released from the hospital as planned, the week did not go as Robin had expected. She had envisioned it as an idyllic time in which she and her son could finally get down to the business of being normal. And, perhaps, therein lay the problem. In her naiveté, she hadn't known how to define *normal*. She hadn't understood that normal constituted a million diaper changes, the application of enough talcum powder to dust down the state and a baby with a bird-like hunger that had to be satisfied every two hours...night and day...day and night. If she had been sleeping poorly before, she now hardly slept at all, and what little she did was nothing more than a series of scattered catnaps.

Add to that a mountain of laundry, a mother who called every ten minutes to ask how everything was going, and Jake, who hadn't called even once. He'd insisted upon driving them home from the hospital, had carried her things into the middle of the living room, had helped her tuck Peter into his new bed, then had left. Not that she'd expected him to call afterwards, not that he should have, but... All right, all right, she'd expected him to! She knew it was illogical, but there it was. She'd expected him to call. After all, they were friends, weren't they?

Friends?

You didn't kiss friends. You didn't intimately place your body next to friends. You didn't tell friends that you missed them...at least not with your heart caught in your throat, afraid that they were about to turn down your dinner invitation. What was happening to her? What was happening between her and Jake? Why was she thinking of him when she should be thinking of Gerald? Thankfully, she was too tired to consider these questions. Or much of anything else...except diapers, laundry and another feeding.

Friday morning dawned with overcast skies that eloquently heralded the finale to a bad week. The washing machine flooded the kitchen while Robin went to the store for the groceries she needed to prepare dinner. Peter, who had been unusually fretful during the night, cried constantly all day long. And dinner fought her every step of the way. At fifteen minutes until seven, the hour designated for Jake's arrival, the roast was underdone, the potatoes were overdone, and the cake...

Robin peered into the oven at the bundt pan of chocolate batter. Shouldn't it be rising by now? It had been baking... She glanced down at her watch. Thirty-five minutes. It had been baking for thirty-five whole minutes. Wasn't that enough time to raise it to the height of a skyscraper?

Her only answer was Peter's whimper from the bedroom.

"You can't be hungry, Peter. You just ate." She sighed when she realized that it had been almost two hours since her son's last feeding. "My, my," she said, switching off the oven light, "how times flies when you're on the verge of a breakdown. Please, Peter, give Mommy just a few more minutes, okay?"

Peter's whimper grew.

Robin turned up the fire under the cake, then made a mad dash for the bathroom. She'd showered following her mop-up of the kitchen, but hadn't had time to comb her hair or apply makeup. She still wore the jeans and red sweater she'd put on earlier, both of which she wanted to exchange for something softer, prettier. First, however, she'd just splash on a little makeup. She reached for the bottle of beige-toned liquid just as three things happened simultaneously: the doorbell pealed, the phone rang, and Peter let out an I've-had-enough-of-this-wait wail.

The bottle of makeup fell from Robin's fingers and crashed into the sink. It broke into smithereens.

"Damn!" Robin said, feeling her composure break into the same small pieces.

The doorbell shouted another peal.

The phone screamed another ring.

Peter now gave a bloodcurdling cry.

Robin longed for a very deep hole to crawl into...or perhaps a strong pair of arms.

When Robin opened the front door, she only marginally noted the colorful bouquet of flowers that Jake was holding. The only thing that really permeated her frayed senses was his arms...his strong-looking arms. Fighting the urge to fling herself against him, she forced her eyes to his.

"Don't step over the threshold," she warned, "unless you're ready to go down with the *Titanic*."

"That bad, huh?" Jake asked, answering his own question with a silent *That bad*. He could see just how bad things were from her frazzled expression, the blank, harried look of her eyes, in the fact that her face was bare of makeup and her hair was pulled back into a sloppy ponytail. He'd never seen anyone more beautiful. He wondered just where he'd found the strength to stay out of her life all week. He also wondered why he hadn't been sensitive enough to realize that this week was going to be difficult for her. He cursed himself for his lack of judgment.

"The *Titanic*'s phone is ringing," he announced quietly. He could hear Peter vying for attention...and marveled at how strong his lungs had grown.

Shoving back a strand of hair straggling into her eyes, Robin said of the phone's strident ring, "My mother...the iceberg."

Jake grinned. The act almost—almost—set the world right again.

Without an invitation, Jake stepped into the house. "You get the phone. I'll get Peter." He tossed both the flowers and his coat on the sofa.

Relieved to have someone take over the helm of the sinking ship, Robin did as ordered. Moving into the hallway, she silenced the phone in mid-ring.

"Hello, Mother," she said blandly into the receiver. "Ohh, just a lucky guess." In seconds, she saw Jake step from the bedroom, Peter in his arms. A now quiet Peter. As Jake passed by her, she heard him murmuring something to her son. Though the words themselves were unintelligible, the tone was not. It spoke of calm and peace and blissful serenity. It loosened the knots tied in her neck. "No, Mother, everything's fine. Truly. Well, I'm sorry I sound upset. No, Peter's fine. Yes, I know he was crying. He's just hungry. Yes, he's stopped crying." As she said this, she glanced over at Jake, who stood before the blazing hearth. Their eyes connected.

She wasn't going to tell her mother that she had company, Jake thought, bringing Peter to rest against his shoulder and patting the child's small back with his enormous hand. The baby made a cooing sound that seemed to ask, "And how would she explain who you are and what you're doing here?" *Good questions,*

Jake thought. *I'm not even sure I know the answers to them.*

No, that wasn't true. He knew the answers to both the questions. Who he was, was simple. He was the man who loved Robin Bauer. As to why he was there, he was there to tell her that he was the man who'd shot her husband. He'd already vowed to himself that he wouldn't leave this house without telling her. And he wouldn't. This time he meant it. Though now, with everything in a state of chaos, was hardly the time to keep his self-promise.

Suddenly, Jake became aware of the charred aroma of something burning. At least that's what he thought it was. "Do you have something on the stove?" he whispered.

"...no, Mother, I..." Robin placed her palm over the receiver and mouthed, "What?"

"Do you have something on the stove?"

As the question reached her ear, the smell reached her nose. "Oh, my God...I've got to go, Mother...I've got something in the oven." Without waiting for a response, Robin slammed down the phone and raced toward the kitchen.

Jake found her standing over the cabinet, her shoulders slumped in an attitude of dejection. Gray-black smoke billowed from the cake pan before her. "The cake burned," Robin said matter-of-factly, her back still to the man she'd sensed had entered the room. "Not that it matters. It's flatter than a Frisbee. Regrettably, the rest of the meal is just as impressive. The roast—the cow probably should have been sold for leather products and not for food consumption— won't be ready to serve until tomorrow, while the potatoes should have been served yesterday."

"It's not the end of the world," Jake said quietly. "The *Titanic*'s not sinking."

"Oh, yeah?" she asked, turning to face him. "Well, you haven't been on board this week." Jake could see the glassy sheen of her eyes. The sight did crazy hurting things to him. "The washing machine is broken—it flooded the kitchen this morning—the only bottle of makeup I had is broken in the sink, my mother calls every ten minutes, Peter's cranky—" as if on cue, the baby whined "—he's constantly hungry or wet or both...not that I really mind changing him or feeding him, it's just that I feel like I haven't slept in weeks...years." She raked back a swath of fallen hair. She felt very dowdy, very plain, very close to tears. "I wanted to at least comb my hair. To at least put on some makeup. I wanted...I wanted things to be perfect for this evening."

A single silent tear crept to the edge of her eye and tumbled over the rim. Behind her, smoke still tunneled ceilingward.

"Come here," Jake said huskily, pulling her against him with his free arm. She went. Not because he hadn't given her a choice, which he hadn't, but because she couldn't have resisted him had she tried. His smile had almost set the world to rights. His touch finished the job.

She burrowed deep within him, wallowing in the comfort he gave. He was solid. So solid. So strong. She closed her eyes, thinking of the countless times during the week that she'd longed for the solace this man offered. She didn't analyze how or why Jake had become important to her. She simply accepted as fact that he had.

Thinking of the miserable week prompted her to say, "I'm an awful mother."

"You're not an awful mother. You're a normal mother and a very tired mother."

"The food's ruined."

"To hell with it."

"I look like the Wicked Witch of the West."

"With or without makeup, with or without combing your hair, you're still gorgeous."

Pulling back, she looked up at him. Her eyes, framed with not so much as a single stroke of mascara, were wet. Jake thought they looked beautiful, like nuggets of gold nestled beneath a shallow green pond.

"You drove over here with that kind of failing eyesight?" she asked. A tiny grin, the first in days, played at her lips.

Jake's eyes moved slowly over her upturned face. There wasn't even a hint of a grin at his mouth when he said roughly, "There's nothing wrong with my eyesight."

His voice, the way he looked at her, sent heat coursing through her. It settled in the pit of her belly. It had been a long time since she'd felt the sensation...and a longer time since she'd felt it with someone other than her husband. Predictably, this last caused her guilt to flare. Even so, she couldn't make herself pull away...nor did Jake seem inclined to push her away. It was Peter who finally forced them apart.

Fretting noises, like miniature fireworks, erupted into the hushed silence. Jake became aware of restless motion. Glancing down, he saw and felt Peter rooting against his broad chest in search of food.

"I think your son's hungry," he said, looking over at Robin and shifting the baby into her arms. "Here, you go feed him. I'll take care of everything else."

"But..."

"Go," he said, urging her in the direction of the door.

The last thing Robin saw was Jake doing battle with a bundt pan. A few minutes later, from the bedroom where she was nursing Peter, she heard Jake working on the washing machine. She next heard him in the bathroom scraping up shards of glass. Then, just as she'd shifted Peter to her other breast, she heard Jake calling to her.

"I'll be back in a little bit! You just rest!"

Sighing, Robin lay back against the soft bed. She closed her eyes. Jake would take care of everything. Jake would keep the *Titanic* from sinking.

CHAPTER NINE

AT THE SOUND OF THE FRONT door opening and closing, Robin came awake with a start. Jerking her head toward the bedside clock, she realized that she'd been asleep for almost twenty minutes. The child in her arms was asleep, too—blissfully asleep if the even sound of his breathing was any indication. Easing from the bed, Robin carried her son to the crib and, laying him gently down, tucked him beneath the quilted coverlet. She then glanced at herself in the mirror...and groaned.

Less than ten minutes later, Robin walked into the living room. Jake sat on the red braided rug before the fireplace, unsacking hamburgers, french fries and milk shakes. He glanced up at Robin's entrance.

She noted for the first time that he wore the fisherman's sweater that she'd seen on him once before. She hadn't remembered it looking that good on him, though, as if it had been personally designed with his brawny physique in mind. The olive-green cords fit just as perfectly.

Jake, on the other hand, noted that Robin, although she hadn't changed clothes, had released her hair from the ponytail and had, instead, plaited it into a braid. Silky wisps curled about her forehead and at her shell-like ears. Both her lips and cheeks wore a hint of scarlet that blended with the crimson of her sweater.

A row of tiny buttons closed that clingy garment. Something about the prim buttons and the way the sweater molded her full feminine form reminded him of her duality. Was she a woman? Was she a child? Or was she an alluring combination of the two?

"I fell asleep," the child/woman admitted with an endearing shyness that arrowed its way straight into Jake's heart.

Forcing his gaze from her soft curves to her eyes, he answered in a voice as thick as the milk shakes sitting on the rug, "That's good. You needed the rest." With a jerk of his head, he prompted her to come join him. "You'll feel even better after you've eaten something." Suddenly, he lowered his voice as though the two of them were mired in a deep, dark conspiracy. "Don't let Peter know we're having Big Macs or we'll have to share."

"Peter's asleep," Robin said, smiling as she folded herself onto the rug. The fire from the hearth stroked her with its shimmering heat, while outside a cold wind had begun to howl. The winter-low temperature was dropping by the hour.

"Good, then our dinner's safe." Handing her a hamburger, he added, "I didn't know how you liked yours, so I got it with the works. I figured you could take off what you didn't want."

"Anything's fine. In fact, anything's wonderful."

"Here's your fries and you can have either a strawberry or a chocolate milk shake."

"It doesn't matter."

"Which one?"

"Uh . . . strawberry."

"Good."

Robin laughed, wondering if the jovial sound could possibly be coming from the woman who had been so upset such a short while before. "Why didn't you tell me you wanted the chocolate one?"

Jake grinned, he, too, wondering if this was the same woman who'd opened the door to him earlier in the evening. "I was trying to be chivalrous."

Robin's smile faded. "I'd say you already have been."

At the softness of her voice, Jake looked up from smearing ketchup on his fries. "I didn't do anything," he said, adding, "Oh, by the way, a sock was caught in the outflow valve of the washing machine. I also turned the fire out from under the roast. You can finish cooking it tomorrow. If it isn't done in a couple of hours, I'd recommend turning it into a purse. The cake, however, was a lost cause. I trashed it."

"Thanks," Robin said, her eyes going to the sweet-smelling bouquet of mixed flowers that Jake had placed in a pitcher of water and set on the coffee table. "For everything."

"Like I said, I didn't do anything."

"You were there."

The words, sweeter than any flower's fragrance, wrapped themselves about Jake's heart like satin ribbons. All too soon, however, when he remembered what he must tell her before the night was through, the ribbons seemed to tighten, choking the very life from his chest.

For seconds, they simply stared at each other. The heated feeling she'd experienced earlier once more snaked through her stomach. Just as before, it confused her.

"Eat," Jake said abruptly, roughly. "Before everything gets cold."

Relieved at his distracting command, Robin reached for her hamburger. Two bites into it, she was certain that food had never tasted so good. By the end of it, she was positively purring.

"I take it 'mmm' means good?"

"'Mmm' means this is the best thing I've had in my mouth all week." She didn't mention the crackers and cheese, the crackers and peanut butter, the crackers and crackers that had been the mainstay of her diet since bringing Peter home.

"You didn't have turkey and dressing yesterday?"

Robin hesitated in bringing the last ketchup-drenched french fry to her mouth. "No," she answered, wondering if her voice sounded as strained to Jake as it did to her. How could she explain that, even if she'd been able to find the time and energy, she wouldn't have prepared the typical Thanksgiving feast... simply because it was the first real holiday she'd spent without Gerald? It had been best to pretend that it was just another day. "So," she added quickly—perhaps too quickly, "did you have turkey and dressing and all the trimmings?"

Jake, who'd removed his boots earlier and now sat leaning against the hearth with his ankles crossed, sucked the last of the chocolate milk shake into his mouth. He noted the way Robin had shifted the conversation away from her. He could even guess why she had. Holidays were notoriously hard to get through if one was alone. He knew. "Yeah," he answered, feeling his usual wave of guilt, this time because he was responsible for her miserable holiday. "I ate at the nursing home."

"How is your father?"

Jake shrugged, his guilt exacerbated. "Okay, I guess. The doctor assures us that his hip is doing fine. Otherwise, we're playing a guessing game as to how he's doing. He won't talk to us. Except to ask us how we could do this to him. The staff is warm and friendly, the food is good, Pop has a private room. We even brought some of his things from the house—a chest, his chair, his television, photos of Mother and his grandkids. Even so, you'd think we'd put him in prison." Jake began to pick up the remains of their meal. "The worst thing," he said, stuffing the milk shake cartons back into the sack, "wasn't putting him in the home, though God knows, that was bad enough. The worst thing is wondering if we've done the right thing."

Robin draped her arms around her knees and hugged herself close. "Guilt's all too easy to buy into, isn't it?"

Jake glanced over at her. Light from the lamp with the pierced tin shade, the only light in the room except for the roaring fire, spewed through the pinpricks and scattered about her like motes of stardust. "I can't imagine there being any valid reason for you to feel guilty about anything." Remembering the confession that she'd made in the garage, of feeling guilty at having wanted to kiss him, Jake added, "Life goes on, Robin."

"Yes, and so does death," she answered, but it was as though she were suddenly somewhere faraway.

"You have a bill for a five-hundred-dollar suit."

"So?"

"We're spending too much money."

"You let me worry about the money."

"But I do worry. I . . . Where are you going?"

"Back to work. Where I won't have to listen to you bitch about money."

As always, the memory hurt. Why wasn't there a Band-Aid one could put on painful memories?

The cryptic remark about death, Robin's vacant stare, ensnared Jake's attention. She looked so small, so defenseless, huddled as she was unto herself.

Tell her. You owe her the truth. Now. Before you chicken out again.

"Robin," he began, praying he could find the words, praying she wouldn't hate him if he could, "I want to talk to you." His voice drew her back to the present. Her eyes, hazy with hurt, found his. "About your husband," Jake added.

"I know," Robin said.

The words kicked Jake in the stomach like an out-of-sorts mule.

"You know?" he asked.

"It was only a matter of time. I knew that time was limited when I realized you were a policeman. As a policeman, you'd have to know what happened."

Jake's stomach, along with his heart, fell to his feet—with relief. She didn't know he was the one who'd shot her husband. And yet, why should he feel relieved? He was only going to have to tell her himself now.

"Not only that," she continued, "but Gerald's death made the newspaper day after day. After a while, you had to figure out who I was. Or, at least, make an educated guess." Looking him straight in the eye, she asked, "You do know how Gerald died?"

"Yes," Jake said, the one word strangled from him. "Robin—"

"I'm glad you know," she said. "I'm not quite sure why, but I'm glad you do."

She still clasped her arms about her knees. Jake had the impression that she was holding herself together.

"Robin—"

"He and I fought that night," she said. The confession was made matter-of-factly, as though she were just admitting that the two of them had had dinner that evening. "Over a suit that I thought he'd paid too much money for." She laughed, mirthlessly. "I buried him in the suit. How's that for irony?"

It was obvious that she was somehow blaming herself for what happened. Because the two of them had fought that night.

"You can't blame yourself," he began, only to be cut off with "Why not?"

"Because you didn't pull the trigger," he snapped. *I did! Dammit, I did!*

"Mrs. Bauer, I'm sorry to inform you that your husband's been killed...killed...killed..."

At the memory of the sorrow-faced police chaplain standing in her living room, tears rushed to Robin's eyes.

The sight of them hacked at Jake's soul. He had to force himself to go on.

"Robin, listen, I have to tell you—"

As quickly as the tears had come, Robin stifled them. Stoically stifled them. Just the way she'd stoically survived by forcing herself to move forward and not backward. "I don't want to talk about it anymore," she said, adamantly ending the subject.

"We have to talk—"

"No!" she insisted, surprising both him and her by placing the tips of her fingers against his lips.

The act was impulsive. It was also intimate. Robin felt the velvet-smooth softness of his mouth, the moist heat of his breath. She remembered, vividly, the way that mouth had melded, on two occasions, with her own. Jake felt the subtle, sweet pressure of her touch, which in and of itself devastated his senses. What destroyed him completely, however, was the fact that she was trembling. He could feel the gentle tremors pulsating against his lips. They spoke to the most basic of his needs—the need to protect.

"Please," she whispered, but she was uncertain just what she pleaded for. Was she pleading for him not to continue with the discussion? Yes, she was sure she was, but she was also pleading for something else. What? For him to blot out all the ugliness of the past few months? For him to make everything in her life all right the way he'd righted her evening? For him to...

"Hold me," she heard herself saying softly, beseechingly. At some point, she'd risen to her knees before him. Something about the prayer-like position strengthened her supplication.

Her command was both heaven and hell, heaven because he wanted nothing more than to do as she asked, hell because his moment of truth was slipping away—further, further away with each breath they both drew, with each heartbeat that crashed against their chests.

"Robin—" he tried one last time, speaking her name against her fingertips.

"Please," she whispered, edging her fingers away in a slow glide that felt like satin being drawn over his fevered skin.

At the removal of her touch, at the sudden emptiness that welled inside him, Jake realized that he'd never really had a choice. Groaning, he pulled her to him, wrapping his arms about her even as she wrapped hers about him.

Strength. She felt his unrelenting strength, a buttress, a fortress, a beacon shining through life's cruel darkness.

Small. She was so small! So tiny! So fragile, yet so brave!

Jake hadn't intended it to happen, any more than had Robin, but the moment they embraced, his head turned in search of her lips. Robin made her mouth available to his sweet, savage plunder. She whimpered as his needy lips found hers—grazing, nibbling, then merging with hers in complete possession. He drank deeply of the senses-stirring sound, of her provocative taste.

Always before, her kiss had been tentative, filled with guilty reluctance, but now, driven by a desperation to flee the night-black memories that had haunted her for months, driven by a need to lose herself in this man, she kissed him fully, freely. Jake moaned, angling his mouth more intimately across hers, forcing her lips to part beneath his. His tongue probed in a nimble ballet, then plunged forward, unleasing a fiery passion in them both.

Robin moaned as razor-sharp need spiraled through her, tunneling lower and lower until she felt herself growing wet and quivery in the hidden recesses of her feminine body. The feeling had startled her before. She now simply allowed it to consume her, relishing it as though she'd just found the heat of a new sun. Jake, too, felt the licking of a white-hot fire in the pit of his belly. It had been a long time since he'd felt the feeling, and never with this intensity. Never! When

Robin's tongue, curiously with both a boldness and a shyness, curled with his, he thought he would burn to cinders on the spot.

"Robin!" he breathed, wrenching his mouth from hers and crushing her to him. Again, he marveled at the way their bodies fit. As if they had been made for each other—she for him, he for her.

"Jake..." She said his name. At least, she thought she had. All she knew for certain was that her head buzzed with air-light sensation.

"Hmm?" he mumbled, confirming that she had indeed spoken. His hands, spread wide, moved over her back, luxuriating in the feel of the soft woolen sweater and the softer woman beneath. Tugging her closer, he could feel her breasts settle against his chest. Just as he could feel the tiny knob-like buttons that kept the ultimate softness from him. "What is it?" he whispered when she said nothing.

"What?" she asked fuzzily, drunk with intoxicating feeling.

"What is it, baby?"

Baby. He called her baby. The endearment further clouded her mind.

"I...I don't know," she whispered, uncertain quite what she'd wanted with him. On the other hand, she was certain what she wanted *from* him. She wanted him to keep doing what he was doing—holding her, molding her to him in a provocative, suggestive way, teasing her ear with gentle nips of his teeth. "I don't remember...I don't—" she moaned as he trailed his lips down the column of her neck "—I can't think clearly...when you're around." She moaned again as he bit gently at her chin.

"Don't think," he whispered as his mouth rolled back onto hers. "Just feel."

This kiss was damp and deep and soul-slow. As though she were being buffeted about in a sensual storm, Robin grasped Jake's upper arms and held on to him. She tried to remember feeling this way with Gerald, this out of control, this I-don't-give-a-damn-what-happens-if-I'm-in-this-man's-arms feeling, but couldn't. Surely she'd just forgotten. Surely...

All coherent thought scattered as Jake's hands, following the trail of her spine, skimmed down her back...and slid beneath the hem of her sweater. Bare skin met bare skin.

Warm. Rough. His hands were warm and stimulatingly rough. And she longed for him never to stop touching her in this way. Except perhaps to touch her more intimately. At the thought, she arched her breasts, her aching breasts, against the wall of his chest.

Warm. Soft. Her skin was incredibly soft! Like her sexy whimpers. Like her lips. Like her breasts molded against him. Gliding his hands upward, he traversed the length of her back, her shoulder blades resting beneath his palms. His thumbs slid over the strap of her bra. What would happen if he unfastened it? The question did hard and thick things to him.

At the feel of his masculinity straining so powerfully against her, Robin's stomach knotted with desire. Painfully knotted. She gasped into Jake's mouth even as her knees buckled and her body sagged.

Sliding his arm about her waist, Jake lowered her slowly to the braided rug. She went, staring up at him with eyes softer than morning dew. Her breath was coming fast and heavy from slightly parted lips, lips still wet from his kiss. Something in the honesty of her reaction awed him. Even the firelight seemed awed by her, for it would flicker a moment, then dart away, then flicker across her ivory skin once more, as though uncertain it had the right to gild her with something as imperfect as its golden flame. Only in her hair did it assume a boldness. There it wove itself within the silken, honey-brown strands until it appeared that the tresses shone with their own fawn-colored flame.

Reaching upward—he couldn't have stopped himself under penalty of death—he brushed back a curl from her forehead. The curl twirled itself about his finger.

"Tell me to stop," he pleaded. "While I still can."

Robin said nothing. She simply turned her head to bestow a kiss against the inside of his wrist.

"Tell me to go home."

Still Robin said nothing.

"Tell me I have no right. Tell me this isn't what you want. Tell me to go to hell."

"I can't," she whispered at last. "Don't you know I can't?"

Her confession gutted his breath. He slammed his mouth back on hers. Each tasted urgency. When breath became a precious commodity, Jake pulled his mouth away and began to rain kisses at her temple, on the tip of her upturned nose, at that sensitive spot just behind her ear.

He groaned. "You smell like baby powder."

"I'm sorry."

"No...no...I like it!" he breathed, his mouth taking hers once more.

Instinctively, her hands slid beneath his sweater. She connected only with his shirt. This time her moan was one of frustration. She wanted to touch him, not the barrier of cloth. Tugging, she pulled the shirttail from his pants and insinuated her hands beneath the fabric. Her palms found the small of his back. The bare small of his back. Just as he had minutes before, she ran her hands the length of his spine.

Jake hissed his breath into her open mouth. "Good. Oh, baby, that feels good. So good!" Ripping the remainder of his shirt from his pants, he guided her hands around his rib cage and to his chest. He eased her hands into the thicket of crisply coiled hair.

Robin spread her fingers wide—she wanted to feel as much of him as possible!—as she slid her hands upward. With each millimeter of skin she caressed, the fire burning within her was banked higher. At the touch of his toned stomach muscles, the fire flared. At the touch of his beaded nipples, the fire blazed. At the feel of his hands molding her sweater-covered breasts, the fire jumped its bounds and sizzled through her bloodstream.

She opened her eyes, realizing only then that they'd been closed, just in time to see Jake's head lower. She felt his mouth at her breast, his breath seeping through the woolen garment to warm her skin. He nuzzled her with his nose, then covered her with his mouth. Her nipple hardened. Its instant tightness puzzled her, pained her and made her blush at her brazen reaction.

The fire in her bloodstream galloped to every limb, wilting each to a state of uselessness, reducing her to a state of will-lessness.

"Jake," she whimpered, but he said nothing. Instead, he began the slow unbuttoning of her sweater. As the halves of her breasts came into view, panic seized Robin. Would he think the blue veins networking her breasts with milk ugly? Would he think her breasts too full, too heavy? Would he think—

Her brain emptied of all thought as he kissed the milk-swollen swells that rose above her practical cotton bra. Conversely, her body became aware of every touch, every graze, every brush. She could feel the jarring of the snap of her jeans as Jake yanked it open. She could feel the tremulous rasp of her zipper. She could feel the opening of her jeans being parted into a V. She could feel Jake's mouth kissing her navel, his tongue swirling deep inside it, his hand edging lower to cup the threshold of her femininity.

She convulsively arched against his massive palm.

"Jake!" she cried, desperately needing to end the throbbing ache consuming her. So desperate was her need that pride, guilt, shyness—nothing mattered. Except the cessation of the raging inferno within her.

Jake raised his gaze to hers. Her eyes were passion-bright and unashamedly begging him to finish the lovers' game they'd been playing. Some last shred of sanity told him that if he made love to this woman, he would only be digging himself a deeper hole, one he couldn't possibly hope to ever crawl from. She would hate him a hundred times worse when he told her the truth. And yet... And yet, the simple truth was, he had no choice. He loved this woman... with an intensity that demanded expression.

Clothes fell away frantically. Robin watched as Jake dragged the sweater over his head, attractively mussing his hair in the process. He set her fingers to unbuttoning his shirt even as he unfastened the remainder of her sweater. Both her bra and his hair-dusted chest came into view.

"The light," she whispered when he reached to unclasp her bra.

He hesitated, then, as a concession to her shyness, he reached for the lamp. The room dimmed, illuminated only by firelight. As the clasp of her bra gave way to Jake's single-minded fingers, her breasts tumbled forward. Jake's breath caught at their magnificence. They rode high, but their fullness was such that they sagged slightly, enticingly. The areolas were large and dark, far larger, far darker than he'd dreamed. Nothing, no fantasy, however wild, could have prepared him for the beauty of the fire painting her in an erotic mixture of light and shadow.

He thought he would surely die of pain, the pain in his love-full heart, the pain in his passion-full jeans. And then she was reaching for him....

In the next few seconds, Jake saw and felt as he'd never seen and felt before. He saw the sensual curve of Robin's hips as her jeans slid from her legs; he saw a scrap of blue cotton panties; he saw feathery curls, the pinkish-white of a cesarean section scar, the sweet parting of her legs. He felt smoothness and heat, fire and wonder. He felt her woman's body stretching to accommodate his steel-hard maleness.

"I don't want to hurt you!" he said, his breath tattered and torn.

Robin said nothing. She simply urged him deeper inside her.

For her, too, the world was reduced to sensation. She heard Jake's rapid breathing, saw his brown hair and bronze skin and the freckles dappling his shoulders and forearms, tasted the wetness of his alternately frenzied and slow, sultry kisses. But mostly, she just felt—the sliding of skin over skin, the filling of her body with his, the feeling of being protectively buried, deliciously smothered, beneath something far bigger than she.

And then there was motion. Sweet motion. Wild motion. Irresistible motion. Motion that swept her higher and higher. Motion that made her burn brighter and brighter, hotter and hotter. Suddenly saturated with sensation, she cried out as ripples of heated pleasure purled across her now sweat-damp body. She cried out something that sounded like Jake's name.

At her release, at the sound of his name spilling from her lips, Jake groaned at the quickening of his own body. He filled her with a warm moistness. Over and over. Until he'd emptied his body, his heart. Easing from her, he rolled to his side. Her face was flushed, from the fire, from their lovemaking. Her eyes were filled with a dream-like haze. A single tear, like a brilliant diamond, hid among her thick brown lashes.

Was it a tear of regret?

At the possibility that it might be, Jake's heart shriveled inside his chest. Catching the tear on the pad of his thumb, he sought her eyes for an explanation.

She clearly heard the silent question.

"No," she whispered, "I'm not sorry."

Relief flooded Jake. Lowering his head, he brushed his mouth against hers.

Robin moaned, then turned toward him, losing herself in his arms. She'd spoken the truth. She wasn't sorry. Yet an infinite sadness drifted over her, dragging guilt in its depressing wake. A guilt that threatened to consume her. The source of the guilt was all too easy to trace. She'd never felt the way she'd just felt with Jake. Until minutes before, she'd never known that kind of ecstasy existed. She'd never known it with any man. Not even her husband.

CHAPTER TEN

AT PETER'S CRY, JAKE came awake abruptly. It took him a second, but only a second, to figure out where he was. He was in Robin's bed. With her warmly tucked in his arms. Her moist breath, still sleep-paced despite Peter's whimper, bled onto his shoulder. Her cheek rested only fractions of an inch from his chin, while her arm lay across his waist. He wished this moment, this night, could go on forever. When Peter cried again, Jake sighed with resignation.

"Hmm?" Robin moaned as Jake disentangled their love-sated bodies.

"Peter," he whispered into her ear.

As though the word galvanized her into action, Robin started to roll from the bed.

"No," Jake said, pushing her shoulders back into the feather-soft mattress, "I'll get him."

Robin did as ordered, primarily because she realized with a start that she didn't have on a stitch of clothes. The night came rushing back at her with its gentle, mellow memories—their lovemaking before the fire, Jake carrying her to bed, Jake crawling in beside her. From there, everything was a blank, which meant she must have fallen asleep instantly. Well, not everything was a blank. She vividly remembered the way Jake had pulled her close, the way her body had curved into his, the way his arms had closed tightly about her—the way she'd wished the night could go on forever.

The bed swayed as Jake slipped from it. In the dark, Robin could hear his muffled bare footsteps on the wood floor. Suddenly, the clown lamp by the crib flashed on. In the wedge of subdued light, Jake's naked form, his broad expanse of back, his trim waist, his slim hips, were provocatively illuminated. Robin's mouth went totally dry. However, she did not glance away.

"Hey, pal," Jake crooned, completely uninhibited by his au naturel state. "What do you mean waking people in the middle of the night?" he asked as he quickly changed the baby's wet diaper. "Hungry, huh? I know, I know, you're a growing boy." Bundling the baby in the fleecy blanket, he picked him up. Peter, who'd fretted through the diaper change, now quieted. Instead of a cry, he made a cooing kind of triumphant sound.

Jake's eyes found Robin's. He grinned.

"The little rascal knows he's gonna eat."

Robin, fighting to keep her eyes above Jake's waist, smiled back—shyly. "He has his mother well-trained," she said, trying to appear as casual as Jake, but not feeling in the least as though she were succeeding. She simply could not be blasé about what had happened that evening. Though perhaps the most unsettling aspect of it was how very natural the whole thing seemed, as if it were meant for her to wake up in this man's arms. Which brought up a whole other unsettling aspect. Gerald. Which, in turn, brought a flood tide of guilt.

Jake saw the dark emotion come from out of nowhere to hook her with its knife-sharp talons.

"Don't," he rasped, leaning down to place her son in her arms. "Don't spoil tonight with guilt." He brushed his lips against hers, intending the kiss to be only a meeting of their mouths. At contact, however, a wildfire blazed through them. Jake could feel it scorching Robin; Robin could feel it roasting Jake. Jake groaned. Robin moaned. Deepening the kiss, he opened his mouth over hers. The rhythm was slow and languid, the texture sexy wet.

Robin melted.

Jake sizzled.

Peter whined, cried, howled.

Jake groaned, this time in abject frustration. Reluctantly, he withdrew his mouth, though his eyes sought Robin's. "Peter's not the only one hungry," he whispered thickly.

Robin had the feeling that the comment referred as much to the state of her appetite as it did to Jake's. If so, it was an assessment she couldn't argue with.

Peter bellowed, his mouth sucking at thin air, his head rooting against the blanket in search of his mother's breast.

Jake drew his thumb across the baby's cheek. "You owe me, Peter Bauer," he said, his voice as gravelly as a riverbed. "You owe me." Almost in the same breath, and as he reached for his corduroy pants, Jake asked, "Where's the thermostat?"

The question startled Robin, making her focus her attention on the room. It was cold, bitterly cold, a fact she'd been slow to note cozied as she was beneath the thick cover. Chill bumps pebbled Jake's bare shoulders, enticingly intermingling with the brown freckles. The brown freckles she'd slid her hands over...and over...and over... Bringing her runaway thoughts up short, she answered, "In the hallway. To the left of the phone."

Jake nodded and strode barefoot from the room. Outside, the wind sang frosty songs.

Robin watched Jake go. She had the sudden crazy notion that tonight wasn't real, that it wasn't really happening at all. Tomorrow she'd awake and realize that it had all been a dream. Would she be glad? Or infinitely sorry?

At the impatient cry of her son, Robin pulled back the cover and nestled him at her breast. His cry ended in mid-wail, replaced by a loud sucking noise as his eager mouth fastened around her nipple. She smiled at his ravenous slurping.

"Greedy," she whispered. The smile faded as she brushed back a swath of her son's silky hair. "Oh, Peter, is tonight real?"

Peter's only answer was to tug on his mother's breast.

"It's getting colder," Jake said minutes later. He'd sauntered back into the bedroom as though it were his own. Unself-consciously, he peeled away his pants and let them lie where they fell. He scooted a hasty return to bed.

"I know," Robin said. "I think it's supposed to...snow." The word faltered as her heart stopped, then jogged forward at the renewed sight of his naked body, at the feel of the bed giving with his weight, at the feel of his body slipping in beside hers.

Pulling the cover up over him, he glanced at Robin. Wayward wisps of hair wreathed her face, while the braid, held together with a simple rubber band, was just long enough to clear her shoulder. Her eyes were still softened by sleep, making her appear even more

vulnerable than usual—as vulnerable as the baby she
held. Stretching, he tugged the cover up over her bare
shoulder, then rearranged the blanket around Peter,
shielding his head from the chill as he nursed.

Robin looked up at Jake. He was leaning on an elbow, a lazy strand of hair strolling across his forehead. An aura of sleep still clung to him, reminding
her that only minutes before they'd been lying in each
other's arms. Her shoulder, which tingled from his
touch, reminded her that she liked the way he took
care of her. And Peter. It was something she could
grow dangerously accustomed to. Jake's hand, cupping the crown of Peter's small head, rested near her
breast. Very near. Disquietingly near. And that she
didn't seem able to grow accustomed to.

*"Your breasts aren't going to get saggy after the
baby comes, are they?"*

Robin could hear her husband's question as though
it had been asked yesterday and not months before the
baby had been born. She readjusted the covers, making certain that Peter's eating was being done discreetly. She hoped that the readjustment had been just
as discreet. Or, more to the point, that it had appeared natural.

"Go back to sleep," she said. "There's no need
both of us staying awake." Her voice sounded
strained, her comment awkward. But what was a
woman supposed to say at a moment like this? What
was the protocol when a...the word *lover* came instantly to mind. It startled her that it was appropriate. What was the protocol when a lover stayed over
and watched as you nursed your baby? A sudden
troubling thought occurred. "You don't have to stay,

at all. I mean, if you need to go...if you want to go...if..."

Jake shifted his gaze from the breast Robin had meticulously concealed beneath the covers to her eyes. "Do you want me to go?"

Robin said nothing. She just swallowed deeply.

"It's a simple question," Jake said, adding, "A simple yes or no will do."

"No," she replied. He'd been right. The answer was simple. All she had to do was listen to her heart. It crossed her mind again that maybe tonight wasn't real.

Relieved at her response, Jake said, "Then I'll stay. And we'll go back to sleep together."

"Sometimes Peter's slow—"

"I'll wait."

They stared, both seemingly unable to look away.

Jake thought of the way the firelight had flickered over her skin...and of the way she'd insisted he turn out the lamp before removing her brassiere. Why? Especially when she was so beautiful she'd taken his breath away?

Robin thought of the way he'd made love to her— tenderly, yet passionately—and of the way he'd filled her...completely.

Does she remember what it felt like to have me inside her?

Does he remember what it felt like to be inside me?

"Are you warm?" he asked, realizing that he was growing more than warm from this last thought.

Robin nodded. "Yes."

"Are you comfortable?"

She nodded again, but, as she did so, she shifted on the pillow.

"Here, let me fix it for you," he said, reaching over and punching the pillow. Robin, careful not to disturb the baby, eased back into the pillow's softness. "Better?" Jake asked.

Without awaiting an answer, and as naturally as night turns to day, then back again, he raked aside an errant curl from her forehead. Possessed of a will of its own, his hand refused to stop there. His impulsive fingers trailed down the braid falling over her shoulder.

"I love your hair braided. It makes you look old-fashioned. And sexy."

The way he said the last word thinned Robin's breath. "H-how can I look both?" she asked, the reedy notes of her voice caught in her throat.

"I don't know, but you do. Everything about you is contradictory. Your nose—" he brushed his finger across her upturned nose "—is cute as a button, while your mouth..." He drew his crooked finger across her full bottom lip. Flesh caught at flesh until the tip of one pearl-white tooth showed. Jake moaned at the sight.

Robin's breath slowed to a snail's pace.

Jake's gaze drifted down the column of her neck to the curve of her shoulder showing above the bed covers. Beneath the shoulder, Peter nursed contentedly. He made snuffling sounds occasionally. Jake dropped his gaze to the baby, and Peter chose that moment to turn loose of his mother's nipple. There was nothing Robin could do to keep Jake from seeing her breast. All of it. Jake sensed her sudden discomfort, but refused to indulge it. Instead, he traced the fullness of her breast with his bent finger, drawing it slowly, brazenly, down...down...down...stopping just short of the knotted nipple. Dark and glistening, it was still wet from Peter's mouth. Jake wished it were wet from his.

Robin simply wished she could breathe.

Peter obviously wished that someone would pay him some attention. Screwing up his face, he began to fuss. And to kick. The *thud-thunk* of the foot that landed in Robin's stomach brought her back to the moment.

"I...I have to switch him," she said, her eyes not on her son, but on the man whose finger was still erotically positioned. If possible, his not touching the crested peak was more sensual than had he touched it fully and a thousand times.

Suddenly, Jake removed his finger. Air rushed back into Robin's lungs.

"Turn over," Jake said, already taking the baby from her and laying him to her other side. He then pulled Robin's back flush with his chest. Like a man staking what was his, he placed his arm about her waist and laid his hand on Peter. With some guidance from his mother, Peter found her other breast.

Little by little, Robin relaxed against the body behind her. The hair of Jake's chest enticingly abraded her back, while the flat of his stomach nestled against the swell of her hips. His masculinity was pressed against her and he seemed in no way embarrassed by that. Even Robin had to admit that the intimate scenario they were engaging in seemed normal...and a lot more appealing than the nights she'd fed Peter alone.

Minutes later, it seemed just as natural for Jake to again take the baby from her, this time to burp him. Peter's little body appeared lost against the hugeness of Jake's shoulder. Similarly, Jake's hand appeared to swallow Peter's teeny back.

"C'mon, fella," Jake urged, "a couple of little burps and I'll let you off."

Peter yawned instead...and tried to stuff his fist into his mouth.

"Yeah, I know," Jake cooed. "It's beddy-bye time for everyone, but you've gotta burp first." The big hand tapped the tiny back. "C'mon."

Peter's eyelids began to drift downward.

From her still cozy-warm position in bed, Robin smiled. "You're losing him."

"Hey, pal, you're making me look bad."

Peter's eyes closed entirely.

"You've lost him."

"Nonsense. They don't call me King of Burp for nothing."

Robin couldn't help but laugh. "King of Burp?"

"Yeah. Marie used to say I could burp a bullfrog."

The name was sobering. At least to Robin. "Marie's your wife?"

From where he sat on the side of the bed, Jake met her eyes with his. "My ex-wife." Their staring at each other might have gone on forever, if Peter, his eyes still closed, had not chosen that moment to burp. Jake grinned. "See, I told you." Peter burped again. Jake's proud look seemed to say, "Oh, ye of little faith."

His hands splayed wide across the baby's back, Jake eased from the bed and headed for the crib. As before, Jake's nakedness seemed of no concern to him. As before, it was a major concern of Robin's. She tried to look away, but couldn't. The dip of waist, the curve of a buttock commanded all of her attention.

When he started to cut off the lamp, she managed to find her voice. At least a sliver of it. "Turn it down to the night-light mode. It'll make getting up easier next time." After a round of trial and error, Jake accomplished what she'd suggested, then turned toward her, his body in full and open view. Robin both cursed and blessed the semidarkness.

The bed sagged beneath his weight and, before she knew quite what was happening, he was reaching for her.

"Mmm, you're warm," he proclaimed, encountering the smoothness of her bare legs.

"You're cold," she replied, confronting the crinkly hair of his legs and the icy-cold of his toes.

"Then warm me," he challenged.

The daring look in his seductively dark eyes was hotter than a midsummer night. Robin felt that heat pooling in the most delicate part of her body and spreading through her suddenly tingling thighs. Unbidden came a specific, and very graphic, image of just how she might warm him...and herself in the bargain. The image was so specific, so graphic, that her cheeks flamed with color.

"You're blushing," Jake teased, running the pad of his thumb across the crimson skin. "I can see it even in the dim light." The grin on his face was one of delicious devilment.

Robin's blush deepened.

Jake's grin broadened. Slowly, the grin disappeared, replaced by a look of utmost seriousness, a look of awe.

"You're beautiful," he whispered.

The reverent hush in his voice, the worshipful way his body was intertwined with hers, prompted her to pose the question she'd already asked Peter, the question she'd repeatedly asked herself. "Is tonight real?"

Was tonight real? Jake considered the complex query. The woman in his arms was real, his feelings for her were real, very real, but was the night they were sharing?

"No," he answered. "That's why we can say or do anything we want."

Curiously, as though the pronouncement had granted her a license to steal, Robin did what she'd wanted to do from practically the first moment she'd met Jake: she traced her fingertips across the worry lines in his brow. They were deeply etched in his bronzed skin, yet her caress almost visibly erased them. The same fingertips trailed downward, inching his eyes closed as they touched warm lids and feathery lashes. His cheeks bore a stubble of beard that provocatively pricked her senses. As though she were blind and had only the sense of touch to make her see, she brushed her folded knuckles across his lips. His parted, breathing lips.

Robin moaned softly as Jake's teeth sank down, worrying the flesh without bruising it. His eyes never leaving hers, he flicked his tongue across her knuckles before snaking, here and there, into the sensitive valleys between her fingers. She whimpered, feeling herself liquefy, then vaporize. As she'd done before, she tried to remember feeling this way with Gerald—she wanted to remember feeling this way!—but she couldn't. God help her, she couldn't! Part of her grew angry, at herself, at Gerald, that she didn't have this memory to fall back on when she needed it.

"You're so soft, so sweet," Jake whispered, edging away the cover and kissing the beginning swell of her breast. He felt her body stiffen slightly. Undaunted, he nudged the blanket lower and brushed his warm mouth across still more of her breast, this time the plump inner fold. Again, he felt her body grow rigid. When he started to push the blanket aside entirely, she reflexively moved her hand to stop him. His eyes met hers.

"Don't," he growled. "Don't ever hide yourself from me!"

As Jake's mouth found her breast, his fingers connected with the cesarean section scar on her abdomen. Some possessive something triggered inside him. He thought of how small she was, how in need of someone to watch over her, how alone she'd been at the birth of her baby.

In a primitive claiming, with a wild guttural sound, he yanked her to him in an embrace that went far beyond anything sexual.

Tonight wasn't real, he reminded himself. Tomorrow he'd tell her the truth about who he was.

Tonight wasn't real, Robin reminded herself. Tomorrow she'd deal with the guilt she knew she'd feel.

Whatever happened in the future, tonight they belonged to each other. Tonight there was nowhere to hide. For either of them.

THE NEXT MORNING, JAKE found Robin in the kitchen. Dressed in jeans and the same red sweater she'd worn the evening before, the sweater he'd unfastened button by button, she stood before the stove. Bacon sizzled in the frying pan, while pancakes bubbled on the griddle. The aroma of freshly perking coffee permeated the room, as did the battery-operated radio's warning of a possible snowstorm.

Robin, a turner in one hand and a dish towel in the other, appeared oblivious to all except the pancakes growing higher by the heated moment.

Don't touch her, Jake forbade himself. *If you do, you'll never tell her the truth. And you have to tell her. Time's run out.*

Even as he thought this, the nape of her neck beckoned beyond denial, and he brushed his hungry lips against her soft, clean-smelling skin. He thought he'd heard the shower running earlier. He now knew he had.

At the unexpected touch of his lips, Robin jumped, then, her body instantly recognizing his, she melted back into him. He slid his arm about her waist and tugged her more snugly into him in a way that said to hell with not touching her.

"Breakfast's almost ready," she said. "I hope you like pancakes."

"Yeah, but you didn't have to go to this trouble."

"Oh, yes, I did. I had to try and save face. I'm really a pretty decent cook. Yesterday just got out of hand." Anchoring the turner at the edge of the pancake, she flipped one, then the other. "See. Not bad, huh?"

As she asked the question, she pivoted in Jake's arms. The only thing he saw was the beguiling hint of shyness in her eyes, the happiness curving her mouth. Her luscious-looking mouth. Her delicious-looking mouth. Her I've-got-to-have-a-taste-or-die mouth. Cursing himself, Jake kissed her. Rising on tiptoe, folding her utensil-and-cloth-laden hands about his neck, Robin kissed him back.

The stubble of his beard scratched her. She liked the raspy feel of his whiskers. She even liked the slightly disreputable way they looked. Earlier, as she'd lain watching him sleep, she'd thought his face looked as if someone had taken a charcoal pencil and shadow-sketched it. As she'd lain there, not daring to move a muscle for fear of waking him, she'd also waited...waited for the inevitable guilt to come. Then and now, she could feel it pacing the perimeter of her conscience, waiting to breach her defenses, waiting to rush forward and attack. But it hadn't yet. It would. She knew that. All she was doing was postponing it. In Jake's arms, perhaps she could postpone it a little while longer.

Abruptly, the kiss ended. Just as abruptly, Jake's arms fell away—almost as though if he didn't release her now, he wouldn't. The look on his face, one of pain, confused Robin. It also caused a chill to skitter down her spine.

"I want to talk to you," he said roughly.

"Now?" *In the middle of a kiss,* she thought, but said, "Couldn't it wait until after break—"

"No. It's been too long a wait as it is." Walking to the stove, Jake dragged the frying pan of bacon off the burner and cut the fire out from under the pancakes. "Here, sit down," he said, motioning toward a straight chair. When Robin continued to just stand and stare, Jake took her arm and guided her to the chair. He removed the dish towel and the turner from her hands and laid them on the table.

"What is it?" Robin asked, sensing that the morning had turned deadly serious. And for a reason she didn't understand at all.

Jake took a deep, unsteady breath. He looked, and felt, as uncomfortable as a man could look and feel. "Robin..." he began, then stopped to rake his fingers through his hair. He started again. "Before I begin, I want you to know that what happened last night...between us...I...I didn't plan that."

A silence ensued as what he said sank in.

"Is that what this is about?" Robin asked. "You're sorry about last night?" The thought that he might be sorry hurt. Badly. To the very marrow of her bones.

The thought that she might think he regretted what happened between them hurt Jake. Badly. To the marrow of his bones.

"No! Never!" he answered quickly, squatting before her and splaying the corduroy fabric of his pants tight across the muscles of his legs. Robin vividly remembered those legs entwined with hers. "I could never regret what happened," he repeated. "Last night was... Last night was special. More special than any night has ever been for me."

Relief bathed Robin. "Then what?" she asked, confused now more than ever.

Still hunched down before her, he said, as though his life depended on making her understand this one point, "I'd never deliberately hurt you. Or Peter. You do know that, don't you?" Before she could possibly answer, he demanded, "Tell me you know that."

The whole tenor of the conversation had begun to frighten Robin. Somewhere in the background, the weather forecaster's predictions grew more grim. Equally distanced from the scene unfolding in the kitchen was the sound of the telephone in the hallway beginning to ring.

Ignoring both—perhaps he didn't even hear them— Jake repeated, "Tell me you know that!"

"I know you'd never deliberately hurt me. Or Peter."

Partially relieved, Jake stood. He threaded his fingers back through his hair. In the furthermost part of his mind, the ringing of the telephone registered for the first time. He conveniently overlooked it. "Robin, I . . . I'm a policeman."

"I know that," she answered. "What has that got to do—"

"I'm a policeman who doesn't go to work."

She still looked bewildered. She, too, had begun to notice the telephone's incessant ringing. She, too, chose to ignore it.

"Haven't you ever wondered why I don't go to work?" Jake asked.

"You told me you were taking some time off."

"A leave of absence. I'm taking a leave of absence. And I didn't take it. It was forced upon me."

Still, nothing made sense. Still, the phone rang. Still, both Jake and Robin let it ring.

"I-I don't understand," Robin said.

"I can't use my weapon."

"Can't use your weapon? What does that mean?"

"It means that I can't draw my weapon. It means that I freeze. It means I'm not worth a damn as a police officer!"

Robin heard the anguish in his voice and, though she understood none of what he was saying, she wanted desperately to comfort him.

"Robin—" the words sounded choked "—I killed a man. An innocent man."

He waited for her to make the connection—God, he prayed she would! That way he wouldn't have to say the words. But he could tell that she didn't. In the silence, he realized the phone had stopped. Suddenly, it began to blare again.

"Will you get that damned phone!" Jake growled.

Wordlessly, Robin rose from the chair and walked from the kitchen to the hallway. She picked up the receiver, fully expecting to hear her mother's voice. Instead, she heard a man's.

"Robin Bauer?" the voice inquired. There was something clipped and professional about the man's tone. Something almost arrogant about it. Maybe even something a little . . . frightening.

"Yes?"

"Thank God," the voice said. "Do you know how hard you are to get in touch with, lady?"

Robin didn't answer. She simply glanced up at Jake, who'd stepped into the hallway.

"This is Phil Markham," the man said.

"Do I know you?" Robin asked.

"I'm a reporter for—" The man mentioned the paper he worked for. Robin recognized the name of the newspaper.

"I'm sorry. I don't talk to reporters," she said, and started to hang up.

"Wait!" the voice yelled. "I think you'll want to talk with me."

At the mention of the word *reporter*, Jake's face drained of all color. "Who is it?" he asked.

Robin answered neither man. A tremendous sense of foreboding crashed around her.

"Are you there, Mrs. Bauer?"

"Yes," she said, now cupping the phone with both hands. "I'm here."

"Do you have any idea why the police have reopened the robbery investigation at Century Aeronautics?"

"What?"

"The robbery investigation. Do you have any idea why the case has been reopened?"

"No," she answered, her eyes still fully on Jake's.

"Who is it?" Jake asked again.

"Did you know that the cop who shot your husband has taken a leave of absence from the force?"

Something in the phrase *leave of absence*, a phrase she'd just moments before heard Jake use, first alerted her to the tragedy that was about to befall her.

"I was forced to take a leave of absence. I can't use my weapon. I killed a man. An innocent man."

No, it couldn't be! some part of her screamed. It just couldn't be. And yet... Suddenly everything made a kind of horrible, hideous sense—everything from the way she and Jake had so conveniently met, to his overwhelming concern for her and Peter, to the fact that he was a policeman...on leave...for killing an innocent man. Even the handkerchief with the initialed *C* made sense. That is, if the initial stood for...

"...Cameron," she heard the reporter say. "Lieutenant Jake Cameron's taken an indefinite leave of absence."

She knew. Jake could see the knowledge in her eyes. In her betrayed eyes.

"Robin, listen—" Jake began.

"How could you?" she asked, no longer speaking into the telephone. It had fallen from her numb fingers and now dangled by the cord.

"Robin—" he tried again.

"You killed Gerald," she said calmly—far too calmly. When Jake didn't reply, her composure shattered. "You killed him, didn't you?" When Jake still didn't reply, she hollered, "Dammit, did you kill him?"

Jake's composure, tenuously held together over the past months, cracked right down the middle, as well. It cracked right down the middle, spilling remorse and grief and a hundred other unbearable emotions at his feet. "Yes, goddammit!" he screamed. "I'm the one who killed your husband!"

CHAPTER ELEVEN

JAKE'S CONFESSION STUNG the still silence.

Even under the circumstances, circumstances he most assuredly would not have chosen for the revelation, he felt relieved, as though a great burden had been lifted from him. Regrettably he saw that burden settle on Robin. Under its weight, she tunneled deep within herself to that place where she, all alone, hid out from her pain.

"I tried to tell you," he said quietly. "A thousand times I tried to tell you."

"You just didn't try hard enough, though, did you?"

Her words held an aloofness, her look a troubling blankness, an emotional vacancy. He thought she looked as though she were seeing him for the first time, that what she'd given of herself the night before, she'd given to a totally different man. Her shutting him out hurt. More than anything in his life ever had.

"I was trying to tell you this morning," he pointed out in his defense. He knew it was a weak defense, but then, it was the only defense he had.

Robin gave a sharp, mirthless laugh. "The old eleventh-hour salvaging of your conscience. I don't suppose it occurred to you that maybe last night, before we...that maybe last night would have been a more appropriate time to enlighten me? Or was sex more important than honor last night? Were you afraid the grieving widow might not put out if she knew you'd murdered her husband?''

The words struck like a well-aimed blow. Jake's senses staggered under the cruel impact. "I don't deserve that," he said, his voice barely audible. "Whatever else you want to hurl at me, yes, but not that.''

Curiously, the pain she had inflicted hurt her as badly as it had Jake. She wanted to apologize, to say she knew he was right, that he hadn't deserved that kind of low blow, but she couldn't. The words just wouldn't come, damned as they were beneath a hurt so severe she thought it was going to crush her. She turned away and, noticing that the receiver hung almost to the floor, she picked it up and dropped it back onto the cradle. She then rested her elbow on the telephone alcove and lowered her face to her hand.

Finally, she glanced up. Her shock was receding, only to be replaced once more by betrayal. As though it were the crux of the whole issue, she said, "You lied to me.''

"I didn't lie, Robin. Technically, I didn't lie.''

Betrayal fell victim to anger. A white-hot, seething anger. She thought of how innocently she'd let him into her life, of how he'd pretended not to know who she was when, all the time, his every move had been coldly calculated.

"Well, you'll have to excuse me," she said, storming past him and heading into the living room. "I'm not thinking very technically right now. It seems to me that silence can be the biggest lie of all.''

She was right. He knew that. "I'm sorry," Jake whispered. As weak as the apology was, it was the only thing he knew to say, the only thing left to say.

Robin whirled, green sparks flashing in her eyes. She was standing before the fireplace, her arms draped about her. The fireplace was cold, void of all but the ashes of last night's fire. Somehow, the ashes seemed appropriate. Just as did the cold emanating from the hearth.

"Sorry? Gee, that's swell of you, Lieutenant. It is Lieutenant, isn't it?" She didn't give him a chance to answer. "It's swell of you to be sorry for killing my husband, swell of you to be sorry for insinuating yourself into my life under false pretenses, swell of you to be sorry for withholding the truth, even if technically you didn't lie. It's swell of you—"

"Dammit, Robin, stop it!"

The air crackled with a negative, angry energy, with two people fighting to maintain some hold on their sanity. "I tried to tell you last night. That's what I came here for, but you wouldn't let me. When I tried to, you said you didn't want to talk about your husband anymore."

Both were keenly aware of what had transpired next. She had begged him to hold her. Helpless to deny her, he had. From there, their bodies, their hearts, had led them. Robin's every bit as much as his. She had the grace to blush. And look away. Back into the fireless hearth.

"For God's sake," Jake said, desperation heavy in his plea, "please try to see the last few months from my perspective. I'm not asking you to forgive me. Just try to understand." When Robin didn't protest, he forged ahead. "There hasn't been a minute of a day or night that I haven't wished I could go back and undo what happened. I've played that night over and over and over and, even though it would have gone against everything I was trained to do, even though I was exonerated, I keep telling myself I shouldn't have shot. My God, Robin, the guilt has eaten me alive! It's the reason I had to see if you and Peter were all right."

She glanced over at him. Her eyes were void of all feeling. "Pardon me for not being able to work up a lot of sympathy," she said, absently twisting the wedding ring upon her finger. "At least you're alive to feel guilt. Gerald isn't."

"Some things are worse than death. Believe me."

"All I believe is that you killed my husband...and that you almost killed my baby."

Once more, her allegation hurt. Once more, he couldn't deny the truthfulness of what she'd said. He was certain, as he'd always been certain, that Peter had been born prematurely because of the stress Robin had endured.

"I never have, I never would, do anything to deliberately hurt you or Peter. Deep in your heart, you know that."

Both knew that less than ten minutes before, she'd admitted to knowing that very thing.

"No," she now said, negating what she'd said earlier, "I don't know any such thing. I don't even know you. Least of all do I know you. Everything that's been between us has been a lie."

"No!" Jake cried, thinking of the way their kisses had spoken only the truth, of the way their bodies had known no prevarication. Beseechingly, he stepped toward her. "Robin, listen. It was an accident—"

"Get out," she whispered unemotionally. In reaction to his stepping forward, she stepped backward.

It was that sole action—her stepping away from him—that drove the final stake through his heart. In that moment, he didn't care whether he lived or died. No, that wasn't true. He did care. He wanted to die. He'd been only marginally alive for a long while and what little life had been left in him, she'd snuffed out with her silent, lethal rejection.

Wordlessly, his heart beating no rhythm he could discern, Jake reached for his coat, which still lay draped across the sofa where he'd left it the evening before. The flowers, still reposing in the pitcher on the coffee table, mocked with their cheerful beauty. Shrugging into his coat, his boots pounding loudly on the wooden floor, Jake started for the door. He didn't look back. He didn't say goodbye. Everything of meaning had already been said...and it had been said silently...in a single step.

THE DAY WAS HELL.

For both Robin and Jake.

Long after he'd left, she sat on the living-room floor, huddled before a cold fireplace. Only hours before, she'd wondered if the night had been real. She now wondered the same thing of the morning. Surely she'd just been locked inside a nightmare, a nightmare from which she would awaken at any moment. As though thinking this thought restored reality, she became aware of sounds. In the bedroom, Peter was beginning to stir. In the kitchen, the radio said that the storm was moving in. In her heart, the same refrain kept echoing.

Jake had killed Gerald.

Jake had lied to her.

Jake had betrayed her.

But most of all, and this was something she would never forgive him for, Jake had made her care for him.

Finally, forcing herself to rally for the sake of her son, she fed Peter, bathed him, then bedded him down again. Instead of sleeping, however, he fretted and cried and fretted some more, as though he sensed something was amiss. Robin rocked him, sang to him, walked the floor with him. At last, he fell asleep. Weary beyond words, Robin dragged herself to the kitchen. She threw out the cold pancakes and the soggy bacon and poured the overbrewed coffee down the sink. She told herself she should eat something, but nothing appealed to her. Moreover, she was afraid that if she tried to eat, she wouldn't be able to keep anything down. Her stomach felt like a squadron of butterflies had been let loose inside it.

She couldn't remember ever feeling more miserable. Not even at Gerald's death had she felt this miserable. That had numbed her until she'd felt nothing. Now, however, her body was ultrasensitive. Every sight, every sound, every smell, brought back a memory of Jake. And every memory hurt. Miserably.

MILES AWAY, in his lonely apartment, Jake couldn't remember ever feeling more miserable. His divorce, seeing his kids on a sporadic basis, being involved in the accidental shooting had all taken an emotional toll that had ranged from hurt to anger to despair, but at each crisis he'd been so concerned about making it through, about the sheer act of surviving, that a good part of his energy had been diverted from feeling. Now, all he did was feel. He could feel Robin's hurt, he could feel the pain his betrayal had caused her, he could feel the misery of knowing that nothing he could ever do would change history.

He should have told her who he was from the very beginning. He should have told her! But how could he when, with each heartbeat, he'd fallen more and more in love with her? Bypassing the chocolate milk, Jake headed straight for a bottle of scotch. Despite the noonday hour, he downed a shot, wiping the back of his hand across his mouth. The liquor burned, seared, scorched, but it didn't even come close to easing his pain. To do that, it would have had to erase the memory of Robin stepping away from him.

ROBIN STEPPED BACK FROM the living-room window. Thirty minutes before, the predicted snow had begun to fall. The lacy flakes, the size of quarters, blew hard and furious, establishing almost zero visibility despite the fact it was only midafternoon. One flake seemed to pile immediately atop another, creating a wonderland that was both beautiful and alarming. If the snow continued to fall at this rate—and the forecast called for just that and worse—by evening the world would be hidden beneath a blanket of white. Even the trees in the nearby woods were beginning to look ghost-like in their filmy, niveous shrouds.

Did she have enough food supplies if she got snowbound? Moreover, did Peter have enough diapers? And what if the electricity went out? She'd heard that electrical power could be unpredictable out of the city limits. This last in mind, she searched through the house for a flashlight. Eventually, she found one that looked as if it had served a tour of duty in World War II. The weak battery corroborated the fact. Despite the potential hardship, Robin was grateful for the worsening weather. At least it was something to take her mind off...

Jake stepped to the window of his dad's room in the nursing home. It was a little after five o'clock. Giant snowflakes swirled by the glass pane. He wondered if it was snowing as violently in Lowell. He wondered what Robin was doing. He wondered if she was hurting as badly as he. Like a wounded cub, he'd felt compelled to return to his parent's den, in hopes his father could somehow ease the hurt. But, typically since entering the nursing home, his father hadn't spoken to him. When he'd asked how he was feeling, the old man had simply shrugged. Interestingly, encouragingly, the nurse said that she'd overheard Hank Cameron engaged in conversation with the man next door. Jake wished to God his father would say something to him. Anything!

"It's snowing," Jake said, looking out over a lake that was frozen solid.

Hank, dutifully eating his dinner, said nothing.

"They're forecasting a storm."

Still, the old man said nothing.

Jake's heart shriveled in disappointment. He tried not to show it, however. Instead, he turned and glanced down at the dinner tray. "Finished?"

His father nodded... once.

Jake removed the tray to the dresser from where it would later be picked up by one of the staff. "Wanna watch television?"

Hank shook his head and turned toward the window and away from his son.

"You want a magazine to look at?"

Nothing.

"What about playing cards?" Jake had no idea how he was going to concentrate on anything but green eyes, soft lips and the mess he'd made of everything, but if his dad wanted to play, he'd somehow manage.

Jake needn't have worried. Hank said nothing.

Something snapped inside Jake. "Pop, don't..." he pleaded, his voice cracking. "Not today. It's been a bitch and I've had all I can stand...." Jake stopped. What was the use? he thought, wearily dropping into the bedside chair and fighting back the burning in his eyes. He lowered his head into his hand. What the frigging hell was the use?

The bedclothes fluttered slightly, almost imperceptibly, as one gnarled hand reached out and closed around the hand that dejectedly lay on the side of the bed. Disbelievingly, Jake raised his head. His father was watching him, as though trying to determine the size of the burden his son carried on his shoulders. Maybe even the why of that burden. Hank Cameron still didn't utter a word. Call it pride. Call it stubbornness. Call it whatever. But there was no doubt that what shone in his eyes was love. His son was hurting—for whatever reason—and nothing mattered beyond comforting him.

The old man's hand tightened.

Jake's hand tightened back.

And for one moment in time, it didn't matter that life was a bitch.

"SHH," ROBIN PLEADED to a whining Peter. "Please, don't cry, baby. Mommy doesn't know what to do." The truth was that she'd done everything she knew to do to placate her son: she'd fed him, or tried to, but he'd mostly resisted the attempt; she'd rocked him;

she'd paced the floor with him. Nothing seemed to help. He just seemed hell-bent on crying.

Just the way the blizzard seemed hell-bent on dumping every single snowflake in the world right at her doorstep. It was now a dark, dreary seven o'clock in the evening and already snowbanks were drifting high. That is, she thought they were. It was almost impossible to see beyond the porch. The woods might as well have been a world away.

"...an updated weather advisory," the woman on the radio said. "Everyone is being cautioned to stay indoors...."

Robin laughed sarcastically. How could anyone get out in this? Which was an unsettling thought, considering that the supply of diapers was lower than she'd thought. And what if Peter was sick? Was that why he was crying?

"Shh," she whispered, patting the baby as he began a new round of wailing. This time the wails turned to outright screams. "Shh, shh," Robin comforted as she paced the floor again. She was somewhere between the sofa and the rocking chair when, without even a hint of a warning, the electricity went out. The house was plunged into an immediate and inky blackness.

At the same instant, Jake flicked on the lights of his apartment. Brushing his hand through his hair, he dusted the carpet in snowflakes. Damn, it was cold! And growing colder. The forecast indicated that the bad weather was just beginning...and that Lowell was getting the brunt of the storm. Throwing his coat on the sofa, he marched into the kitchen, jerked the phone off the hook and started to dial the heart-familiar number. In mid-dial he hung up.

He sighed heavily, hurtfully. She'd told him to get out of her life. And that's precisely what she'd meant. He'd never been more sure of anything. He had nothing left to give her except heartache, which, in reality, was all he'd ever had to give her. Besides, he'd accomplished what he'd set out to do: he'd seen for himself that she was all right. In the bargain, he'd learned that she was a strong, capable woman—a survivor. She'd be all right, storm or no storm. Wouldn't she? Yes, yes, she would! Jake repeated this mental dialogue a dozen times during the course of the next few hours.

Wrapped in her coat, Robin sat in the dark before the fire. With the failing of the electricity had gone not only the lights, but also the heat. The hour was ten after ten. It seemed more like ten after forever. She'd dragged, literally and laboriously, some cords of cut wood to the back of the house, no small feat in and of itself in the bone-chilling blizzard. The flashlight had waited—thankfully—until she'd accomplished this task, then died in her arms like a fallen comrade. Not a single candle had she been able to find. She was cold, tired, hungry. And if she were honest with herself, she was scared. The storm, along with Peter's crying, was growing steadily worse.

"Shh," she whispered, herself near tears.

Her thoughts, as they had all day, went to Jake. It was so easy to think of him in time of crisis. It was so easy to think of him period. But she mustn't. He had shot her husband. She was being disloyal to Gerald to think about Jake.

Yet . . .

. . . it was Jake who always seemed to be there when she needed him.

...it was Jake whose shoulders seemed broad enough to carry the world.

...it was Jake, whether he'd shot her husband or not, whose lovemaking she couldn't strike from her mind.

Then, because she was cold and tired and scared, she hugged her crying baby close and wept.

AT A FEW MINUTES PAST midnight, a Jeep crept into what the driver thought was the driveway of Robin's house. Covered in white as it was, it was impossible to tell exactly where the driveway ended and the yard began. The vehicle's two headlights fought their bright way through the dense curtain of falling snow, highlighting the cottage. The driver noted two things immediately. A column of smoke curled from the chimney, and there wasn't a single light on in the house. Maybe she'd gone to bed. Then again, maybe the electricity was out. Ever since Jake had heard that parts of the area had an electrical blackout, he'd paced his apartment like a caged animal. At last he hadn't been able to withstand not knowing another minute. She could throw him out, she could tell him to go straight to hell, but he had to satisfy himself that she and Peter were all right. It seemed to be an old, familiar story. It seemed to be the story of his life.

As he slung open the Jeep door, he thought again of his father's hand as it had comfortingly slid over his earlier that afternoon. The single act had motivated Jake's nocturnal mission. When you loved someone, you reached out your hand to them—no matter your differences, no matter the unscalable mountains that lay between the two of you, no matter the hurt and pain you'd caused each other, no matter the unwelcoming reception you might receive. Grabbing a sack, Jake trudged toward the cottage.

His coat collar turned up, his head bent low, he squinted his way through the hurting cold. Even breathing was a painful task, making his lungs feel as if they might crack if he took more than a shallow breath. And snow was everywhere—scrunching underfoot, sailing into his hair, sneaking down his collar, stinging his face in frigid punishment.

As he drew near, Jake heard Peter's cry. He had just started to pound on the door when said door opened. Jake's hand halted in mid-knock.

Robin had seen the headlights as they'd slashed across the driveway. She hadn't even wondered who'd be showing up at such an ungodly hour on such an unholy night. She knew. In the few moments it had taken Jake to reach the doorstep, she went over all the reasons she ought to send him away. Each point had been valid. Each point had also been moot, for when she opened the door, her relief was so profound that no reason, however valid, stood even the smallest chance of competing.

Though each was wreathed in darkness, neither had the slightest trouble finding the other's eyes. Jake was almost certain she'd been crying. The realization tore at his heart.

"Are you all right?" he asked, using all of his willpower to keep from pulling her into his arms.

"Something's wrong with Peter," she said, heaving the squalling baby, who'd been carried so much that he now seemed to weigh a ton, from one shoulder to the other. She fought the urge to fling herself into Jake's arms.

"What's wrong with him?" Jake asked, stepping into the house uninvited and depositing the sack on the nearest chair.

"I don't know. He's cried all day. He slept a little bit about an hour ago, but then he woke up crying again."

Peeling off his fur-lined gloves and throwing them at the coffee table, Jake reached for the baby, taking him from his mother as if he had every right to do so. Robin didn't put up the slightest resistance.

Deducing from the dark, cold house that the electricity was indeed out, Jake said, "There're some candles in the sack." When Robin, so tired she looked ready to drop, just stood in the same spot, he urged, "Light some, huh?"

Scrounging around in the paper sack filled with two large boxes of diapers and a sundry assortment of food, Robin found the candles, two of which she lit from the fireplace and anchored, via drops of candle wax, to saucers. She set one on the end table, the other on the coffee table. She then dropped to her knees on the floor before the sofa. Jake sat on the sofa's end, unbundling the baby from his warm blanket.

"Have you taken his temperature?"

"It's normal. At least it was an hour ago."

"What is it, fella?" Jake asked calmly, soothingly. He watched as Peter, bawling doubly hard since he'd been laid down, screwed up his beet-red face. He drew his legs upward in what looked like a little jerk. "Shh, it's okay, pal," Jake said, asking Robin in the same soft voice, "Has he eaten?"

"He seems hungry, but then he won't eat. He takes just a little bit of milk, then stops. He acts like something's hurting him. Jake..." her voice was unmistakably filled with concern "... what's wrong?"

"I think he has colic," Jake said, smoothing his large hand over the baby's small turgid stomach. The baby bellowed pitifully. "Is that what's wrong, fella? You got a tummyache?"

"Colic? That's not serious, is it?"

Jake glanced over at Robin, who was still kneeling on the floor. "He's just got gas on his stomach."

"But for so long?"

"You haven't lived until you've walked the floor all day and all night."

"You're sure? I mean, about it being nothing more than colic?"

"As sure as I can be after walking the floor with two daughters."

Robin gave a sigh of relief and raked back her hair. Jake noticed she'd released it from the braid. She'd obviously combed it, but mostly with her fingers as she was now doing. The effect was one of gypsy-wild disarray. It was an unfettered, provocative portrait that spoke directly to Jake's masculine senses. He had to force himself to pay attention to what she was saying.

"So what do we do for the colic?" she asked.

We. She has used the word *we.* Not *I,* but *we.* And the usage had come so naturally that she hadn't even noticed. But he had.

"Did the doctor send home any drops?"

Robin shook her head.

"It won't do any good to call him," Jake said, adding, "Even if we could find a pharmacy open, it'd take all night to get there, and we need something now."

Peter's cry confirmed the urgency.

Rising from the sofa, Jake grabbed a candle. "What do you have in the medicine cabinet?"

"Not much. I don't take much medicine." This last she said to Jake's back. "Shh," she whispered to Peter, wrapping the blanket back around him and scooping the squirming infant into her arms. "It's okay now." She said nothing more. In fact, she didn't dare comment further. But then she didn't have to. She knew that what she meant, but couldn't bring herself to say, to think, was that everything was okay now that Jake was here.

In seconds, he returned carrying a laundry basket, a pillow and a brown bottle. "I found some paregoric."

For a moment, Robin had no idea why the paregoric had been in her medicine cabinet. It wasn't hers. Of that she was certain. Suddenly, she remembered. When her mother had come up for Peter's birth, she'd developed a stomach virus. The doctor had wanted to prescribe some other medication, something newer, but her mother had insisted that the older medicines were best. Just the way she'd insisted that Robin never would have had a difficult pregnancy if she hadn't had to endure the stress of Gerald's death.

"It's Mother's," Robin said, pushing aside this last painful thought. It was more than she could cope with that the man standing before her, the man helping her through yet another crisis, was the same man responsible for the stress she'd undergone, the stress that had almost cost her her baby's life . . . and very nearly her sanity.

"Get a bottle and put about a quarter-inch of water in it," Jake ordered. "Then let's try to get him to take a little bit with this mixed in it." Explaining neither the laundry basket nor the pillow, he dropped both to the floor before again taking the baby from her.

As if Peter were his own. The thought crossed Robin's mind. It was yet something else she chose not to dwell upon.

When Robin returned from the arctic-cold kitchen, a small baby bottle in her hand, Jake had already fitted the pillow into the wicker laundry basket. It made a perfect cradle for Peter, whom he'd now laid inside it. Peter's cries had intensified to screams.

Robin, her nerves stretched almost to the breaking point, felt herself on the verge of screaming along with him.

Taking the bottle from her, Jake unscrewed the top and mixed a few drops of the medicine with the water. Recapping the bottle, he fitted the nipple into Peter's mouth. Peter sucked, cried, then sucked again.

"See if you can get some of it down him," Jake said, indicating for her to take the bottle. Swaddled in coats, they were both now kneeling on the floor. Robin reached to do as she'd been bade. There was no way that their hands could keep from touching. Each glanced sharply at the other. An avalanche of memories assailed both. She thought of intimate caresses tenderly painted with the bristly rough pads of his fingertips. He thought of skin softer than an angel's wings. "I'll get some more wood for the fire," he said, his voice smokier than the flames blazing in the hearth.

Robin divided her attention between Peter, who fought at the bottle, and Jake, who battled with the cords of wood. His nose red, his hair flecked with snow, Jake closed the door for the final time and tossed yet another log onto the fire. Greedy flames ate at the wood, the hungry, sizzling tongues licking and lapping at the offering. A burst of heat, like a gust of wind, blew through the cold room. Jake held his hands before the fire, letting his palms bask in the red-orange warmth.

Robin watched him. In truth, she was unable to stop herself. Who was this man? The play of the firelight answered her in the language of symbolism. Part of him she saw in vivid and clear light. This illuminated part she knew as her friend, as Peter's friend, as the man who'd made the past few weeks bearable. This man was capable, with arms that could fight away the demons of the dark, with broad shoulders that could hold the world at bay. She also knew this light-bright part as her lover—as her sensitive, caring, unforgettable lover.

Yet there was a part of him concealed in shadow. Who was this unclear, this shrouded man? Of this man, she knew that he'd taken something precious from her, from Peter, something that could never be given back. He'd also been duplicitous. And in a way she could not explain, that seemed worse than his having taken her husband from her. Both men, the man of light, the man of shadow, had one thing in common. They confused her, leaving her unable for the first time in her life to ferret through her feelings.

His hands warmed, Jake turned. His eyes met Robin's. He could see everything that she was thinking and feeling—every confused thing. It hurt him to see her wrestling with her emotions, for he sensed her pain as clearly as he sensed the fire's warmth.

"I want to hate you," she said, quietly, simply, as honestly as she'd ever admitted anything. Beside her, the bottle still off and on in his mouth, Peter whimpered and whined.

Though it took every ounce of strength he possessed, Jake said, with an evenness that surprised him, "If it's easier for you, then hate me."

The snowflakes, fragile victims of the fire, had melted in his hair, making them look like moist diamonds scattered amidst the wind-tossed strands. She wanted to rake back the wayward strands, wanted to feel the wet snowflakes on her suddenly thirsty fingertips. "I wish it were that easy," she answered.

"Why isn't it?" he asked.

She shrugged. "I don't know. It should be. You killed my husband—"

"Accidentally, Robin."

She chose to ignore his clarification. "You killed my husband, you forced yourself into my life under false pretenses, you . . . you confuse me. I don't know what I think or feel." She pushed back her own hair, which had tumbled onto her forehead. "I don't know what I'm supposed to think or feel." This last was said in total exasperation.

"Just let it be tonight. There'll be plenty of time in the morning to sort out how you feel. There'll be plenty of time to hate me then. For tonight, just let me help you."

Robin said nothing. She just stared at the man silhouetted in the golden firelight. Ultimately, it was Peter's crying that drew their attention.

Stepping forward, Jake knelt down and took the bottle from Robin. He held it up to determine how much the child had drunk. "He got some of it down," he said, turning the baby over on his stomach and patting the small back. To Robin he said, "Try to get some sleep."

"No, I'll—"

"Go to sleep," Jake said, using his free hand to drag a throw pillow from the sofa. A blanket that she'd obviously used for warmth already lay on the rug.

Tired and weary, Robin stretched out before the fire, facing the roaring blaze. "I'll rest just a minute," she said, her tear-tired eyelids already shutting.

Jake pulled the blanket up around her shoulders.

"Shh," he whispered to Peter, who still fussed and fretted. "It's okay. Everything's okay, pal."

Robin listened to Jake's softly spoken assurances. Little by little, Peter quieted. Though she knew that the medicine must in part be responsible, she knew also that Jake, and his reassuring voice, had a way of soothing the savage breast. A part of her was irritated that Peter responded so positively to this man. Another part of her was equally irritated that she did, too.

Fighting to hang on to this irritation, she fell into a fast and blissful sleep.

CHAPTER TWELVE

THE NIGHT WAS A BLUR, a blend of shallow sleep and deep dreams. More than once, Robin came instantly awake. Always, it would take her a second to orient herself, to come to the realization that she was uncomfortably stretched out on the rug before the crackling fireplace…and why. The sound of the wind howling, the quavering candlelight, the frigid cold of the room despite the roaring fire quickly reminded her of all that had transpired. Each and every time she awoke, she searched for Jake. She always found him jamming another log into the fireplace or pacing with a whimpering Peter or just sitting on the floor, leaning back against a chair, watching her. Each and every time, in a quiet, calm voice, he'd tell her to go back to sleep. Each and every time, she would.

At twenty minutes past a cold and frozen four o'clock, a burning log snapped in two. In the almost surreal silence, the sound was deafening. Robin jackknifed to a sitting position.

"It's only the fire," a soft voice said from out of the darkness.

Robin peered through the murky shadows. She found Jake standing at a window, staring out into the snow-white night. He had turned toward her, his hand, now once more encased in a glove, still holding back the lacy curtain. She could feel his eyes on her, just as she could faintly make out the growth of beard stubbling his face. Instead of the latter making him look unkempt, it simply made him look rugged, attractive, desirable.

"Go back to sleep," he repeated.

By brute force, Robin dragged her eyes from him. "Is it still snowing?" she asked.

"Yeah."

She speared her fingers through her hair. Bringing her hand from the relative warmth of the blanket, she was acutely aware of the cold room. She'd always heard that not only was it darkest right before dawn, but also that it was coldest. At the moment she didn't doubt it.

"God, it's cold," she said, her breath puffing into a frosted vapor. Suddenly concerned for Peter's warmth, she shoved back the cover and crawled to where the wicker basket sat before the fire—not too close, yet close enough to soak up the heat. She noted that Peter now wore a woolen cap upon his head and that another blanket had been placed over him.

"He's asleep," Jake said unnecessarily, for Robin could tell immediately that the baby was resting soundly. And warmly.

Why does this man have to take such good care of us?

Why does he have to be the man who killed Gerald?

As these questions tormented her, Jake stepped forward and, sliding back the grille, piled another log on the fire. The flames devoured it.

"Get back under the cover," he ordered, squatting and yanking back both the blanket and the heavy quilted coverlet that she used as a bedspread. This last hadn't been there when she'd first fallen asleep. It had been added. By Jake. Probably at the same time he'd spread more cover over the baby.

Why does this man have to take such good care of us? Dammit, why?

And why does the denim of his jeans have to splay so arrestingly, so sexily, over his thighs?

"C'mon," Jake said. He was still squatting, one knee now levered against the floor. He'd thrown back the bedclothes in a sign of invitation.

Drawing her eyes from the V of his legs, Robin crawled back beneath the covers. With a flick of his wrist, she was once more swaddled in warmth. At least in a measure of it, for she could still feel the room's chill penetrating through to her goose-pebbled flesh and chill-brittle bones.

"Go to sleep," Jake said, his eyes one with hers.

"I don't know if I can," she whispered, clutching the cover close. "It's cold." As though to prove the point, she shivered.

"Try," he said, pulling his eyes away, for there was something in the way her shoulders shook that disarmed him. He'd felt an overwhelming urge to take her in his arms. The night before, she had let him; she had even asked him to. Tonight, however, she wouldn't welcome him near her . . . even though near her was the only place in the world he ever wanted to be.

As if distancing himself physically would also help to distance himself emotionally, he slid across the floor and to the furthermost chair. Seated on the rug, he propped his back against the chair and crossed one ankle over the other. He folded his arms about him and tucked his gloved hands beneath the pits of his arms.

He closed his eyes and tried to go to sleep.

So did Robin.

Sleep, however, was as elusive as a quick thief in a slow night.

Robin tossed and turned, turned and tossed. My God, she thought, why hadn't she noticed before how hard the floor was? Or how cold? God, it was cold— the floor, the air, her very blood!

At the sound of rustling bedclothes, Jake cracked an eyelid. Robin's restlessness stirred him. He wanted to do something to ease her discomfort. He also vividly remembered what she felt like moving beneath him. The memory hacked at his heartbeat. As the bitter-sweet remembrance assailed his body in a specifically physical way, he squirmed. My God, he thought, when had this floor become so damned hard?

Robin was acutely aware of Jake's every move-ment. Opening her eyes, she glanced briefly at him, then away. Something in the spread of his legs, the slump of his spine, reminded her of the night they'd shared. She could feel his body sprawled atop hers. Negligently, masculinely. Grabbing the sofa pillow beneath her head, she pounded it, hoping to pulver-ize some of the knots, hoping to squash some of the memories. She lay back down, the cold moving through her like sleet. She shivered again.

Jake cursed the way her bedraggled but sexy-looking hair fluffed about the pillow, about her face. He also cursed the way she shook from the cold, the way she tugged the blanket and coverlet closer around her neck, the way her teeth chattered silently.

Don't even think it, he warned himself, hugging his arms more tightly to him as if chaining them from their own free will.

Robin turned again.

No! he reminded himself.

She tossed.

No, dammit!

She trembled, balling herself into a tight, fetal knot.

Jake growled and pushed himself from the chair. Yanking back the cover, he slipped in beside her, face to face, pulling her flush against his chest. He could feel the coiled surprise in her body; he could hear the gasp as air spilled from her lungs.

Without hesitation, he worked open the buttons of her coat. At his gloved clumsiness, he uttered a profanity before teething the leather from his hands. He then finished unbuttoning her coat. He followed with his own. Again, as though exercising his right, he opened the woolen garments and tucked her body next to his—chest to chest. Their body heat mingled and merged. He felt the shivers sluicing through her. She felt his warmth neutralizing her cold. She also felt the strength of his masculine body, the protective, possessive strength. She knew it was wrong—this man had killed her husband—but she could not fight this temptation. Tomorrow, perhaps. But tonight she was tired and cold. Colder than she could ever remember being. So cold that she felt she'd never be warm again. Her body bypassing her brain, she closed her eyes and melted into Jake.

Neither spoke a single word.

The dream was warm and fuzzy, and Robin felt as if she were floating on a thick, spongy cloud. Intuitively, she knew she didn't want to wake up. She wanted to stay here in the sleep-foggy world where you didn't have to think or feel anything you didn't want to.

Feel.

She wanted to continue to feel the hard body pressed against hers. In fact, she wanted to feel more of it. The hand draped about Jake's waist fluttered to life, slowly drifting between their two bodies and up the wall of his solid chest. Robin splayed her fingers wide, seeking flesh, but all she found was fabric. She moaned in disappointment.

As though in compensation, she felt Jake's hand, warmer than any glove, smooth across her back. Her bare back. When had his hand worked its way beneath her sweater? It didn't matter. It mattered only that it had. Only that his skin was intimately caressing hers. This time her moan was one of pleasure.

Of their own volition, her hips rolled forward, seeking something. She wasn't quite sure what. But she was certain that it was some sweet something she'd found before with this man. Her thighs nudged his; in answer, his nudged back. His leg also slid between hers—as naturally as the sun slipping into a morning sky.

A restless tingle skipped through Robin, making her whimper, making her hungry. Raising her head, she nuzzled her lips at the hollow of Jake's throat before cozying her cheek against his. She felt the scratchy-roughness of his beard, smelled the faint scent of his aftershave, felt him roll his head toward hers, felt his mouth poised above her, ready to—

Alarm bells went off within Robin's head. Sleep instantly fell away as reality crowded in. Her eyes had flown open...only to find Jake's eyes wide and watchful.

The dream had been warm and fuzzy, and Jake had felt as if he were lazily bobbing on a sun-drenched sea. He didn't want to wake up. There was too much pain to be felt when awake.

Feel.

God, what was he feeling? A hand trailing up his chest? A woman's hand? Whatever it was, it felt good...except there was a barrier between that hand and his skin. That didn't feel good. It made him feel cheated out of something he intuitively knew was soft and warm and wondrously sexy.

As if to compensate for this deprivation, he tunneled his hand beneath the layers of fabric, searching for the back of the woman in his arms, searching for her bare skin. When he found it, he heard her moan, a sultry sound that quickened his male pulse.

Something told him to wake up, but he ignored that something. Which was more than easy to do when her hips rolled toward his. In truth, he thought of nothing but rolling toward her, pressing thigh to thigh, an action that produced yet another reaction. He slid his leg between hers...which she willingly, eagerly parted.

Wake up, he told himself when he heard a moan that he strongly suspected was his own.

Even as he ordered himself to wake up, he fought against it. My God, what was she—he was aware now that the woman in his arms was Robin—doing? Her lips brushed his throat, as her cheek snuggled next to his. Her skin was soft, so damned soft! He rolled his head toward her, seeking more of what she was so sweetly offering. With the same certainty that he knew it was getting hard for him to breathe, he knew her lips were near his, deliberately positioning themselves just beneath his, in anticipation of—

Jake's eyes had flown open.

He stared down into slumberous green eyes. They were more than slumberous, however. They were hazy with passion. She wanted his kiss. Despite who he was, despite the hell he'd made of her life, she wanted him to kiss her. The thought elated him; the thought pained him. It pained him because it pained her. He could see that pain, accompanied by guilt, existing side by side with her passion. While she might not have clarified her hatred of him, it was obvious that she had no trouble hating herself for this clear-cut betrayal.

Even so, she begged for his kiss.

He was uncertain where he found the strength, but he rolled from her and got to his feet. Threading unsteady fingers through his sleep-tangled hair, he walked to the window...and away from temptation. Drawing back the curtain, he looked out.

The first rays of dawn were brightening the world. Although the wind had quieted, it still blew with a primitive harshness, creating snowdrifts and snowbanks that made the landscape look like that of another planet. It was still snowing, and huge icicles hung from the house like the fangs of some wild beast.

Jake turned, his eyes meeting Robin's. She continued to sit in the middle of the floor, the cover draped about her. Her eyes were still hazy... just the way his body was still drugged with need.

"Jake—"

"Nothing happened," he interrupted.

But something had happened, and Robin knew it, something that was every bit as confusing as all that had gone before it. Within the honest confines of sleep, her body had responded to him. And while they might not have kissed, the fact that they hadn't was solely thanks to him. Even now, her lips tingled for what might have been, which pushed her guilt to astronomical new heights. Her confusion soared off all emotional charts. And through it all, Gerald Bauer stared condemningly at her from his photo.

Her confusion didn't clear within the next hour. Obviously worn to a frazzle, Peter continued to sleep, a blessing that Robin was more than grateful for. Tending to personal needs, she returned to the living room to find Jake boiling a pan of water on a newly stoked fire. Unable to resist the blaze, Robin crossed to it and stood warming her hands. In the background she heard the radio advising listeners that the storm had been worse than expected and that electricity was out in many areas.

Jake glanced up from rummaging through the sack he'd brought the night before. "Hungry?" he asked.

Robin considered. "Yeah, I think so. Actually, I know so. I'm famished."

"I have some instant coffee and some sweet rolls," he said. "You want a Danish or a cinnamon roll?"

"Either."

Jake handed her the first one he came to—a gooey Danish. He also set out the coffee, next to the mugs and spoons he'd earlier brought from the kitchen. She sat on the hearth, he cross-legged on the floor, while they ate. The food was quite simply the best Robin had ever eaten, and the coffee, hot and black, was perfection.

Would he be leaving this morning? Robin wondered as the coffee heated her stomach, the cup her hands. She hoped he would leave, yet, contrarily, she

hoped he wouldn't. Rather than try to reconcile these
two opposing points of view, she said, "Thank you.
For showing up last night, I mean. I don't know what
I would have done with Peter if you hadn't."

"You'd have managed."

"Yeah," she said, thinking, *But, as always, you
made the managing easier.*

They were still staring at each other—it seemed to
be what they did best—when all of a sudden, as unexpectedly as it had died, the electricity sparked to life.
The lights flashed on, while the central heating
hummed through the vents.

"Thank God . . . thank goodness," they both said.

Almost in tandem with the rebirth of the electricity, as though in every way the world had come alive
again, the phone rang. Robin rushed to catch it before it woke Peter.

In seconds, she returned with the announcement
"It's for you."

Jake glanced up with a more-than-puzzled look.
"For me?" He couldn't imagine who would be calling him at Robin's. No one knew he was here.

Robin nodded, repeating, "For you."

"Who is it?"

"He didn't say."

He? Who the hell was he? Certainly not yesterday's reporter or Robin would have recognized his
voice. Anyway, how could Phil Markham—and Jake
was almost positive the bloodhound reporter who had
called Robin was Phil Markham—possibly know that
he was here? How could he possibly even make a wild
guess that he was?

With an unaccountable sense of foreboding, Jake walked into the hallway and picked up the receiver. "Hello?"

"Have you lost your mind?"

It was by and large the same question that his sister had asked him weeks before. The overworked question had been asked this time by Daniel Jacoby. Jake sighed. He felt weary...and it had little to do with the fact that he'd had only bits and pieces of sleep.

"How did you find me?"

"Well, let me assure you it wasn't easy. I called your apartment so many times that I was ready to have you declared missing. I finally decided to call your sister, and she told me where you might be. Reluctantly told me, I might add." There was a pause, then, "Man, have you lost your mind?"

"Yeah," Jake said, his voice sounding as if it weighed a ton.

"Why?" The question was laced with concern. It was also obvious what the question referred to.

Jake answered his friend the way he had his sister. "I don't expect you to understand. It was just something that I had to do. I had to see if they were all right."

"And is that all you've done?"

Give or take falling in love, Jake thought, but said nothing.

Daniel Jacoby cursed. "I knew it! I could tell from what your sister didn't say that you'd gone and gotten yourself involved. You're a dumb bastard, aren't you, Cameron?"

"Gee, Jacoby, keep talking like that and people are gonna think you think I'm stupid or something." Which he was. Lord, was he ever!

Ignoring his friend's sarcasm, the psychologist asked, "How did you find out where she was?"

"I snooped through your files."

Daniel Jacoby cursed. "You do know that's unethical? And that I could haul your ass up on charges of—"

"So haul," Jake interrupted.

His friend cursed again. "Does she know who you are?"

"Oh yeah," Jake drawled, rubbing his hand over his beard-shadowed chin. He felt very much on the inside as he did on the outside—rough and prickly. "Compliments of Phil Markham. At least, I think I have good ole Phil to thank. Talk about bastards, he beat me to telling her by all of five minutes. Five friggin' minutes. Ever have one of those days, Jacoby?"

Again, Daniel ignored the question. "How'd she take it?"

"How do you think?"

There was a moment's silence, then a genuine "Man, I'm sorry."

"Yeah," was all Jake answered.

"I'm not sure now how you'll take what I called to tell you. I thought it might help to relieve that guilt you've been walking around with, but now I don't know."

Jake's interest was piqued. Intuitively, he knew that the reason Daniel had called had to do with the case being reopened. It was something he'd deliberately not mentioned to Robin the day before. "What have you found out?"

"That Gerald Bauer wasn't as innocent as we first thought."

Jake closed his eyes. He knew that was what Daniel was going to say. He'd just known it. The way he knew that the information would tear Robin apart. "How guilty are we talking about?" he asked, choosing his words carefully.

"As guilty as sin. It seems our golden boy was planning a major heist . . . plans to a new secret aircraft. He'd already approached a competitive firm about buying the goods."

Jake swore, low and hotly.

"As controller," Dan went on, "he didn't normally have access to the plans, so the police think he took them that night and hid them in the back of his desk. His plan, everyone now believes, was to slip them past the guard the next day. Probably amid some accounting papers."

"He certainly had enough brass, didn't he?" Jake was angry. Dammit, he was angry at this creep Gerald Bauer for leaving his wife and son such a legacy!

"Yeah. He had brass, all right, but not an ounce of luck. The dumb jerk picked a night when Century Aeronautics was robbed."

"Then the rest of it went down just as we thought?"

"Apparently. As he was leaving, he found the guard dead and, fearing for his life, took the gun and shot at what he thought was a burglar. Namely, you."

Jake fought to keep the malignant memories of what happened next at bay. It didn't matter that he'd been exonerated, it didn't matter that Gerald Bauer had been guilty of theft, the fact was that he'd killed a man. And he'd never take that lightly.

"You all right?" Dan Jacoby asked.

"Yeah. I guess. I'm not real sure how to tell, anymore. Look, you're sure about all this?"

"Yeah. It all adds up. Gerald Bauer was living beyond his means. Well beyond. Apparently, he had a real taste for the finer things."

"Yeah," Jake said, thinking of the man's finer-than-fine wife. That wife in mind, he added, "There's no way to keep this quiet, is there?"

"You know there isn't."

Jake had known it, but had felt compelled to ask.

"The police are gonna need to question her," Daniel said. "Plus, Phil Markham somehow got wind that the case was being reopened, and he's putting two and two together and coming up with a pretty accurate four."

Jake called the reporter an unflattering name.

"So," Daniel said, going right to the crux of his friend's dilemma, "she hears it from rank strangers or she hears it from you."

This time Jake swore, giving his dark impression of the situation.

"I hear you, man," Daniel said. "I hear you."

Jake found Robin sitting on the edge of the brick hearth. She looked up when he entered the room, unable to hide her curiosity. Instead of indulging it, however, he pulled his gaze from hers and walked to the window. He stared out, knowing that he was only postponing the inevitable, knowing that he was momentarily taking the coward's way out.

Outside the snow was recklessly falling, further blanching an already white world. Inside, for the first time since the electricity had come back on, honest-to-goodness warm air gushed from the vents.

"... it's been reported that electricity has been restored to some of the outlying areas," the radio stated, "but the storm is still very much active and weather advisories are still in effect...."

Robin's curiosity finally drove her to ask about the phone call. "Who was it?"

Jake turned. He wished he didn't have to tell her. He wished he didn't already feel sick to his stomach over the hurt he knew he was going to inflict. He wished she didn't look as in need of protection as the child peacefully sleeping at her feet.

"It, uh, it was the department's psychologist, Daniel Jacoby. He wanted to bring me up to date on the robbery at Century Aeronautics."

The mention of Century Aeronautics wiped out all Robin's interest in how this Daniel Jacoby had known to reach Jake at her house. It also jogged her memory about something the reporter had said the day before, something about the case being reopened. She'd entirely forgotten about it in the face of the turmoil that had followed—finding out that Jake had shot Gerald, the storm, Peter's incessant crying.

"Does it have anything to do with the case being reopened?" she asked.

Jake's forehead creased into a frown. "How did you know about that?"

"That reporter mentioned it yesterday."

Jake's frown deepened. "What else did he say?"

"Nothing." *Except that you'd killed my husband.* "He wanted to know if I knew why it had been reopened. I told him no." She worked her fingers through her hair and repeated her question, "Is that why this Jacoby guy called?"

As though the blow would be more merciful delivered at close range, Jake slowly crossed the room. He stopped in front of her. She had to tilt her head back to maintain eye contact.

"It wasn't a simple robbery, Robin."

In the silence that ensued, the radio stated, "... police are cautioning drivers to stay in if possible...."

"What do you mean?" Robin asked, finding her voice at last. She was aware of being uncomfortable. Perhaps it was the hot fire at her back; perhaps it was the growing suspicion that she wasn't going to like what she heard next.

"Let me rephrase it," Jake said, fumbling for a tolerable entrée. "There were two robberies that night. One was a simple robbery, the kind of break-in we see a dozen times a week. The other robbery falls under the heading of white-collar theft."

"I...I don't understand. You mean someone at Century Aeronautics was stealing from the company?"

"Yes. Plans for a new aircraft."

Robin's discomfort reached unbearable proportions. She stood, removing herself from the heat of the fire. She couldn't however, remove herself from the feeling that she didn't want to hear what was going to follow.

"I don't understand what any of this has got to do with Gerald's death."

For a fleeting second, it crossed Jake's mind that Robin feared what he was going to tell her, as though she sensed the truth, but couldn't bring herself to admit it. That ludicrous idea fled as quickly as it had come. She wouldn't be looking at him with such a puzzled expression if she had any inkling of Gerald Bauer's guilt.

"The police think that . . . they think that your husband stole the plans."

Jake wasn't certain what he expected her reaction to be. It certainly wasn't what he witnessed. First, Robin stared at him. Just stared. As if she were trying to make the words compute into something intelligible. Second, she turned, as though he'd said nothing more upsetting than that it was snowing, and walked to the laundry basket doubling as Peter's bed. She dropped to her knees and checked the baby, ending with "shh, shh," as she unnecessarily patted the back of the sleeping child.

Taking a tentative step toward her, Jake stopped short of touching her and said, "Did you hear me?"

She said nothing.

The radio said, " . . . just been advised that we have a new update concerning the storm. . . ."

"Robin . . ."

Slowly, she stood. Slowly, she pivoted toward him. The cold, silent-seething fury in her eyes froze Jake in his tracks.

"How dare you?" she whispered with a frightening calmness. "How dare you take from me, from Peter, the last thing that Gerald has to give. How dare you maliciously smear his good name."

Something snapped inside Jake. Unlike hers, his voice was not calm. In fact, it was so loud that Peter stirred. "Do you think I'd make something like that up? Do you think I'd enlist the department psychologist's help in starting an ugly, unfounded rumor?"

Robin's eyes flashed with a frigid fire. "I'll tell you what I think, Lieutenant Cameron. I think you'd say, do, believe, anything to ease your guilt. Anything!"

"You're right about my wanting to ease my guilt. More than anything I want to ease my guilt, but I wouldn't do it at the expense of an innocent man...or at the expense of an innocent child." His voice lowered to a hoarse whisper. "Nor would I do it at the expense of the woman I love."

Faster than lightning, Robin's hand snaked out of thin air, her palm crashing against Jake's cheek. "Don't you *dare* say that to me. You don't now, nor will you ever, have the right to say that to me!"

A huge and heavy silence followed. Jake's cheek stung. Robin's hand ached. Neither noticed. Both were too aware of the pain in their hearts.

"...I repeat the weather update. Many roads are now impassable due to the snow and ice. Everyone is being urged to stay indoors...."

Without a word, in defiance of the weather warning, Jake, who still wore his coat, grabbed his gloves and headed for the door. He didn't hesitate in slinging it open. Flurries of snow rushed in, defying the warmth to melt them. And then, in an eerie scenario of déjà vu, he was gone, slamming the door behind him, stalking out into the raging storm.

He never once looked back.

But then, there was nothing to look back to.

CHAPTER THIRTEEN

IN THE LATE AFTERNOON OF THE same day, the storm blew itself out. Robin stood at the cabin window, staring out at the virginal-white world. A snowdrift, like some great, grounded bird, banked high to the right, while the woods looked like a beautiful but bleak wilderness in some fairy tale of winter adventure. There was no motion anywhere. Nor any sound. It was as though a plague-like stillness had descended upon the land. Robin hated this unnatural stillness, this silence, for within it she repeatedly heard the scream of her tortured thoughts and the thud of her lonely heartbeat. She also told herself that she hated Jake Cameron.

Within the oppressive quietude, Robin could hear the sound of her hand striking Jake's cheek. She'd never hit another human being; she'd never been that angry. Without conscious awareness, she rubbed the palm of her hand with her thumb, reliving the pain of the blow. Curiously, she felt the pain most deeply in her heart. That, too, was where she felt the cold. Even though the house was warm, she was shivery-cold, far colder than she'd been at the peak of the storm with the electricity shut down. Motivated by that frigid feeling, she stepped from the window over to the fire. Hugging herself, she closed her eyes as the warmth surrounded her.

How could anyone believe Gerald guilty of theft? There had to be a logical explanation. If the police thought him guilty, then someone had set him up to look that way. Jake? No, not even she could believe that of Jake. Yet was that any more vile than what she'd already accused him of doing? Hadn't she accused him of lying to exonerate his own guilt?

Sweet heaven, what had she said?

But then, how could he have said what he did?

How could he blatantly accuse Gerald, dead and unable to defend himself, of taking aircraft plans?

Robin felt her anger building again, boiling higher and higher until it scalded her with its heated force. Yes, she hated Jake Cameron for his brazen accusation, for the way he'd shot her husband, then callously lied his way into her life, for making her worry about whether he'd gotten home all right.

She opened her eyes and looked at her watch; it was a quarter to five. He should have been home long ago. That is, if he hadn't run into any trouble. Her imagination going wild, she saw him in all sorts of grim situations, ranging from stranded on the side of the snow-draped road, where he froze to death slowly, to a sickening crash of vehicles, where everyone involved died instantly.

Maybe she should just call and see if he got home. She wouldn't have to talk to him. If he answered, she'd hang up. She'd— *Stop it!* she commanded herself. *For the love of Pete, do you hear what you're saying?*

At five o'clock, she again glanced at her watch. She glanced again at ten minutes after the hour. Then again at nineteen after. Then again just before the hand reached six. She knew she was acting like someone waiting for something to happen. What? For Jake to call and apologize? For Jake to call and say that he was simply checking on her? For Jake to call and make everything all right just the way she'd come to expect him to salvage her wrecked moments? No, he wouldn't be calling. Not ever again. If she wanted to know if he'd gotten home, it was she who'd have to call.

"Then, for heaven's sake, call and get it over with!" she seethed, as angry with herself as she was with him.

She marched to the phone, dialed the number of his apartment, then, listening over the pounding of her heart, heard the phone begin to ring. It rang and rang and rang. Somewhere past a dozen rings, Robin hung up. She told herself that his not being home meant nothing, that he could be out shopping, that he could be out visiting his father, that he could be out . . . with a woman. She told herself that the latter was none of her business, even though the empty feeling in the pit of her stomach suggested that it might be.

Amid tending to Peter, whose colic had thankfully disappeared, Robin repeated the call at thirty-minute intervals. Always with the same negative response. By ten o'clock, she was growing seriously worried. By eleven o'clock, she was fit to be tied. By midnight, she was pacing the floor, pictures of how bad the storm had been when he'd left, how impassable some of the roads still were, flashing through her head. Worn and worried, she nonetheless fell into a restless sleep at three-thirty.

At six-thirty the next morning, the first thing she did upon awakening was dial Jake's number again. There was still no answer. Nor was there any at seven. Panicked by the sinister images now playing out in her head, Robin grabbed the telephone and proceeded to ruin the information operator's day. Robin could remember only the last name she sought a number for. At least she thought she remembered it. Luckily, there was a listing for a Dr. Ames. Robin prayed that Jake's sister's husband, who she thought she recalled Jake, at some point this week, saying was a professor at Harvard, had a doctorate.

The phone was answered by a woman on the fourth ring. "Hello?"

Robin paused, then plunged. "Is this Jake Cameron's sister?"

At the unusual greeting, there was a hesitation, then, "Yes. I'm Whitney Ames. Who's this, please?"

Nervously shifting the phone to her other ear, Robin replied, "This is Robin Bauer. We met several weeks ago," she hastily added. "Outside a restaurant. I was with your brother."

There was another pause. "Yes, I remember."

Robin was certain she could hear the surprise in the woman's voice. When Robin said nothing, surprise was joined by concern.

"Is everything all right?" Whitney asked.

"I've been trying to reach Jake all night, but he doesn't answer his phone. I was just wondering if he's okay. I thought maybe you'd heard from him...maybe that he'd called...or you'd seen him...or...or something." Robin leaned back against the hallway wall and closed her eyes. She shouldn't have called. Dammit, she shouldn't have called!

"Robin, are you okay?"

Something in the quiet, sensitive question, in the way the woman had intuitively sensed her mood, reminded Robin of Jake. It also told her that she would have liked to be this woman's friend. If things had worked out differently. If she hadn't been the sister of the man who'd betrayed her, the man who'd irreparably shattered her life.

"Look," Robin said, fighting at tears she would have been hard-pressed to explain. "Jake left here yesterday morning...in the middle of the storm. He, uh, was upset. The radio had advised against travel and...well, I was worried...I've called his apartment a dozen times, but—"

"I haven't heard from him," Whitney interrupted.

Robin's heart sank.

"But that doesn't necessarily mean anything. He can be an overly private person at times. We don't speak every day."

Even though Whitney was calm and collected, Robin sensed her concern. It did nothing to abate her own, though she told herself that Whitney's not having heard was a good sign. Surely she'd have been notified if... Unable to complete the painful thought, Robin let it drift away.

"Why don't I check around for him?" Whitney said, adding, "When I get in touch with him, I'll have him call you."

"No!"

The word slammed into the conversation, bringing it to a sharp halt.

"I, uh, I'd prefer instead if you'd just call me back," Robin said finally. "If it isn't too much bother."

"No, of course it isn't. What's your number?"

Robin told her, then added, "Thank you. I really need to know that he's all right."

They were, almost verbatim, the words that Whitney had heard once before, when Jake had tried to

explain why he'd become involved with Robin and her
son.

"I, uh, I'd also appreciate it if you wouldn't tell him
that I called," Robin said. "Please." The last was delivered so passionately that it was obvious her request
was sincere.

Nonetheless, Whitney asked, "Are you sure?"

"Yes," Robin returned in an unequivocal tone,
adding, "I'm very sure."

AT A FEW MINUTES AFTER eight o'clock, a knock
sounded on Jake's door. Sprawled out on the sofa, his
head at an awkward angle, his feet dangling over the
arm, he dragged himself awake. Well, sort of awake.
As awake as one could get after a night of one too
many beers and too few hours of sleep. He sat up
slowly—easy, easy, man!—swinging his bare feet to
the floor...the cold floor. His shoulders slouched, he
grabbed his head...the one whose skull was being vi-
ciously drilled in half by some maniac.

The knock came again—louder, more persistently.

"Yeah, yeah," Jake muttered.

He stumbled to his feet, trying to focus bleary eyes
that really preferred not to cooperate. His mind
equally fought at focalization. He sensed that there
was something he didn't want to remember, some
threatening thing hovering just outside his blurred
mind. As he brought his hand to his unshaved, bristly
cheek, the memories rushed back like a hostile tidal
wave.

*"I wouldn't try to ease my guilt at the expense of the
woman I love."*

He could still hear the smack of Robin's hand as it
sliced through the air and connected with his face. He

could still feel the pain—the numbness, followed by a stinging, followed by an all-out fiery burning. No one had ever slapped him before—a couple of rowdy, resisting criminals had landed punches on his jaw—but he'd never been slapped. It hurt. But not nearly as much as what she'd said.

"Don't you dare say that to me. You don't now, nor will you ever, have the right to say that to me!"

Something inside Jake died, just as it had when Robin had hurled the cruel words at him. This new death surprised him. He hadn't known there was anything left to kill.

The knock came once more.

"All right already!" Jake cried, tearing open the door. His gaze collided with that of his sister.

He watched as she took in his tousled hair, his red glazed eyes, his whiskered chin and cheeks. From there, her gaze lowered to encompass his rumpled clothes—his wrinkled jeans, his shirt hanging half in, half out, his bare feet. He wondered inanely if she could tell that his mouth tasted like yesterday's garbage. And that his head felt like the site of a nuclear explosion.

"What are you doing out in this lousy weather?" he asked as he turned and walked back into the small living room.

Whitney followed, closing the door behind her. She shed her coat, though she left on a red beret. Its cocky tilt seemed to define her extroverted personality. "You obviously haven't looked outside lately. The storm's over. The sun's out."

Jake displayed not the least curiosity. Instead of checking out the weather, he plopped himself back on the sofa, leaned his elbows on his knees and again cupped his head with both hands as though trying to hold it on.

"I take it you don't care that the sun's out."

"Not much."

"You want an ice pack for your head?"

"No. I want to hurt."

"Suit yourself," Whitney said, sitting down beside her brother.

Jake winced at the slight, jarring motion.

"Wild evening of carousing, huh?" Whitney said, baiting Jake for an explanation.

"Wrong, wench lady. I didn't leave the house last night."

"Then why didn't you answer the phone?"

"Was that you?" he asked, trying to hide his disappointment. In his heart of hearts, he'd hoped that it had been Robin, calling to say... Calling to say what? That all was forgiven? What a jerk he was! What a stupid, damned jerk!

Lost in his own misery, he didn't notice that Whitney conveniently ignored the question. Instead she fingered the neck of the nearby beer bottle—there were five bottles in all sitting on the cluttered coffee table. "I didn't know you were this crazy about beer," she said.

"I'm not. It's all I had after I finished off the scotch."

"Ah, the old need to lose touch with reality."

"You got it."

He'd never been an abuser of alcohol. In fact, he could remember only one other hangover—when he was a teenager succumbing to peer pressure. He hadn't even turned to the bottle when his wife had non-

chalantly asked for a divorce. Well, he had a hangover now, he thought. A real doozy.

Jake leaned back, laying his head against the sofa.
His eyes were closed. Still he could see scrambled
images playing across the screen of his mind, images
of Robin snuggled close to him, images of Robin's
cold fury, images of Robin slapping him.

Long quiet moments passed before Whitney asked
quietly, "You want to talk about it?"

"No." The word was delivered in a dismissive tone.

Whitney persisted. "Does it have anything to do
with Daniel Jacoby calling and wanting to know where
you were?"

Jake said nothing.

"He told me that it was important he talk to you
and that he couldn't reach you. I took a wild guess at
where you might be." There was a hesitation before
she asked, "Did I do wrong by telling him?"

Jake glanced over at his sister. He could see her
concern. It was there in the way she was hanging on his
answer. "No. It was all inevitable. It was all just a
matter of time."

When Jake offered nothing more, Whitney began,
"Jake—"

"It's okay, Sis. It's not your problem."

"Not my problem?" Whitney said in disbelief.
"You're hurting and it's not my problem?" When
Jake still said nothing, she roared, "Talk to me, Jake!
For heaven's sake, talk to me!"

Jake grabbed his head and groaned. "Don't do
that," he pleaded.

"Then talk to me."

Giving a deep sigh, he said, "It's very simple. Robin found out who I was. To add insult to injury, I had to tell her that her husband was a thief."

At this last announcement, which came as a total surprise, Whitney was rendered momentarily speechless, a state she suffered from only on rare occasions. "A thief?" she managed finally, then, when the full implication registered, she whispered, "Oh, my God."

"Yeah, a thief. And, yeah, oh, my God."

Getting to his feet, Jake walked to the window. He opened the drapes and peered out, squinting. Just as his sister had said, the sun was peeking through the blue-gray skies, causing the snow to glimmer like a cluster of shiny diamonds. Jake resented the opulent beauty of the scene...and the fact that the world seemed to be going about its business as usual despite the emptiness he felt. The emptiness was curiously painful, he mused. One would think that hollow wouldn't hurt, but he was beginning to believe that it hurt worst of all.

"Gerald Bauer was stealing aircraft plans, which he was going to sell to a rival company," Jake explained. "He got caught in a simple robbery that was going down at the same time."

Jake spent the next few minutes highlighting what had transpired over the past couple of days. He omitted the fact that he and Robin had become lovers.

"How did she take everything?" Whitney asked.

Jake snorted. "Let's put it this way, she's not exactly singing my praises."

"But surely she can't blame you for her husband's being a thief?"

"Right now she's fighting believing that he was. Hell, I'm not sure she knows what she's thinking, or feeling, except I do know that the old parable about the messenger is true. She'd have my head in a New York minute if she could."

"Jake, give her time. In the heat of the moment, people say and do things that they don't mean."

Jake felt his cheek burn anew with the force of Robin's slap. He heard her telling him never again to declare his love for her. As always, the words cut deep.

"Yeah," he said, the memories almost more than he could bear, "then again, they sometimes say and do exactly what they mean."

"Jake, listen to me. I know she still cares. I—" At the authority in her voice, he turned. His look was piercing, as though questioning this authority. His look additionally begged her to make him believe what she was saying. Whitney moistened her suddenly dry lips as she grappled with her moral dilemma. At last, she said, "I just know it. Trust me. People don't stop caring that easily."

Wrong, Jake thought. Robin had. He had finally managed to make her do what she had apparently been having trouble doing. He had finally managed to make her hate him.

ROBIN'S PHONE RANG at a few minutes after ten o'clock. Balancing Peter on her shoulder, she snatched the receiver on the first ring.

"Hello?"

"I spoke with him," the feminine voice said without preamble.

Relief flooded Robin, leaving her knees watery-weak. "Then he's all right." It was a statement, not a question.

"I wouldn't exactly say that," Whitney said, pulling no punches. "He survived the drive home in the storm, but that's about all."

Robin felt her relief fleeing, though she hardened herself to what the woman had said. She couldn't afford the luxury of caring beyond this point.

"Robin, he's hurting."

In spite of her resolve, Robin's heart cleaved in half. Tears gathered in her eyes.

"So am I," she whispered, then gently recradled the phone before Whitney said anything else, before Whitney demanded that she say anything else.

Robin just stood in the hallway, clutching her baby to her. The tears she'd been fighting would be denied no longer. They trickled from her eyes and rolled down her cheeks. She wasn't certain why she was crying, any more than she was certain what she was feeling. One thing she was feeling, one reason for the tears, was her relief at knowing that Jake was all right. She'd been petrified when one silent hour had bred another. But that relief confused her. Why should she care what had happened to him? But then, everything about Jake confused her, everything about their unorthodox relationship confused her. She didn't know what she was supposed to be thinking or feeling.

Wasn't she supposed to hate the man who'd killed her husband? Wasn't she supposed to hate him for accusing Gerald of thievery?

Yes, it would be so much simpler just to hate him. That in mind, she told herself that that was precisely what she'd do. She'd hate Jake Cameron. And she'd pour her heart and soul into the effort. Never mind that she'd been inordinately relieved that he was all right, never mind that something deep within her hurt at the idea of his hurting, never mind that something even more deeply hidden inside her regretted what she'd said to him, regretted that she'd slapped him. Never mind all this, she would hate him.... If it was the last thing she ever did.

IN THE DAYS THAT FOLLOWED, Robin learned something that she heretofore hadn't known about herself: she wasn't very good at hating. When the police showed up, apologies on their lips for the questions they must ask, Robin had tried to hate them. But she couldn't. They were only performing the job they were paid for, and in her case, that job consisted of laying before her irrefutable proof that her husband had, indeed, been a thief. They then asked personal questions such as, Had they been in serious debt? Did she and her husband ever quarrel about money? Did she realize that he had a savings account in a bank that Robin had never heard of?

At this point, she'd tried to hate Gerald. Again, she couldn't. All she could do was pity him. All she could do was feel a sorrow as profound as anything she'd ever felt. They'd started out on the same road together, but somewhere along the way he'd changed to a fast lane. Somewhere along the way, his destination had no longer matched hers. When had this change occurred? And why hadn't she noticed that it had? And what, dear God, would she tell Peter about his father?

And then there was Phil Markham. She almost succeeded in the dark art of hating when this reporter relentlessly pursued her for a story. She lost count of how many times she hung up on him and, when he repeatedly showed up on her doorstep, she simply refused to answer the door. After all, she could be just as stubborn as he. She even toyed with the idea of going to Arizona to visit her parents, but ultimately decided that, as with Gerald's death, this was something she must see through alone. Fortunately, Phil Markham eventually moved on to a hotter, more current story.

Ironically, the person she came closest to hating was herself. The reason was simple: she had treated Jake abominably. She realized that it had been much easier to blame him than herself. The truth was that she'd always viewed herself as Gerald's murderer, believing that, if they hadn't fought that night, he might never have gotten killed. When she'd suddenly been faced with a real live scapegoat, someone who had actually pulled the trigger, it had been easier, more emotionally comfortable, to blame that someone.

It had also been easier to blame Jake than to sort through all the ambiguous feelings she was experiencing. On the one hand, she tried to remind herself that Jake had killed her husband, while on the other hand, it was Jake's kiss she remembered and not Gerald's. That state of affairs confused her, as did a hundred other conflicting emotions. Her guilt had mushroomed when she'd realized that she'd never really made love to the father of her child, that never had she felt with him what she'd felt in Jake's arms. Again, it had been easier to blame Jake than to confront the truth.

She knew, too, that even as she'd denied Gerald's being a thief, a part of her had known that Jake was speaking the truth; that was why it had been so difficult to hear. In fact, there were times when she could

almost believe that she had known what Jake was
going to tell her before he'd said a word. Maybe that
had even been why she'd slapped him. Because the
word *love* had shamed her. He was being honest and
forthright, while she could only lie and play games
with herself.

Love.

He had said he loved her. In the dark of the night
she would hold that close—cherish it, worship it—but
by the light of day she would see how tattered and
tarnished the word was. And it had become so by her
own hand. She had told Jake that he would never have
the right to love her. The dreamer in her longed to go
to him, apologize, beg his forgiveness, but her pride
always stopped her from doing it. After all, she told
herself, as the wife of a thief, she had little to offer a
man of honor.

And so it was that Robin learned that she knew
nothing of how to hate. She couldn't hate the police,
Gerald, the reporter, or herself. Most particularly, she
couldn't hate Jake. In fact, she was very sure that she
felt the exact opposite in regard to him. She was very
sure that she was more than a little in love with him.

CHAPTER FOURTEEN

IT WAS THE CHRISTMAS holiday, not that Jake could tell from any peace and joy he felt within himself. Rather, he was reminded by everything from blinking colored lights to silvery tinsel to the jangle of Salvation Army bells. If truth be told, it wasn't only peace and joy that Jake didn't feel. He didn't feel much of anything except that god-awful hollowness that, ironically, seemed to fill him to the brim in a way that no emotion ever had. The emptiness hurt, making him feel as though he'd been gutted of all his insides and brutally left to bleed to death. But he didn't die. He wanted to. Lord, how he wanted to! But he just kept on breathing, kept on walking around empty and gutted, kept on hurting.

The only thing that seemed even remotely like Christmas was his two daughters' impossible-to-curb excitement and their forever-long lists of what they wanted Santa to bring them. He forced himself to mask his own unhappiness for the girls' sakes. He even forced himself to act as though he were enjoying taking them shopping, which he traditionally did for Christmas since the divorce. After all, he didn't know anything about buying clothes for his daughters, and clothes were the only thing they wanted.

The girls had found a "really neato, really primo" boutique on Newbury Street to which they dragged their father. After trying on everything in the store, they decided on two sweaters, both with staggering price tags. When Jake paled, the salesclerk explained that the sweaters were made exclusively for the shop by a woman who lived nearby in Lowell, that no sweater had a duplicate anywhere in the world. The clerk went on proudly to display the designer label, which read simply, and facetiously, Rags by Robin.

Robin.

The name was like a gigantic fist in Jake's stomach. For a moment, he actually thought his knees were going to buckle. Right there. In the shop. With everyone watching.

"Daddy?"

Jake ran his big hand over one of the sweaters, as though worshipping the delicate stitchery. The softness of the sunshine-yellow yarn reminded him of Robin—the smoothness of her ivory skin, the incomparable perfection of her lips, the tenderness of her touch as her hands had lovingly caressed his body.

"Daddy?"

What was she doing? What was she feeling? Did she ever think of him? It had been ten days since he'd stormed out of the cottage, and he could say, unequivocally, that she was the only thing he thought of. Her and Peter. A million times a day. A million times a night. A million times a million.

"Daddy?"

Suddenly aware that he was being paged by his younger daughter, Regan, Jake glanced up. He also self-consciously pulled his hand from the sweater, which he was now stroking like a lover. Regan was looking at him strangely. The look was mirrored by her sixteen-year-old sister, Rachel.

"Are you okay, Daddy?" Regan asked.

"Yeah, are you okay?" Rachel repeated.

"I'm fine," Jake said, shoving his hand into his coat pocket. He could still feel it tingling, though. Tingling with warm memories. He'd give anything to ease the tingling with one sweet touch of one special lady.

"Look, we can find other sweaters," Rachel began.

"Yeah, cheaper ones," Regan added.

"No!" Jake saw the startled look jump into his daughters' eyes and lowered his voice. "We'll get the sweaters."

ON THE FIFTEENTH DAY OF December, Jake returned to work. It was either that or go stark raving mad. Besides, he knew the time had come. He had tried continuing to work with the preemie babies in the neonatal unit, but found too many painful memories there. Each child reminded him of Peter, which, in turn, reminded him of Robin. Curiously, considering all that had happened, he still felt that the two of them belonged to him . . . just the way that he belonged to them. It was a crazy notion, but one that he couldn't dislodge, so he'd said a farewell to the hospital and a hello to the police station.

It felt good to be back . . . good and right. The latter he proved within two hours of being on duty. A massive drug bust called for the participation of nearly a dozen police officers. Without hesitation, Jake had drawn his weapon. But then, he had known that, when the occasion arose, he'd be able to pull it . . . just the way he'd known before that he couldn't. The moment was one of the most exhilarating of his life. And

one of the most satisfying. If only this victory had
eased the hollowness within him. But instead, the
emptiness was magnified. He had wanted to share the
moment with Robin.

That night, several of his fellow patrolmen insisted
upon buying him a drink in celebration. Jake didn't
want to go—he wanted to slink off into the night and
simply be left alone to lick his wounds—but there was
no way he could refuse their generosity. And so he let
himself be talked into a little Irish pub, a foamy stein
of beer and false joviality. After the one drink, against
the protestation of his friends, he said a good-night
and went back to his lonely apartment. There, he ate
a TV dinner, took a shower and tumbled into bed. He
then did what he did every night. He prayed that he
could sleep. As always, though, sleep eluded him,
leaving him with memories that seemed more alive
than life itself.

MILES AWAY, ROBIN FACED the same sleepless night.
But then, what was new? She hadn't slept well in so
long that she could almost believe she'd forgotten
how. Each night she tossed and turned, more often
than not wide awake when it was time for Peter's next
feeding, which meant that the following day she was
dead on her feet. Tonight, she was particularly tired.
She knew the fatigue was coming primarily from the
day she'd had, the emotional day.

For a reason she hadn't been able to understand,
she'd gone to the cemetery. Despite the cold, she'd sat
for a long while . . . just staring at the gravestone . . . at
the hump of earth . . . at the poinsettias she brought to
brighten the grave. Somehow she'd thought visiting
the grave site would perhaps clarify her feelings to-

ward Gerald. But it hadn't. It was as though she'd been emotionally overloaded, and all her circuits were blown. She no longer felt anything for Gerald—neither love nor hate.

Stretching restlessly on the bed, she sighed. It was funny, if one cared for irony, that the man who'd shot Gerald still produced feelings within her. She'd half hoped—no, wholly hoped—that Jake would call, but days, weeks, a lifetime had gone by and he hadn't. What was he doing? Had he gone back to work? Did he ever think about her? And what did he think of her when, and if, he did? All uncharitable thoughts, she was certain. For what else could they be?

She thought of him every second of every day...and of the fool she'd been. The first-class, incomparable fool. Reaching out, she ran her hand across the side of the bed where he'd once lain. The space was empty, barren...just the way she felt inside. The space was also cold. Empty and cold. Those were the conditions her life had been reduced to.

COLD. THE DAMNED STATION was cold, Jake thought from within the little cluttered cubicle he called an office. His desk was littered with balls of paper and the remnants of lunch and dinner—a coffee cup, a milk shake carton, an empty bucket that had held fried chicken.

"Hey, somebody want to turn up the heat?" Jake shouted.

He still wore his leather jacket, the fur collar turned up to frame his face. Beneath it, he wore a shoulder holster and gun. He also wore jeans and boots. He was working a second shift, back to back. One of his buddies had asked someone to cover for him because it

was his wife's birthday. Jake, who didn't sleep at night
anyway, volunteered. He'd figured he might as well get
paid for staying awake.

"What's wrong, Cameron, you growing soft?"
someone shouted back, although that someone was
fiddling with the thermostat.

"Yeah, well, call me soft if you want. I just don't
want frostbite on my butt."

"Did you guys hear the one about the traveling
salesman who got frostbite when his car broke
down...."

This came from another policeman, who had the
room hollering with laughter in minutes. Even Jake
grinned. Mostly because it was expected of him.

Plopping down in his swivel chair, he rolled a sheet
of paper into the typewriter and began to peck out one
of the dozens of overdue reports on his desk. In seconds, his eyes had strayed to the framed photos of his
daughters. They had left that morning to go skiing in
Colorado with their mother and...stepfather. The
word stuck in his throat! They'd stopped by his
apartment the evening before to leave their Christmas
presents. Because Jake didn't have a tree, they'd simply left the gifts on his coffee table. When they hugged
him goodbye, Jake hadn't wanted to turn loose of
them. When he had, he'd fought hard to keep back the
tears. Maybe his daughters' being gone was the reason he felt so cold...and empty. Well, maybe it was
one of the reasons, anyway.

What was Robin doing? Feeding Peter? Knitting?
Hating him? He glanced over at the telephone. He had
an overwhelming urge to grab the receiver and dial her
number and bluntly ask her if she hated him. What

would she say if he did call? Would she be surprised? Pleased? Displeased—

The phone rang, startling Jake and effectively ending his stupid speculation. Angry with himself, he scooped up the phone.

"Lieutenant Cameron!" he barked.

There was a slight pause. "Uh-oh, I called at a bad time."

Jake let out a stream of a sigh. "Hi, Sis. No, now's a fine time."

"You sure?"

"Positive." He switched the phone to his other ear and continued to search out and strike keys on the typewriter. "What's going on?"

"I called your apartment several times and finally decided you must still be at work."

"Yeah, I'm pinch-hitting for a buddy." Jake depressed the wrong key, silently swore and reached for the erasure ink.

"The week's gone well, huh?"

"Yeah," Jake said. "It's good to be back."

"The girls get off okay?"

"Yeah."

Something in his delivery of the word prompted Whitney to say, "I know it's hard. Divorce sucks."

"Tell me about it."

"You are still coming to the house for Christmas, aren't you?"

Jake thought of Robin. How would she spend the holiday? Alone?

"Michael said you have to come," Whitney added before Jake could answer. "He's got some toy for Mike, Jr., that has to be put together. Some sort of robot. He said to tell you that you have to help."

Jake forced aside his thoughts about Robin; it was none of his business how she spent the holiday. "The man must be desperate to want my help, but I'll be there." Though he would have preferred to spend the day alone, he knew he couldn't turn his sister down. She would only worry about him, and he couldn't put her through that.

"Great. Oh, by the way, Dad asked about you today. Said you hadn't been around much this week."

Jake was so intent on defending himself that he didn't hear the sudden lilt in Whitney's voice. "Look, I know I should have stopped by, but I've been working longer-than-usual hours this week. After all, it was my first week back. I'll make it up to him in the next day or two. I'll—" Jake stopped abruptly, both his speech and his hand upon the typewriter, as what his sister had said filtered through to him. "What did you say?"

Jake could hear Whitney's smile. "I said that Dad asked about you."

There was a moment's silence as Jake assimilated the announcement. "You mean he actually spoke to you?"

Whitney could contain her laughter no longer. "Oh, Jake, I couldn't believe it," she bubbled. "I stopped by the nursing home on my lunch hour, right? Expecting to find him grim and silent as usual, right? Well, he was playing poker with the man who has the room next door. Sol Weemer...or Wymer...or something like that. Anyway, he's a nice guy. Well, in I go and Dad looks up from his cards and says, as though he'd never been on a silence strike at all, he says, 'I can't talk now. I'm whipping the pants off this cheating card shark.' I about passed out. Anyway, five minutes later, the game ended, Dad introduced me to the guy, the guy shuffled back to his room, and Dad talked to me as big as you please. Like nothing had ever happened. Asked how Mike, Jr., was and Rachel and Regan and you. Said you hadn't been by all week.''

Whitney stopped, fully expecting her brother to say something. He didn't.

"Jake?"

"I...I'm speechless." But he was pleased, and that pleasure clearly showed through. It was the best news he'd had in a while...a long while.

Whitney laughed again. "Can you believe it?"

Jake grinned. "Yeah, it sounds just like Pop. Hell, he might even have forgotten he wasn't speaking to us."

Whitney's tone became more serious. "No, I think he remembered. At least he remembered some things. He remembered that something was troubling you. He said that the last time you were there, you said you'd had a bitch of a day."

Jake's grin faded. "Yeah."

Whitney dared to ask the unaskable question. "Have you heard from her?"

"No." The word encouraged nothing more.

Whitney, however, was undaunted. "Jake, call—"

"No."

"What have you got to lose?"

"No."

"Jake—"

"No, Whitney!" He hated himself for the roughness of his voice, so he repeated, this time with a forced quietness, "No, Sis. I appreciate your concern, but no."

"Suit yourself," Whitney said, her attitude deceptively dismissive. She'd already decided to give the two silly lovebirds the remainder of the month to work out their differences before taking matters into her own hands.

Despite his vehement denial, once his sister had hung up, Jake studied the recradled phone.

"Call her."

No, he whispered, yet the cold, empty part of him, the heart part of him screamed yes!

"What have you got to lose?"

What *did* he have to lose? He already hurt as badly as anyone could.

Like a magnet, the phone drew his hand. Snatching up the receiver, he quickly dialed her number... before he changed his mind. He held his breath. For a split second, there was a world-stopping silence as he waited for the phone to ring. Instead, he received a busy signal. He muttered something profane and banged down the phone. In retrospect, he was glad things had turned out as they did. The last thing he needed was to make a fool of himself again.

ROBIN LISTENED TO THE ringing of Jake's apartment phone. She had no idea how many times the phone had rung... nor if she would actually have said anything if Jake had answered. But he wasn't going to. He obviously wasn't home.

She didn't know why she'd even dialed the number. Why was this evening any different from the countless lonely evenings that had gone before? Actually, she did know why she'd dialed the number. It had to do with the completion of a brown sweater. A brown fisherman's sweater. A sweater she hadn't even realized she'd been knitting for Jake until it was finished. Driven by a sudden desperate urge to hear his voice, she'd recklessly dialed his number. Now she was glad he hadn't answered. What would she have said? Anything? And would hearing his voice only have made her misery worse?

Peter made a cooing sound, drawing Robin's attention from the hallway to the crib in the bedroom. She crossed the room and glanced down at her son. His navy-blue eyes alert, he looked wide awake for nine o'clock at night.

"Not sleepy, huh?" she whispered, picking him up, moving toward the bed and laying him down. She lay down beside him. Her finger automatically went to his tiny hand. He made another gurgling noise as her skin touched his. "I called him," she said, as though the child understood her every word. "He wasn't at home."

The baby's hand fluttered, his feet kicked.

"Oh, Peter, do you miss him?" The baby made a sound that Robin chose to interpret as yes. "I know. Me, too."

She laid her cheek against the bed as Peter held on to her finger with his hand. A thousand bittersweet memories assailed her.

"Has he been hitting you up for Big Macs, too?"

"C'mon, go out with me. Just ask Peter for a character reference."

"Don't let Peter know we're having Big Macs or we'll have to share."

Slowly, like a fluffy white cloud gathering in a clear blue sky, an idea formed in Robin's mind. Part of her said forget it, that it was stupid and idiotic. Another part of her asked what she had to lose. How could she hurt any worse than she did?

THE DAY AFTER JAKE TALKED with his sister, he went by the nursing home. He found his father propped up in bed, eating dinner.

"Hi, Pop," Jake said, hoping that Whitney had been right and that the silence strike had been settled.

Hank glanced up from his bowl of bread pudding. He said nothing. Instead, he slowly set the dish down and just as slowly reached for his napkin. He blotted his lips. "Where've you been?" he asked finally.

At the words, reproachful though they were, Jake experienced a profound sense of relief. His hands buried in his jacket pockets, he stepped deeper into the room. "I'm sorry. I've been busy at the station." At his father's unflinching stare, which raked him from head to toe—did he look as weary as he felt?—he added, "I know it's not much of an excuse, Pop."

Hank leaned back in the bed, and nodded toward a chair. "It's a good enough excuse. Sit down," he said.

Pulling his hands from his pockets, Jake eased into the chair. For a moment, neither spoke. At last, Jake asked, "How've you been?"

The senior Cameron shrugged. "Okay, I guess."

"How's the hip?"

Wordlessly, Hank repeated the shrug.

"If you're in any pain—" Jake began.

"The hip's okay," his father interrupted.

Just as silently, Jake nodded in acceptance of Hank's reply. The silence stretched on, however, and he realized that his father was openly evaluating him again. Jake glanced over at the tray and asked, "How's the food?"

"Not bad."

"Looks pretty good."

"It's not bad."

"How was the pudding?"

Not bad, Jake mentally mouthed as Hank repeated the phrase once more.

Another silence, seemingly interminable, surrounded them. It was Hank who shattered this one. "How are my granddaughters?"

"They're in Colorado. With their mother."

Hank made a sound of disapproval. "A father needs to see his kids."

"I know, Pop," Jake said, rushing ahead to change the dreary subject. "Whitney said you've made a friend."

Hank shrugged again, as if his new friend were no big thing. Jake, however, saw the light that jumped into his father's eyes. "Worst poker player I ever saw. And a cheat to boot."

Jake gave a half grin, the best he could manage these days. "You can beat him, huh?"

Hank snorted. "I can clean his clock. And only have to use a few of the cards up my sleeve to do it."

"How much does he owe you?"

"More than he's going to live long enough to pay back, more than I'm going to live long enough to spend."

Jake's smile widened.

"Maybe you can play with us sometime," Hank said with a deceptive nonchalance.

The words squeezed Jake's heart. This was probably the closest thing to an apology that he was going to get. And it was probably the closest Hank Cam eron would ever come to acknowledging that the nursing home wasn't so bad, after all.

"Pop—"

"Course, be forewarned. I can probably clean your clock, too."

Hank looked at his son. Jake looked at his father. The apology had been made, along with the plea to avoid a head-on discussion. Jake accepted one and respected the other. He grinned, though once more the humor never quite reached his eyes. "Don't spend my money, Pop, until you win it."

On the heels of that comment, a nurse burst into the room, bearing a paper cup of medicine. She acknowledged Jake with a smile as she spoke to her patient. "This is for you, Mr. Cameron."

"I just took those pills."

"No, sir, that was at lunch."

"Are you sure?"

"I'm positive," she said, pouring a glass of water and urging Hank to take it. He did and dutifully swallowed down the pills around a muttered "Sometimes I forget."

Hearing the admission knifed at Jake, reminding him that Hank was getting old, reminding him that he wouldn't be around forever, reminding him of just how much he loved his father. Jake stood and walked to the window. The wind was blowing, causing a nearby tree to bend almost double. He shoved his hands back into his jacket pockets as the familiar coldness swept through him.

"What's wrong, Boy?" Jake heard his father ask softly.

Jake turned, his eyes immediately meeting those of the man studying him so thoroughly. A denial sprang to Jake's lips, yet that denial simply would not come forward. Instead, he heard himself say, in a voice thick with feeling, "What do you do when you're at the end of your rope?"

"That's simple," Hank said to his son. "You tie a knot in the end and hang on."

"For how long, Pop?" Jake asked with thinly concealed desperation. "How long can you keep holding on?"

Hank's bleary eyes glowed with wisdom. "For however long it takes, Son. For however long it takes."

Two DAYS LATER, and only days before Christmas, Jake prepared to leave the station at the end of his shift. It had been a particularly rough day, with every thug in Boston trying his best to outdo his lawless compatriots. Someone had even mugged Santa Claus. Grabbing his jacket from the back of his chair, Jake started to throw his arms into it just as Daniel Jacoby stepped from his glass-enclosed office.

"Got a minute?" the psychologist called.

Jake halted the jacket. "Sure," he answered, ambling toward his friend, the jacket now slung over his shoulder by an index finger.

As he moved into the office, Daniel closed the door behind him. Jake plopped into the nearest chair and squared ankle to knee. He looked up. His friend, who always wore a vest and carried a pipe, looked about as tired as *he* felt, Jake thought. There were those who said that Dan Jacoby lived at the station. Jake wondered how he managed the miracle of holding his marriage together, but somehow he did. And he obviously did it well. He and Carolyn, an executive for a department store, had one of the best marriages he'd seen.

"How was your day?" Dan asked, propping himself against the edge of his desk.

"Santa Claus got mugged. Does that give you an idea?"

Dan took a puff on the pipe. The aroma was a fruity one that reminded Jake of apples. Dan, himself, reminded Jake of the personification of cool and unruffled. He idly wondered what it would take to get the guy upset.

"Ah, the holiday crazies are out," Dan commented.

"In full force."

Both men knew that the holiday season was a lot like a full moon; it brought out every loony. It was also the time of year with the highest suicide rate.

"So, how are you personally handling the holidays?" Dan asked.

Ah, Jake thought, we've arrived at the heart of the conversation. He shrugged. "The girls are with their mother and stepfather in Colorado. Skiing."

"And how does that make you feel?"

"Did anyone ever tell you that you sound like a psychologist?"

Like a psychologist, Dan made no response. He just puffed on his pipe and continued to stare at Jake, patiently awaiting an answer.

Jake squirmed in his chair. "How the hell do you think I feel? I resent it."

"Good. That's normal. Now, what about Robin Bauer?"

The name, delivered with such unexpectedness, stole Jake's breath. "What about her?" he managed to ask.

"Have you talked to her?"

Jake thought of the moment of madness when he'd dialed her number. Thank God, the phone had been busy! He'd thought at the time that he couldn't hurt any worse than he did, but he doubted that was true. Hearing hate and disdain in her voice again would just about finish him.

"No," Jake answered, "I haven't talked with her."

"Why not?"

"Are you forgetting, Jacoby, that she told me to kiss off?"

"You think she meant it?"

"Yeah," Jake said hoarsely, "I think she meant it."

"Maybe, maybe not," Dan responded. "People don't always say what they really mean. And even if she did mean it at the time, what about now? What do you think she's feeling now?"

"I don't know," Jake answered, giving Dan a dose of his own medicine by asking, "What do you think she's feeling?"

Dan nonchalantly took a long draw on his pipe. "Shame," he said. "I expect she feels shame by association. After all, her husband was guilty of a crime. I think she's probably also feeling guilty over the way she treated you. She in essence called you a liar for suggesting that her husband was guilty of theft. Actually, she accused you of worse than that . . . of implicating him to get yourself off the hook. I suspect that she's thinking, after everything turned out as it did, that you probably don't want to see her again."

"That's crap," Jake said, restlessly coming to his feet and stepping over to a wall of glass that allowed him a view of the squad room. As always, the station was a madhouse. "She knew exactly how I felt."

"How do you know?"

"Because I told her!" Jake spat, turning toward his friend. He didn't notice that the officer at the nearby desk glanced up toward the psychologist's office. "Because I damn well told her!" Jake hadn't realized until just that second that he was angry with Robin, angry with her for rejecting the only thing he had to give her, angry for doubting him if, in truth, that's what she was now doing.

"You don't think—" Dan began, but Jake cut him off.

"Dammit, Jacoby, don't you understand? I try not to think!"

AS JAKE DROVE HOME, his mind was filled, as always, with nothing but Robin. Nothing but Robin and everything that Dan had said. Was his friend right? Was Robin experiencing shame and guilt? Was she now uncertain about his feelings? Was the next move up to him?

No, he sadly feared that the next move would have to come from her. He could still remember too clearly the disdain, a disdain bordering on hate, in her eyes. He could still hear her barbed words ringing too loudly in his ears. He could still remember too vividly what it felt like to have his heart stop beating with life.

And yet, with a blatant disregard for his bloodied fingers, he could not let go of the rope he so precariously clung to. Instead, he continued to tie knots and hang on.

JAKE SAW THE BOX THE SECOND he started down the hallway to his apartment. It leaned against the wall as though it had had the same tiring day he had. He knew the UPS delivery man had brought it because the guy, an Italian with a heart of gold, always delivered Jake's packages right to his door instead of leaving them downstairs at the mailboxes.

Mildly curious—after all, he wasn't expecting anything—Jake unlocked the apartment door and, repocketing the key in his jeans, stooped to pick up the package. It was small, but heavier than he'd anticipated. He glanced at the return address. Lowell.

Jake's heart thumped.

Shutting the door behind him, not even bothering to remove his jacket, Jake tore open the package... or attempted to... with hands that had become unsteady. A thousand disconnected, disjointed thoughts whirled through his mind with the same speed that the paper fell away. It dropped to the floor unheeded. He lunged at the box, but finding it taped, he swore. Using his nail, he sliced through one strip of tape. The contents poured out—one chocolate-brown sweater, which he caught, and one small white envelope, which he did not. The sweater was soft to the touch, incredibly soft. It was also a fisherman sweater, done in similar stitchery to another he owned. The simple label read: Rags by Robin.

His heart thumped again.

The sweater still in hand, Jake bent and picked up the card. With no finesse whatsoever, he ripped the envelope open and flipped open the card.

My momma made this for you. I hope you like it. I miss you. My momma misses you, too. Hope you have a Merry Christmas.

The card was signed: Love, Peter.

Jake's heart was thumping so rapidly that the beat reverberated in his ears. The sound was deafening. He read the note again, absorbing every word, luxuriating in nothing more than the fact that he was reading Robin's handwriting.

My momma misses you, too.

Yes, it said what he thought it said. But he read it again just to confirm it.

Suddenly, the day's fatigue dropped away. Suddenly, the hurting hollowness was filled. Suddenly, he hurled the sweater at the back of a chair and rushed from the apartment. He was behind the wheel of the Jeep, and already en route to Lowell, when he realized that he still held the card, now crumpled, in his hand.

IT WAS A LITTLE AFTER seven o'clock, and nightfall, when Jake pulled into the drive. The house looked exactly the same—a thin curl of smoke climbed into the jet-black sky, the curtains were drawn in an embrace of privacy, the nearby trees hugged themselves from the chill. The only thing different from the morning he'd stormed out of there was the snow; it now lay in isolated drifts that the sun hadn't yet melted entirely. Since that day there had been snow flurries, even an occasional accumulation of the fairy-white powder, but no more major snowstorms. Everyone was praying for a white Christmas.

Jake was just praying, praying that he hadn't misinterpreted the note, praying that he wasn't dreaming recklessly, praying that his heart would slow down before he had a heart attack. Cutting the lights, he threw open the Jeep door, slammed it behind him and rounded the hood all seemingly in a heartbeat. The night was cold and silent, making his breath a smoky vapor, making the sound of his boot striking a patch of snow a loud crunchy noise. He leaped over one step entirely, pushed the doorbell... and waited. No wait had ever been as long.

Robin, who was standing at the kitchen sink, whirled when the doorbell rang. The dish towel fell from her hands and to the floor. At the same time her heart sprinted forward. Could it be Jake? He'd probably had enough time to receive the sweater and the note. Was it logical to assume he'd show up on her doorstep...the way she prayed he would? Or was that just wishful thinking? Perhaps it was more likely that he'd discarded both the sweater and the card as painful reminders of something he didn't care to remember. She couldn't blame him if he had. Yet, neither could she stop herself from praying that it was he at the front door.

If it were, what would she say? How could she possibly apologize for all she'd said and done? How could she explain that she felt tainted by Gerald's misdeed? How could she explain to Jake how very much she needed him, how very much she loved him?

The doorbell rang again. The impatient sound scattered her thoughts to the four winds. She headed for the living room.

Jake heard her approach, faint footfalls on the wooden floor that were suddenly drowned out by the pounding of his heart as the door opened. And then, as neither had thought would ever happen again, they were looking at each other—staring, assessing, visually devouring.

She appeared tired, he thought. Tired and worn, as though she were sleeping as badly as he. He had the sudden urge to scoop her into his arms and take her to bed so they could simply curl themselves around each other and sleep. Maybe for a hundred years.

Then he noticed she was no longer wearing her wedding ring.

He looked tired, she thought. Tired and weary, as though the last few weeks had been just as hard on him as they'd been on her. In a perverse way, she was glad, but it also hurt her to think of him suffering. She could see that suffering clearly in the dullness of his eyes, in the shadow-dark circles smudged beneath them, in the gaunt and hollow look of his face. Slowly, suddenly, and with a total unexpectedness, his face blurred. It took her a moment to realize that her eyes were awash in tears.

Jake saw her eyes glaze. It was the final straw. On a deep groan, he stepped into the house and hauled her to him. It seemed, to them both, that she'd never been out of his arms. He tightened his hold, knowing that he was hurting her, but unable to stop himself. He needed to absorb her into his very being, to make her one with him. But then, she needed no less. Even as he sought to merge their bodies, she stepped closer, closer, trying to lose herself in his nearness.

Fire.

His touch was like the brush of fire, his breath like a heated breeze blowing at the hollow of her throat. When his lips found hers, the world exploded into a firestorm of feeling. On some subliminal plane Robin wondered why she'd ever thought words would be necessary to express her apology, to declare her love, when it was so easy to do with kisses and caresses. And why had she worried about his feelings for her? His lips, his body eloquently expressed his love. They also absolved her of any associative guilt that she might foolishly feel. Yes, words had become inadequate, untrustworthy, superlatively superfluous.

His mouth eased away from hers. Silently, he drew the back of his hand across her tearstained cheek as he looked deeply into her golden-green eyes. Her eyes said everything he wanted to hear. Every sweet and wonderful thing. Slowly, as though they now had all the time in the world, he lifted her into his arms. She burrowed her cheek against his broad shoulder as he started for the bedroom. Once there, they would lie on the bed, curl their bodies together and sleep.

Maybe for a hundred years.

A LONG WHILE LATER, though nowhere near a hundred years, Robin gave a sigh that greatly resembled a contented purr.

"Me, too," Jake whispered, the gentle words buffeting against her temple.

They lay naked, satiated, between the warm covers of the bed. They lay within each other's warmer-than-warm arms. They had made love, slept, then made love again.

Robin turned toward Jake, her arm encircling his lean waist. It sounded as though it was all she could do to summon the strength to speak. "Peter'll be waking up soon," she said.

"Mmm," Jake answered. He, too, sounded drained of all energy.

Suddenly a shiver raced over Robin as she recalled how miserable she'd been before Jake had reappeared on her doorstep, how frightened she'd been that he wouldn't respond to the note she'd written. She never wanted to be that miserable, that frightened, again.

"What is it?" Jake asked as he tightened his hold. He'd sensed her subtle mood change.

Robin swallowed. "I thought I'd never see you again. I thought I didn't deserve to see you again. I thought..." Her eyes found his. "...I thought I'd die."

Tunneling his fingers through her hair, he arranged her mouth so that it was directly beneath his. He kissed her.

"I missed y—" she began.

"Shh," he whispered, taking her mouth again.

"I thought—" she tried once more when his mouth lessened its pressure.

"Shh," he said, his lips touching hers.

"I'm sorry—"

"Shh."

She'd been right to think that words were going to be superfluous. She'd been right to think that apologies were not going to be necessary. Yet there was one thing she had to tell him, one thing that would not bow to a bid of silence.

"I love you," she breathed, pouring her heart at his feet.

"That you can say," he answered.

"I love you."

"Over and over..."

"I love you."

"...for the rest of our..."

"I love you."

"...lives."

And then there was silence. A soft silence. A sweet silence. The kind that has no need to be filled.

CHAPTER FIFTEEN

TO THE DELIGHT OF ALL, it snowed on Christmas Day.

Robin watched the fat flakes, looking for all the world like delicate Battenberg lace, drift by the enormous bay window of Whitney Ames's living room. A huge fir tree, almost reaching to the ceiling, was strung in hundreds of blinking lights, while wooden ornaments, all hand-painted by Whitney and Jake's mother, Robin had been informed, nested in every bough. The presents beneath the tree had been opened an hour before. Torn paper and ravaged ribbon still lay strewn about. In the background, a tape of Christmas music played. The current song urged listeners to have themselves a merry little Christmas.

Bringing a glass of nutmeg-sprinkled eggnog to her lips, Robin sipped, wondering when, if ever, she'd felt this happy. She glanced over at her son, who was being held and pampered by Hank Cameron. Earlier that morning, Jake had brought his father from the nursing home to spend the holiday with the family. The plan was for Whitney to return him that evening. Hank had already made it clear that he had to be back by six o'clock because he and Sol had a big poker game scheduled. As Robin now studied the older man, she decided that she liked him immensely. Maybe that was because he'd taken one look at her and said that she was exactly what the doctor had ordered for Jake. He also seemed to adore Peter.

Hank and Peter. The very old, the very young. Both had struggled for life from opposite ends of the spectrum, Peter to survive the spring of birth, Hank to live out his winter years with dignity. It had been Jake who'd helped them both and, in so doing, had revealed his own attitude toward life—that it was precious at any age. How could she ever have thought that he could take the life of another human being and not be deeply scarred by it? She now knew that that was the sadness she'd seen in his eyes from the start. She still saw it there, but given time, she'd ease his pain just the way he was daily easing hers. They would heal each other. Together, they would mend their broken lives.

Together.

As husband and wife.

Husband. It was still impossible for her to believe that she and Jake were married, that they'd been married for—she checked her watch—all of about twenty-six hours. They had married as soon as the law allowed, with Jake vowing that he wouldn't wait a minute longer. The wedding had been simple, with only Whitney and Michael present. After treating the newlyweds to a sumptuous brunch at a local restaurant, Whitney and Michael had taken their leave amid congratulatory hugs and kisses. Jake and Robin had then returned to his apartment, where they'd proceeded to make love all day and through most of the blissful night.

As though what she was thinking had silently transmitted itself to Jake, he glanced up from where he sat on the floor. He, and his brother-in-law

Michael, were surrounded by nuts and bolts and robot parts. Jake wore the chocolate-brown fisherman sweater...and a smoky look that said he, too, was thinking about what they'd spent the night doing.

Robin suddenly felt as if a sweltering sun were burning down on her, heating her body to a molten glow. She could feel his large hands moving over her, could feel his lips pressing against hers, could feel his body tightly filling hers. She could also see his now naughty grin and feel the fevered flames igniting in her cheeks.

"How much longer?" When eight-year-old Mike, Jr., got no response, he repeated, "Uncle Jake, how much longer?"

Jake reluctantly dragged his eyes from his wife. "I don't know, buddy."

"Son, your uncle and I are dancing as fast as we can."

"Yeah," Jake said, "and right now we're doing a good old-fashioned waltz." Without missing a beat, he held up a strange-looking screw. "You got any idea where this goes?"

"My guess is another planet," his brother-in-law answered. "Is that Part A or Part B?"

"It's Part C," Jake answered, checking with the instructions that the manufacturer had guaranteed were simple and easy to follow. "It goes in Slot D."

"Where's Slot D?" the communications professor asked.

"Beats the heck outta me," Jake replied.

"It goes here," Mike, Jr., said, pointing to a spot on the robot.

"Now, Son, you're going to have to get out of the way if you want this thing put together," his father said.

"How are they doing?" Whitney whispered to her new sister-in-law as she journeyed from the kitchen and sat down next to Robin on the sofa.

"They're looking for Slot D. Without any luck, I might add."

"Gee, you'd think a Slot D would be easy to spot," Whitney returned.

"You'd think," Robin agreed.

Two husbands glared at two wives.

"It goes here," Mike, Jr., repeated, but no one paid him the least attention.

"If you two think you can do any better..." Michael began.

Whitney looked over at Robin. "What do you think?"

"I think we've been challenged," Robin returned.

"Sort of what I thought," Whitney agreed.

As both women set down their glasses of eggnog and slid onto the floor, the two men smiled smugly.

"Excuse me," Robin said, leaning over Jake to get the instructions. She brushed his jeans-clad thigh with her hand—deliberately, unnecessarily, Jake was sure. He hid the grin trying to tweak the corner of his mouth, and thought of the sensual payback he'd give her later that day.

"Certainly," he said with mock formality.

"Okay," Robin said, studying the plans and muttering, "Part A... Part B... insert at right angle... see Figure 3... Slot D..."

"Should be right about here...." Whitney said, following the diagram.

"Um-huh," Robin agreed. "Right about . . ."

"It goes right here, Mom," Mike, Jr., said.

Both women looked at the child and at the spot he indicated.

"Why, Mike, I think you're right," his mother said.

"I think he is, too," Robin said. "Way to go, Mike. Okay, now what next?"

Jake and Michael watched in total disbelief as the two women, assisted by the child, methodically, competently, assembled the toy.

"You're pretty smart, Aunt Robin," the eight-year-old said in praise.

"Not really. I have to be able to follow instructions to knit."

"Uncle Jake and Daddy couldn't read the instructions cause they can't knit, huh?"

"Hey, now," Jake began. "Aren't you three forgetting an important point here?"

"Like what, little brother?"

"Like we had the thing three-quarters put together before you geniuses ever took over."

"Three-quarters?" the women parroted.

"Yeah," Michael jumped in.

"I'd have said more like half put together," Whitney said.

"Or one-third," Robin said.

"One-third?" Jake said.

Both men now stood, their hands on their hips, trying to appear vexed.

"Even Peter knew where Slot D was," Hank tossed in from his wheelchair. Peter made a sound that said he agreed wholeheartedly.

Everyone grinned. Including the men...though they fought it.

"Why don't you two go baste the turkey while we finish up here?" Whitney asked.

"Gee, Michael," Jake said, "you think we can handle that?"

"Gee, Jake, I don't know. Do you know what a turkey looks like?"

"Yeah, like the two of us," Jake returned as the men disappeared into the kitchen.

Thirty minutes later, after the robot had been assembled, Jake found Robin in Whitney and Michael's bedroom. She was nursing Peter.

"Hi," he said, closing the door behind him and squatting in front of his wife. Automatically he stroked Peter's head. "How you two doing?"

"Okay," she said, breathless as usual at this man's nearness.

"Whitney said that dinner's ready when you are."

"I think Peter's finished. He's playing more than he's eating." Robin grinned. "Which is what you've been doing, isn't it? Playing with the robot?" All through nursing Peter, Robin had heard the two grown men putting the toy through its paces...and Mike, Jr., begging for the chance to play with his Christmas present.

Jake grinned, too, just like a little boy. "Michael and I had to work out the bugs."

"Yeah, sure," Robin added, her smile growing broader.

Jake's grin slowly disappeared, and rocking forward onto the balls of his feet, he did something that was totally unboyish. In fact, it was the consummate act of an adult man. He kissed her. At first so lightly that it reminded her of the snowflakes falling drowsily outside the window. But then, the kiss deepened, with his nimble tongue rimming her lips before sliding into her mouth. At the feelings that instantly stirred to life, Robin moaned.

"See," he whispered, his mouth still at hers, "I know where to put all the important parts."

Robin giggled. "And without any instructions."

"You're darned right."

Both were grinning again. It was about all they'd done for days. It was what happiness was all about.

Robin's smile faded. She suddenly felt afraid, as if everything were simply too wonderful to be true. "We really are married, aren't we?"

Jake brought her left hand to his lips. He kissed the gold band. This band was far simpler than the elaborately engraved one she'd shared with Gerald. It was what she had asked for; it was what Jake had given her. There was nothing simple, however, about the commitment it stood for.

"We're really married," he whispered. "Really, really married."

His mouth found hers again, with an irresistible combination of both gentleness and passion. Robin sighed as she sank her lips into his, hoping to drown in the exquisite feelings engulfing her.

"Hey, dinner's ready!" Whitney shouted up the stairs.

Jake simply changed the angle of the kiss and started in all over again.

"Hey, you two lovebirds," Whitney called again a few minutes later.

"What's a lovebird?" her son asked.

"Never mind. Just carry the cranberry sauce to the table. Michael, will you get that robot out of the kitchen?"

"I think we'd better go down," Robin whispered, literally forcing her mouth from Jake's.

Jake groaned in protest. "If we have to," he said, taking the baby she offered him. A ritual had already been established. It was Jake's duty to burp Peter after she fed him. Placing a cloth across his shoulder, he laid the baby in place and patted his back. Robin rearranged her bra and began to refasten the buttons of her sweater. Jake's gaze lowered to the rounded swell of her breast. Her full, ivory, dark-centered breast. A breast that perfectly fit his hand, his mouth. Robin's hand stopped. For moments, neither he nor she could breathe.

"Hold that thought," he ordered hoarsely.

After a prayer of thanksgiving, during which Jake's fingers entwined with his wife's, dinner was served. It was delicious, with the cook being complimented frequently. Whitney insisted that the turkey was good because of the excellent job of basting the last two chefs had done. The two chefs heartily agreed. Robin couldn't remember Jake ever looking more handsome. Nor could she ever remember feeling warmer than she did in the arms of his family.

"Jake said you called Rachel and Regan this morning," Whitney said to Robin an hour later as the two women cleaned up the kitchen. The men, a talkative Hank included, had returned to the living room to watch a football game. Peter slept on the sofa beside Jake.

"Yeah," Robin answered, drying the turkey platter that was too big for the dishwasher. "Jake wanted to tell them about our getting married. He wouldn't admit it, but I think he was a little worried about their reaction—what with everything being so sudden and all. I know I was."

What she didn't say was that she'd been equally worried about her parents' reaction, but unbelievably, they'd seemed unqualifyingly pleased. Obviously, the happiness in her voice had persuaded them that the marriage had been right, even if her and Jake's relationship had started out on bizarre terms.

"I'll bet the girls were excited," Whitney said, picking up the threads of the conversation as she stacked the dinner plates into the dishwasher rack. "But bear in mind that you can't always tell with Rachel. She's a little on the quiet side."

"They were both surprised, of course. And Rachel was a little more subdued than Regan, but I sensed...I don't know, I sensed that they were pleased for their father. Actually, I thought they were very adult about it. I sensed that they realized things hadn't been easy for him since the divorce."

"No," Whitney said, candidly adding, "Marie really did a number on him."

"So I gathered."

Jake still hadn't talked much about his former wife. Robin suspected that the wound hadn't completely healed. But she would help it along. Without question she didn't fear the past memories, the past relationship. She knew that what she and Jake shared went far deeper than anything either had ever felt before. Neither had said as much. But then, it was the sort of thing that neither had to. It was felt by both.

"So what did the girls think about your being *the* Rags by Robin lady?"

Robin smiled. " 'Neato.' I believe that's an exact quote from Regan."

Whitney laughed. "I'll bet they have visions of an unlimited supply of sweaters."

"They seemed more pleased with my promise to teach them how to knit. And with having a new baby brother." Suddenly Robin's hands stilled while drying a thin-stemmed wine goblet. Deep emotion, deep concern, clotted her voice. "I want them to like me," she said, surprising even herself with this intimate verbalization.

Whitney laid aside her dish towel. She placed her hand on Robin's. "They'll adore you...just like Jake does...just like we all do."

Whitney smiled.

Robin smiled.

A bond was formed.

Following the football game, Jake bundled up his new wife and son and drove them back to his apartment. Though still snowing, the apartment was toasty-warm. It was also cluttered. Too small to accommodate both Jake's things and Robin's, particularly with the baby's included, the small rooms looked like a warehouse. It was an inconvenience that neither Robin nor Jake cared about. Their being together was the only thing that mattered. They would start looking for a larger place to live, possibly even a house, as soon as the holiday was over.

"Be careful of the boxes," Jake cautioned as he opened the door and allowed Robin, who was carrying a sleeping Peter, to enter.

Dodging the cartons, she nodded and made her way toward the bedroom.

"Hey, Robin?" Jake called out.

She turned at the bedroom doorway. He stood in the middle of the living room, his arms still laden with opened Christmas presents. Her cheeks were flushed a rose color from the chilled weather, while the wintry wind, like a mischievous zephyr, had played through her hair. He thought she looked very much as she had the first time he'd seen her up close—deliciously disheveled, and an intriguing combination of child and woman.

"I love you," he said.

Robin's heart grew heavy with feeling. She remembered a time when she'd slapped him for saying that. She remembered a time when she'd told him that he'd never have the right to declare his love. Her heart still ached at how she'd hurt him. Her only consolation was that she, herself, had hurt far more. "I love you, too," she whispered.

Jake could see the contrition in her eyes. It was the same contrition that he'd lived with daily since the shooting, the same contrition that he would live with until the day he died. But there had to come, if not an ending to, at least a burial of their guilt. On this foundation, they would build a marriage. It was something they had already agreed upon. There would be no more apologies. From either of them.

That in mind, she didn't apologize. She simply smiled softly, lovingly at her husband before disappearing into the bedroom.

The crib had been carted from the cottage and set up in the corner of the room. Drawing back the covers, Robin gently laid the baby down. Peter fretted at being disturbed.

"Go back to sleep," she whispered, patting the little rump, which was hiked in the air. When the baby drew his fist to his mouth and sucked until bubbles appeared, Robin smiled. It wouldn't be long before he'd be demanding to eat again. At this rate, he'd soon make up for his small size. Why, he might even someday be as big as Jake.

Jake.

Not Gerald.

How odd the mind was, she thought. How soon it forgot. Or was it that the mind rewrote life as one wistfully wished it to be?

Robin felt Jake's arms sliding around her waist milliseconds before she heard his breathy voice in her ear. "What are you thinking about?"

"I was just wishing I never had to tell Peter that you aren't his father," she answered honestly.

Jake tightened his arms about her, pulling her more closely to him. "In all the ways that count, I will be his father. I'll be the man who changes his diaper, the one who walks him at night when he can't sleep, the one who teaches him how to catch a ball. I'll be the one who disciplines him, praises him, loves him. That'll make me his father."

Robin turned in her husband's arms, flattening her hands against his chest, her eyes seeking his. Everything he'd said she knew to be true, yet...

"How will I tell him about Gerald?"

"*We* will tell him. And what we'll tell him is the truth. That the man who was responsible for his birth was a man, who like all men, was good and bad. We'll tell him that he was a man who would have loved his son deeply. And together, we'll find a way to make him understand that I accidentally took that man's life." Jake lowered his head, brushing his lips across his wife's. "We will find a way, Robin. I promise."

She believed him. Just as she believed that his kiss, his touch, could magically restore peace to her heart, her soul. He called her name softly. She answered by breathlessly calling his.

And then his mouth claimed hers.

Outside, snow peppered the windows as night, Christmas night, Holy Night, closed gently around the city. Inside the world was warm, serene. The tigers of the night had been vanquished—forever tamed by love.

Harlequin Superromance®

THEY'RE A BREED APART

The men and women of the Canadian prairies are slow to give their friendship or their love. On the prairies, such gifts can never be recalled. Friendships between families last for generations. And love, once lit, burns hot and pure and bright for a lifetime.

In honor of this special breed of men and women, Harlequin Superromance® presents:

SAGEBRUSH AND SUNSHINE
(Available in October)

and

MAGIC AND MOONBEAMS
(Available in December)

two books by Margot Dalton, featuring the Lyndons and the Burmans, prairie families joined for generations by friendship, then nearly torn apart by love.

Look for SUNSHINE in October and MOONBEAMS in December, coming to you from Harlequin.

MAG-C1R

Take 4 bestselling love stories FREE

Plus get a FREE surprise gift!

PASSPORT TO ROMANCE
SWEEPSTAKES RULES

1. **HOW TO ENTER:** To enter, you must be the age of majority and complete the official entry form, or print your name address, telephone number and age on a plain piece of paper and mail to Passport to Romance, P.O. Box 9056, Buffalo, NY 14269-9056. No mechanically reproduced entries accepted.

2. All entries must be received by the CONTEST CLOSING DATE DECEMBER 31 1990 TO BE ELIGIBLE

3. **THE PRIZES:** There will be ten (10) Grand Prizes awarded, each consisting of a choice of a trip for two people from the following list:
   i) London, England (approximate retail value $5,050 U.S.)
   ii) England, Wales and Scotland (approximate retail value $6,400 U.S.)
   iii) Carribean Cruise (approximate retail value $7,300 U.S.)
   iv) Hawaii (approximate retail value $9,550 U.S.)
   v) Greek Island Cruise in the Mediterranean (approximate retail value $12,250 U.S.)
   vi) France (approximate retail value $7,300 U.S.)

4. Any winner may choose to receive any trip or a cash alternative prize of $5,000.00 U.S. in lieu of the trip

5. **GENERAL RULES:** Odds of winning depend on number of entries received

6. A random draw will be made by Nielsen Promotion Services, an independent judging organization on January 29 1991 in Buffalo, NY at 11 30 a.m from all eligible entries received on or before the Contest Closing Date

7. Any Canadian entrants who are selected must correctly answer a time-limited mathematical skill-testing question in order to win

8. Full contest rules may be obtained by sending a stamped, self-addressed envelope to "Passport to Romance Rules Request" P.O. Box 9998 Saint John New Brunswick Canada E2L 4N4

9. Quebec residents may submit any litigation respecting the conduct and awarding of a prize in this contest to the Régie des loteries et courses du Québec

10. Payment of taxes other than air and hotel taxes is the sole responsibility of the winner

11. Void where prohibited by law

COUPON BOOKLET OFFER TERMS

To receive your Free travel-savings coupon booklets complete the mail-in Offer Certificate on the preceeding page including the necessary number of proofs-of-purchase and mail to Passport to Romance P.O. Box 9057 Buffalo NY 14269-9057 The coupon booklets include savings on travel-related products such as car rentals, hotels, cruises, flowers and restaurants. Some restrictions apply The offer is available in the United States and Canada. Requests must be postmarked by January 25, 1991 Only proofs-of-purchase from specially marked "Passport to Romance" Harlequin® or Silhouette® books will be accepted The offer certificate must accompany your request and may not be reproduced in any manner Offer void where prohibited or restricted by law LIMIT FOUR COUPON BOOKLETS PER NAME FAMILY GROUP ORGANIZATION OR ADDRESS Please allow up to 8 weeks after receipt of order for shipment Enter quickly as quantities are limited Unfulfilled mail-in offer requests will receive free Harlequin® or Silhouette® books (not previously available in retail stores) in quantities equal to the number of proofs-of-purchase required for Levels One to Four as applicable

OFFICIAL SWEEPSTAKES
ENTRY FORM

Complete and return this Entry Form immediately—the more Entry Forms you submit, the better your chances of winning!
- Entry Forms must be received by **December 31, 1990**
- A random draw will take place on **January 29, 1991**   3-HS-1-SW
- Trip must be taken by **December 31, 1991**

YES, I want to win a PASSPORT TO ROMANCE vacation for two! I understand the prize includes round-trip air fare, accommodation and a daily spending allowance

Name_____

Address_____

City_____ State_____ Zip_____

Telephone Number_____ Age_____

Return entries to **PASSPORT TO ROMANCE**, P.O. Box 9056 Buffalo NY 14269-9056

COUPON BOOKLET/OFFER CERTIFICATE

Item	LEVEL ONE Booklet 1	LEVEL TWO Booklet 1 & 2	LEVEL THREE Booklet 1, 2 & 3	LEVEL FOUR Booklet 1, 2, 3 & 4
Booklet 1 = $100+	$100+	$100+	$100+	$100+
Booklet 2 = $200+		$200+	$200+	$200+
Booklet 3 = $300+			$300+	$300+
Booklet 4 = $400+	____	____	____	$400+
Approximate Total Value of Savings	$100+	$300+	$600+	$1,000+
# of Proofs of Purchase Required	4	6	12	18
Check One	____	____	____	____

Name_____

Address_____

City_____ State_____ Zip_____

Return Offer Certificates to **PASSPORT TO ROMANCE** P.O. Box 9057 Buffalo NY 14269-9057

Requests must be postmarked by **January 25, 1991**

ONE PROOF OF PURCHASE   3-HS-1

To collect your free coupon booklet you must include the necessary number of proofs-of-purchase with a properly completed Offer Certificate

See previous page for details